(147)

(1107)

EVIL STAR

БЕДА́

Also by Logan Robinson

An American in Leningrad

*The Russian Republican (RSFSR) Code
on Marriage and the Family (translation)*

EVIL STAR

БЕДА

Logan Robinson

W · W · NORTON & COMPANY
New York   London

The text of this book is composed in Baskerville, with display type set in
Antikva Margaret Black. Composition and manufacturing by The Maple-
Vail Book Manufacturing Group. Book design by Jacques Chazaud

First Edition

ISBN 0-393-02293-5

W. W. Norton & Company, Inc., 500 Fifth Avenue, New York, N. Y. 10110
W. W. Norton & Company Ltd., 37 Great Russell Street, London WC1B 3NU

1 2 3 4 5 6 7 8 9 0

For Edrie Baker Sowell,
who, during the course of this
writing, consented to become
Edrie Sowell Robinson

ACKNOWLEDGMENTS

The first spark of the idea for this book kindled while reading the 26 October 1982 "Science Times," the Tuesday science supplement of the *New York Times,* and I remain indebted to that fascinating publication. A special thanks to Ron Hansen *(Desperadoes)* and John Irving *(The World According to Garp)* who provided guidance and encouragement when I worked with them at the Bread Loaf Writers' Conference of Middlebury College in August 1983. I had valuable conversations on some scientific points with Leonid Rivkin of the Stanford Linear Accelerator and on some medical points with Dr. Henry Pollack of New York Hospital, both old and dear friends. I thank Eric Swenson, my editor at W. W. Norton, a man of many interests, from Russia, to sailboats, to high-tech spy thrillers. My greatest thanks must again go, as they did in my previous book, to my wife, Edrie Robinson, without whose tireless research, editing, cajoling, and comforting this book would not have been possible, and certainly not any fun.

EVIL STAR
БЕДА́

Беда́! Беда́! Бегите все сюда!

Bedá! Bedá! Begite vse syuda!

Disaster! Disaster! Everybody run faster!
(A Russian children's rhyme)

AUGUST

"A MIG-23?"

"No, it's a Sukhoi."

"*Chort*, the devil, Ivan Voinovich, how can you be so sure? It's two kilometers away!"

"It's not difficult, look how it flies, like a big triangular kite. It has to almost stall to keep abeam of us. Come on, Petya, it's no great skill. If you'd flown in the war, you could do it, too. They used to say I could smell a Messerschmitt at four kilometers," yelled the old Russian flyer over the noise of the cockpit.

"Yes, the war, I wasn't even born then. By the way, these noisy military transports must be almost as 'experienced' as you, Ivan Voinovich."

"That's right, and this Ilyushin is almost as dependable. Something to think about when you're over territory this barren. See the Caspian Sea coming up ahead? There's nothing else around here but heat and desolation. I wonder where that Sukhoi is based?"

"It's nice anyway that they gave us an escort. I didn't think this mission rated it. You know, just picking up old scientists outside Leninsk and taking them for vacation on the Black Sea. Pretty unimportant stuff it seems to me. Should I radio the fighter to say hello?"

"No, we have orders to maintain strict radio silence until we're near Yalta. I don't know why. Petya, did they say anything to you about an escort?"

"No, Captain, I thought you would be informed, as always. I'm surprised nothing was said. But anyway, there he is—on our tail for the last twenty minutes."

"And only one plane, that's what's strange. They almost always fly in squadrons."

"Maybe those old physicists we're carrying don't rate a whole squadron."

"Petya, it embarrasses me to have to remind you that those 'old physicists,' as you keep referring to them, were responsible for launching *Sputnik,* back in 1957. You may not remember it, but we were ahead of the Americans in space then. Having a few gray hairs does not mean that you know less, it means that you know more. Among our forty passengers are the finest minds in Soviet deepspace rocketry, and it's an honor that we were asked to fly them back to civilization after their long work."

"Come on, Captain, they're just a bunch of quarrelsome old Volga Germans and Jews. No wonder the government has had them in the desert for the last eighteen months. They may have gotten us started in space, but now there are younger scientists, Russian scientists, *loyal* Russian scientists."

"You've got a lot to learn, Petya. If the leadership has had a group of that caliber working together in iso-

12

lation all this time, it's an important mission and you'd be well advised not to mock them. They built that special facility way out in the desert, and did you see how from the air it was disguised to look like an oil field? This mission must be so secret they didn't even want these big pine cones mingling with the other scientists at Leninsk. By the way, what's become of our friend the Sukhoi?"

"He must have circled around behind us. Here comes the shore of the Caspian. Look at how blue it is against the desert. Still, I really don't like flying over it; I mean water in general. Most anywhere else you get into trouble and a good pilot can put her down and walk away from it. But ditching into the waves, that's another matter."

"That sounds like something I taught you."

"Yes, I suppose it is. You know, Captain, I'll be sorry when they finally pension you out next month. Just think of it—over forty years in the air. You must be about the last of the old combat fliers."

"I myself can't believe it. The only reason they didn't push me out ten years ago is that no one else wanted to fly these long transport runs across Central Asia. I hate to give up flying, but I guess even I'm ready to retire."

"Yeah, piloting these ferry missions sure gets monotonous. When you leave I'm going to transfer to reconnaissance. You know, I think that when we get down to the Black Sea, I'll . . . *My God!* Captain! What was that!"

"It's cannon fire! We're hit! Who is shooting! Forget orders. Radio our position. God, there it is again! We've lost all engines."

"Dawn, this is flight Dawn calling anyone. Over . . . Over . . . We are in trouble, cabin pressure falling."

13

"Damn! Petya! It's the Sukhoi! The hell! He's one of ours!"

"Over . . . Over . . . Oh momma . . . anybody! This is it! We're going down! . . . Lord . . . We're going . . .

SEPTEMBER

When it came to the Russian language, Griffin's devotion was that of the convert who out-orthodoxes the bishop. He didn't have a drop of Slavic blood. By heritage he was just an indiscriminate British Isles mélange; his ancestors had come to America generations earlier. Griffin had started studying Russian in grade school in an experimental language program; part of the "Sputnik reaction," when American educators were convinced overnight that young Ivan could read better than young Johnny. Almost everyone who had started a foreign language in those early sixties' programs had eventually dropped out, but Griffin had gone the distance. His Russian was better than most natives'. It had throughout his life been the one thing he could do really well.

Piled up on Charles Griffin's desk was the morning's background reading: *The Red Fisherman*, the *Sovflot Maritime News*, and *Evening Murmansk*, Soviet trade papers, and regional dailies, available at kiosks in Russia to anyone who was interested. His copies had come courtesy of the American Embassy in Moscow.

"Hey, Griffin. You're wanted down in Sigint in forty-five. They want you to listen to a satellite intercept that no one else can figure out. O'Dwyer himself called. Beats the shit out of me why he asked for you. I'm supposed to be the supervisor around here."

Griffin winced whenever he heard the sarcastic voice of his intimidating supervisor. As always, he said nothing aloud, but to himself he muttered, "It's because you're incompetent, asshole. They wouldn't want your opinion if the tape was in goddamn English." His supervisor wasn't the only aggravation in his job. His pay envelope was no horn of plenty. He didn't even have a proper office; just a modular cube, with half walls that could be rearranged on any bureaucratic whim. And this after all those years of fancy Russian instruction.

Maybe he should have listened to his parents and gone to law school. His college classmates were making $50,000 to start at New York law firms, and it had taken them only three years to get their degrees. Whereas he had starved for four at the corner of 113th Street and Amsterdam Avenue and still hadn't finished his doctorate in Slavic languages. At the end it just didn't make any sense to continue. There were no jobs, no jobs at all in teaching, even if he did write his dissertation. Finally, reluctantly, he had decided to do the only other thing he could with "his" language, the rich Russian language, with its exotic-looking cyrillic characters and its byzantine grammatical complexity. Griffin had gone to work for the government. One year after dropping out of Columbia, he was with NSA, the National Security Agency, earning $26,530 a year as a Russian linguist in

16

the "A" group of the Office of Signals Intelligence Operations.

"Jesus, O'Dwyer about a satellite intercept. I'm moving up in the world." Griffin just skimmed the headlines of the *Sovflot Maritime News*. It was the least interesting of the three papers and forty-five minutes wasn't much time. Griffin read Soviet newspapers to provide context for the intercepted transmissions he would monitor later that day. To track current developments in his specialty, he indexed articles by a computer recall code and kept alert for anything relating to topics that appeared on a "watch list" he received every Monday morning.

Griffin's specialty was the Russian Arctic littoral, the northern seacoast of the Soviet Union. It was important militarily because the Soviet navy had no other Atlantic Ocean access that did not require passing through the territorial waters of the NATO allies. As big as the Soviet Union was, spanning eleven time zones, it had little seacoast. Russian ships on the Black Sea had to pass through Turkish waters, and ships on the Baltic had to navigate through Norway's and Denmark's islands. Only from the Arctic ports of Murmansk and Archangel could the Russian navy move rapidly into the sea-lanes of the Atlantic. Even here, they were monitored by Norwegian listening posts along the North Cape, and much of Griffin's intelligence data was gathered in this area.

Griffin was not exactly mesmerized by the Soviet Arctic littoral. It was as good as any of the other specialties; Central Asian petroleum development was no show-stopper, either. Griffin was largely indifferent to the subject matter anyway. He was using and improving his Russian daily, and this for Griffin meant everything. He even used his Russian out of work. It was the only talent he had for impressing the career girls he met at the bars in Georgetown. They were intrigued to see their names spelled in cyrillic and would ask if it hadn't been difficult to learn the alphabet. Griffin would laugh and explain that it could be learned in an evening or two if you had a good teacher—and then proceed to offer them lessons. This sometimes led to some vodka drinking and other developments, but they were usually short-lived. Most of the time, it seemed to Griffin, they would soon lose interest in this washed-up academic turned newspaper-clipper and jilt him for some lawyer. All but Leana, of course, but he didn't know how long that would last either.

Tiring of feeling sorry for himself, Griffin opened the September 2, 1985, edition of *Evening Murmansk* and began scanning the headlines. Griffin didn't mind reading the Russian newspapers. They were the visible tip of Soviet reality; the official record of "progress" that the Party wanted to communicate to the people. They made a telling contrast to the private conversations that Griffin eavesdropped on later in the day. More often than not these intercepts would contradict everything he had read that morning.

The newspapers were more than paeans to life under Soviet socialism; there were nuggets there for the careful reader. Griffin's favorite section was the letters to the editor, where the ubiquitous "simple worker" would write in to complain about some bureaucratic snafu. Griffin laughed at the Western misconception that the Russians were not allowed to complain. If his countrymen could read a Russian newspaper, they might conclude that complaining was the Russian national pastime. There were limits of course. One could never criticize in print the Politburo, the KGB, the Red Army, or other fundamentals of the Soviet state. But editors were happy to publish respectful letters that focused on isolated problems of distribution or particularly indolent foremen. *The Red Fisherman,* for example, always carried complaints about catches that were left to rot on the docks because of the unexplained late arrival of a refrigerator car or the drunkenness of a loading crew.

On page three of the four-page *Evening Murmansk* there was a typical article about the groundbreaking ceremony for a new cannery to serve the Arctic fishing fleet. The proper Communist Party officials from the *oblast* and *krai* were there, saying the proper things about the hard work of the Soviet fishing fleet and its contribution to the nation's economy. There was a review of the modern methods and large scale of the plant that would make three other canneries in the Murmansk area redundant. To Griffin it was just another example of the waste of resources in the Soviet economy. He knew that one of these three waterfront Murmansk canneries was completed only eighteen months earlier, amidst much ballyhoo about how its huge capacity would provide for the needs of the Soviet citizens for decades to come. Since then, poor fishing in the Arctic waters had never permitted this cannery to be fully utilized. Now the inefficient Russians were building another one. When he checked the location of the new facility in his atlas, he couldn't suppress his amusement. The site for the new cannery was not even on the coastal plain, but almost twenty miles inland. Ships would not be able to unload directly at the plant, but would have to transfer their catches to refrigerator cars for the trip inland. Soviet state planning at its finest, thought Griffin. Leana would be sure to get a kick out of this one. He filed the article under the computer recall code for "canneries" and for "Arctic littoral industrial development," and pulling his

19

customized headset from his desk drawer, headed down to the headquarters block of the signal intelligence facility, known in the trade as Sigint.

When Griffin reached the proper wing of the sprawling facility, he put his hand into a recessed cipher lock and punched in a series of numbers on a ten button electronic pad. If the numbers had been wrong, alarm bells and red lights would have come on, guards would come running; but the numbers were right, the double steel door popped open and Griffin stepped through. Reaching the headquarters office, Griffin briefly greeted another linguist, then went into a small reception area. The room was thickly carpeted, soundproofed, and vibration-free. He gave his name and showed his badge to the smiling brunette receptionist. She compared the badge to his face and announced him on the intercom. Before he could take a chair, Stanley O'Dwyer, Deputy Director of Signal Intelligence, threw open the inner office door and practically bowled Griffin over.

"Griffin, my boy. What took you so long?" O'Dwyer, known as Big Stan in the trade, threw an arm around Griffin, engulfing him. "I've been on the edge of my chair, yes I have. I told them you'd have this little puzzle solved in no time. Didn't I tell them that, Kathleen?" O'Dwyer beamed and the receptionist just giggled. "I've got a tough one for you. Oh yes, you're going to love it."

"I'll do my best, sir," said Griffin, trying to recover his balance.

Despite O'Dwyer's chumminess, he and Griffin had scarcely met. O'Dwyer was among the most powerful men in the NSA, using his expansive style and well-known bearhug both to intimidate and flatter. He was a genius at getting the most out of his people. Some months before he had heard that there was a new Russian linguist around who was pretty damn good. Today Big Stan needed a damn good Russian linguist, so today he and Griffin were suddenly old friends.

"Come right this way, Charlie. Great to see you. Have you done much satellite work?"

"Not as much as I'd like, Mr. O'Dwyer."

"Now, Charlie, have you done *any* satellite work?"

"No, sir."

"That's more like it. Don't forget that Big Stan knows all. 'Omniscient.' Isn't that the word for it? Still, no time like the present to start. You know how it is, the most sensitive thing about satellite reception is that we can get the stuff at all. As soon as the Sovs know we can hear 'em, they shut up! Not so dumb those Reds, hey!"

The two men went from the reception room into a corridor where Griffin had never been. No matter how much of NSA he saw there always seemed to be more. They came to a group of soundproof cubicles, and O'Dwyer led him into one with two comfortable padded chairs. The door gave a solid click behind them. The booth was perhaps ten feet by eight and similar to the one Griffin used every day, except for the presence of a TV camera in the corner. There was a control panel along one side of the room, with buttons marked fast forward, pause, and rewind. Other buttons permitted a listener to change the speed of the recording, faster or slower, to change the tone, to dampen background noise on a tape, even to change the pitch of a voice without changing the speed. On the wall behind the control panel was a wall-size map of the Soviet Union. Below the map was a small library of Russian dictionaries and reference books.

"Looks just like home, doesn't it?" said O'Dwyer.

"Yes, pretty much."

"Well, I wanted you to be comfortable, because I'm not letting you out 'til you figure this intercept, ha, ha." Big Stan roared with laughter, and for a second Griffin thought he might mean it. "Seriously, Charlie, we've got a real bastard in this one and some other fellows just couldn't seem to put it all together. Now, I'm no linguist myself, but folks around here say you may be the best we've got and by God this is where we find out."

O'Dwyer pulled a 12 by 15 inch photo from a plain brown envelope and handed it to Griffin. His manner suddenly turned grim and penetrating.

"Let me give you some background, and this one I don't even want discussed with your supervisor."

"That won't be a problem, sir," said Griffin in earnest.

"Do you know what that is?" asked O'Dwyer.

Griffin tried to make something of the large black-and-white photograph. There was a contrast in two areas that appeared to be a shore line; near the change in shading, between what Griffin thought was land and sea, was a tiny blur that looked like a little shack.

"A coastline?" ventured Griffin.

"To be exact, the coast of Soviet Kazakhstan on the Caspian Sea. Now how about this object?"

"A little house?"

"That is the crashed tail section of an Ilyushin18," said O'Dwyer triumphantly. "We've got guys here as good with their eyes as you are with your ears."

"Wow," said Griffin, staring at the grayish spot.

"The rest of the plane went in the soup. And now I've got another little surprise for you. We just happen to have the one and only radio transmission that Ilyushin ever made. A fifteen-second ditty that I just know you're going to love." Big Stan pulled over the mike.

"Control, O'Dwyer here in booth twelve, run that item B15-F42, if you would."

Over the room monitor came "Yes sir, Mr. O'Dwyer," and a few seconds later the crackling voice of a panicked Soviet flyer. "Zarya, ya Zarya—otvette kto-nibud'. Priyem . . . Priyem. U nas avariya, davleniye v kabine padayet." There was static and a confusion of sounds, then the voice came back. "Priyem . . . priyem. Mamochka maya, kto-nibud'! Vse! My padayem vniz . . . Gospode! My padayem . . ." There was a zipping sound and then silence.

"Jesus," said Griffin, "that's pretty brutal stuff."

"Do you need to hear it again?" asked O'Dwyer.

"It's not necessary, sir. The first bit was the identifying call for the aircraft, in this case the word 'dawn,' then he said 'Come in anybody . . . over . . . over . . . we are in trouble, cabin decompression.' Then comes that sound of popping and then, 'Over . . . over . . . Oh momma . . . Anybody. This is it . . . we're going down . . . Lord . . . we're going . . .' And that's it. I guess they crashed at that point."

"Very good, my boy, very good," cheered O'Dwyer, clapping his hands.

"But really sir, that intercept is as clear as they ever are. None of the linguists would have had trouble with that."

"Nope, that's right, none of them did."

"Then I don't understand."

"Charlie, there's another man in that cockpit. He's not speaking into the microphone. He's seated next to the man who is. And even though you shouldn't be able to hear what he says over the radio, he's yelling so loud, it just may be possible. Now listen again when you hear what you called that 'popping sound.' "

The recording came back on again, and Griffin acknowledged that there might be a voice among the other sounds in the din of the background noise of the airplane's cabin. He thought he could hear a curse word and then perhaps the name Petya.

"I'm going to make it a little easier for you," said O'Dwyer. "We've been able to dampen just a bit that primary voice on the radio so you can concentrate on what's going on in the background. I want you to listen to that modified tape until you can tell me what the other man says. Spend the rest of the day on it, spend the rest of the week if you think it will help. Then call me when you have the answer." Big Stan leaned back over to the mike and said, "Control, run the enhanced version of that tape for my friend here. And if there's anything else he needs, you boys see to it that he gets it right away." O'Dwyer got to his feet, picked up the satellite photograph, and with a final "You can do it, son," he was gone.

Griffin asked control to attach the tape to the machine in the booth and pulled his chair over the thick carpet to the panel. He had brought along his own headphones, especially molded for him when he joined the Agency. The earpiece was a work of art; formed from a cast of his ear to fit perfectly, it was acoustically designed to absorb any supplementary vibration between the microphone and the bones of his ear. The set was so light and comfortable that he had to concentrate even to be sure he had it on. Griffin settled back into the thick, upholstered chair and picked up a finger grip with a pause and playback button, then clearing his mind of all thoughts, he closed his eyes and began to listen.

For the next four hours Griffin concentrated on a staccato burst of phrases that could not have taken more than four seconds to say. The electronic dampening had helped, but even without the primary voice there was the roar of the engines, and some incessant thudding that Griffin could not identify. He worked with a long yellow sheet, every so often noting a phoneme. Sometimes he slowed the tape down, sometimes he said words out loud. He leafed through a linguistic guide on regional speech patterns and another book devoted exclusively to Russian *mat,* or cursing.

Griffin felt that he had most of it; all of it really, except for one word. But as was so often the case, that word was the key. He even had a good guess at the missing word, but if he was correct, the whole thing didn't make any sense. The utterances begán with something like "damn Petya" but then it seemed the man said *"eto sukhoi,"* meaning "it's dry." Then there was some more cursing and then *"eto nash,"* or "it's ours." But what of theirs was dry? The gas tank? But then they could have sputtered and glided, not just fallen out of the air like a shot mallard. Was the man talking about the desert? If so, then how bizarre, in your last seconds of life on earth, to remark that the desert was dry, but damn it, it was ours.

Griffin glanced at his watch and realized he had completely missed lunch; it was late and he was starving. He called control to say he was breaking for a snack and began the trek to the cafeteria. During the long march past an array of stores, banks, and service centers that would have done a small town proud, Griffin tried to make himself relax. He thought that perhaps he should let his mind wander, and think about something else for a few minutes besides the four seconds of tape. After he ate he could return to it refreshed. As he swung on to the nearly thousand-foot corridor of NSA's Headquarters-Operations building, the longest unobstructed hall in the country, and stared at the long mural, he forced himself to reflect on the first time he had seen it, this pathway into the Alice-in-Wonderland world of electronic spookery.

The NSA was the biggest employer of foreign language specialists in the country, and Russian, not surprisingly, was at the top of their list. Their recruiters were often up at the Russian Institute at Columbia. He couldn't deny that Leana had been a factor in his decision to take the NSA exam. Even though she worked for the library at Columbia, Leana was not a university type. To the contrary, she laughed at people in academics, holding her admiration only for those who left the university and tried to have some impact in the outside world. To the graduate students, she spoke of the professors in the Russian Institute in a mildly disparaging way, laughing at their foibles, seeing any reversal, from a parking ticket to a missed flight, as further evidence of their inability to deal with the real world. The higher up the academic, the deeper her scorn. All the graduate students knew she held these views about their chosen vocation, but Leana was so good-natured, and so good-looking that nobody gave it a second thought. But over time Griffin had come to agree with her; Leana praised his change of heart and encouraged him to get a job. Government was the obvious choice. Actually Griffin didn't know which had come first, his deciding to leave Columbia, which had impressed Leana, or his desire to impress Leana, which had made him decide to leave Columbia.

The Russian language part of the NSA exam had been a walkover for Griffin. He had done little else besides Russian language and linguistics in the last eight years. In the oral portion, he had spoken Russian so much

26

better than his examiner that it had gotten a little embarrassing. Interestingly enough, he hadn't done that badly on the other part of the NSA test either, even though he had never taken a test quite like it. It looked benign enough. The exam was called the Professional Qualification Test and was administered by the Educational Testing Service, just like the SAT and Graduate Record Examinations he had taken earlier in his academic career. But the questions were most curious. One had asked him to imagine that he was an anthropologist sitting on a high cliff in the South Pacific overlooking a series of islands. Between the islands, natives in canoes carried messages, stopping often at some islands and rarely at others. Meanwhile, smoke signals were sent between certain of the islands. Each canoe trip and smoke signal was detailed in the question. At the end, Griffin was asked to figure out where the chief was.

Apparently he had figured out where the chief was well enough, because he was soon invited down to NSA's Friendship Annex at Fort George C. Meade, halfway between Washington and Baltimore. Naturally they had made it sound more exciting than it was. The National Security Agency was the largest secret service in the free world, but it didn't have a single cloak in its inventory, not one dagger in its arsenal. That function, to the extent it was done at all, was the job of the CIA. For the NSA, it was all just electronic dishes, satellites, interception equipment, and—putting all the bits of overheard conversations together—cryptanalysts, telemetry specialists, logisticians, and linguists, such as himself.

They had really gone over him during those forty-eight hours at the Annex. He had a medical exam, psychological testing, personnel interviews, and most intense of all, a full-scale polygraph test. The examiner had sat him down in a swivel chair, attached electrodes to his fingers, strapped a broad, black belt around his chest and a blood-pressure pad around his upper arm. Even though he had nothing to hide, Griffin soaked his undershirt just waiting for the questions to begin. The polygraph examiner had psychologically stripped him bare. He would pursue some embarrassing line of questioning, drugs or sexual experience, then as Griffin answered, the examiner would stare at the graphing needles, then suddenly interrupt and yell, "What was that, I didn't quite get that," or "Wait, wait, something's wrong here." Several times during the session, the examiner would suddenly tear off the graph paper and gruffly command Griffin to wait. He would then disappear behind a door that just happened to be near a large mirror in the wall directly in front of Griffin. Griffin was sure it was a two-way mirror and that the examiner and others perhaps were just sitting behind it quietly watching him sweat. Griffin spilled out his darkest secrets and fears, and afterward he was an emotional wreck.

After that interview, Griffin had returned to New York to wait for the results of the Special Background Investigation that the Pentagon would do. The SBI was a fifteen-year background check on everything Griffin had ever done. His employers, teachers, even his former neighbors were questioned about his behavior and his beliefs. The screening was complicated by the fact that Griffin had spent one college semester at a language program in Leningrad. It wasn't exactly feasible for the Pentagon's Defense Investigative Service to go snooping about his old neighborhood on the Petrograd Side asking about him in the shops. But, after all, it wasn't unusual for a Russian linguist to spend some time in Russia.

Griffin hadn't liked his semester in the Soviet Union at all. He had always had a sensitive stomach and had contracted a water parasite common in Leningrad. He had diarrhea for most of his stay. Leningrad was as far north as Juneau, Alaska, and by December it was dark, damp, and cold all the time. His diet had been black and white: potatoes, cabbage, black bread, tea, and vodka. His salient memory of that semester was of his frequent visits to an unheated, seatless, dormitory toilet stall. There was no toilet paper in the city, and as the toilets clogged easily, there was always a heap of crumpled *Pravda*s and *Izvestia*s, smeared with the defecation of previous occupants, on the floor in front of him. Griffin knew that if he went to work for the NSA he would never be able to return to the Soviet Union. This suited him just fine.

At first, Griffin convinced himself that while he waited to hear from the NSA he would continue work on his dissertation. But it was summer by then and New York was ungodly humid. In June, the "City" fled to the Hamptons. It was cool on the Island and there were parties. Griffin went out there sometimes and even had a good time once or twice—but he found the girls a little vapid, and anyway he always felt guilty about the research he should have been doing on his thesis. It all seemed such a waste to him now that he hadn't even submitted the damn thing. On the other hand, it hadn't been so bad that summer in New York—it was that summer that he had finally gotten Leana to notice him. She hadn't shown any interest in him during his graduate student days. She was cordial, of course, even friendly, but his early advances had gotten him nowhere. Even when he'd just ask her to do something in a group, like going to a Russian movie playing on campus, she would have some cute little reason for refusing. "Enough of Russia for one day," she would say. "Don't you students ever tire of that dreary country?"

Leana's lack of intellectual interest in things Russian was as curious to Griffin as Griffin's infatuation with the subject was to other people. Although she was a full, green-card resident alien now, Leana was Russian by birth. She was a natural for her job of Slavic bibliographer at the Russian Institute. Her Russian was of course native, and she knew something of other Slavic languages as well; she had even begun a degree program in library science at Moscow State University. Leana had been permitted to emigrate to join a long-lost and distant Jewish relation. She had told Griffin that she had been ecstatic to discover a possible Jewish forebear; it was her ticket out of the country. She had applied at a time when the Soviets were trying to impress the Western Europeans with their human rights record and weren't checking emigration petitions too closely.

When pressed, Leana revealed a wide-ranging knowledge of Russian life and culture. After only one semester she seemed to know everybody at the Institute. She was of tremendous value to the program. Many people needed her help, and even those who didn't looked for some excuse to meet her. She was, thought Griffin, what the Russians call a *krasavitsa*, a beauty, but in a warm, strong Slavic sort of way, not like some distant Scandinavian, or high-fashion Parisian snob. She was certainly the most attractive woman Griffin had ever been involved with.

Reaching the cafeteria, Griffin collected two chicken pot pies and went outside to sit in a large courtyard. Maryland was finally getting a little more tolerable after the long, muggy summer. He removed his sport coat and took a seat next to an old gazebo, from an age when oral communication was limited to the number of people who could stand in the town square.

Halfway through his first chicken pot pie, Griffin began fidgeting with his napkin. The anguished voices of the two pilots crept inexorably back into his thoughts. It was really some epitaph. The whole thing was so grisly—that mangled tail section on the northern shore of the Caspian. Griffin wondered how many passengers had been in the Ilyushin—thirty, forty, or maybe it was empty. The damn Soviets never reported their crashes unless there were foreigners on board. Probably the NSA was the only one even trying to figure out what happened to that flight. If he couldn't piece together what they were trying to say, the incident would be forgotten forever.

Griffin folded his place mat into the shape of an airplane and, holding it in his right hand, pretended it was flying. He became totally absorbed. He began saying the final words of the two pilots over and over in Russian as he made the hand-held plane bank and soar in front of him. Several people avoided his table. *"Eto sukhoi,* it's dry," he said, *"eto sukhoi."* He imagined he was that pilot in the doomed plane, screaming out *"eto sukhoi."* It was almost as if, if he concentrated hard enough, he could bore right into that pilot's thoughts. Griffin rotated his paper plane in front of him and stared at its broad triangular wing. *"Eto sukhoi?"* He jumped up. "Of course," he said out loud. *"Eto sukhoi!"* He ran from the cafeteria.

When Big Stan O'Dwyer arrived at the listening booth, he found Griffin calmly leafing through *Jane's All the World's Aircraft.*

"What have you got there, Charlie?"

"The answer, Mr. O'Dwyer. It's going to sound pretty far out, but I'm sure I'm right."

"I want to hear it."

"What the other pilot says is, 'damn,' then he says in Russian *'eto sukhoi,'* which means 'it's dry.' Well, it does mean that, and that hung me up for the longest time. I thought for awhile he couldn't have said that, maybe something similar, because 'it's dry' just didn't make sense. But just as the word *griffin* is the name of a mythical creature, but it also happens to be my name, *'Sukhoi'* is a Russian name. *'Sukhoi'* means 'dry,' but it also means the airplane designed by the Russian aeronautical engineer whose name is Paval Ossipovich Sukhoi. You know they name their planes after their designers; Mig is named for Mikoyan and Gurevich, for example. Well, the only plane flying designed by Sukhoi is the SU-15, a big triangular-wing job, the most deadly interceptor they've got."

"It was an SU-15 that downed the Korean 747 in 1983."

"Right. And then the pilot curses again, a curse difficult to translate—literally something like 'what are you,' then a derivative of the word 'prick.' But anyway, the sense of the expression is 'what the hell?' said in shock and surprise, and then he says 'it's ours.' Well, Mr. O'Dwyer this sounds crazy, but the only thing I can make of all this is that that Ilyushin was attacked, attacked by an SU-15, one of their own fighters."

O'Dwyer started to say something and then checked himself. He was no longer slaphappy Big Stan, but a deadly serious Deputy Director of Signal Intelligence. "Just a small detail, but, you know I don't speak Russian, how could 'it's dry' be confused with 'it's *the* Sukhoi'?

32

What happened to the 'the'? How come nobody heard that?"

"Because there is no 'the' in Russian, no 'a' or 'an' either, no articles in the language whatsoever."

"I see," said O'Dwyer. "I guess I had heard that at one point." After a silence, he continued, "I should tell you that you've done a fine piece of work here, and frankly your conclusion is not at all 'far out,' as you said, but more like right on target. The truth is it confirms what I already suspected. I didn't mention this before because, naturally, I didn't want to influence your translation, but some of the boys in ballistics think that that popping or hacking noise you heard in the back of the transmission could be the sound of a Soviet fighter's cannon burst, *incoming* rounds mind you. Also, the way the tail section was severed from the aircraft, and the short interval between the time they radioed and the time the radio died, both indicate some midair explosion. Of course there could be many causes for an explosion. Frankly your piece is the most important in the puzzle in my view. Nothing like an eyewitness' testimony as they say. Don't the lawyers give some special weight to dying declarations?"

O'Dwyer sat for a moment and then said, "Well, I guess that wraps it up. Charlie, you've done a hell of a job," and rose to go.

"But wait," said Griffin impetuously, "we're ignoring the most important part. Why did a Soviet combat aircraft shoot down its own unarmed transport plane?"

"Oh that, yes, you young guys are always concerned about the 'whys.' I try and constrain myself to the 'who-what-where-when' stuff." O'Dwyer was slipping back into his 'Big Stan' personality. "Charlie, who knows what evil lurks in the hearts of men."

"Please, sir, I've been racking my brains on this translation all day. You must have some idea, some speculation what's behind it."

"Okay," O'Dwyer sighed. "I guess you do deserve some of old Stan's speculations for this analysis you've done. I'll admit, a couple of things do come to mind, but they won't exactly sate your curiosity. Anyway, here goes. For one thing, I'm convinced it was not an accident. My best argument for that is that the pilots maintained radio silence on this flight from the beginning. They didn't even radio the tower when they took off, wherever they took off. If they had radioed earlier, we would know about it. The only reason we know about them at all is that snippet of intercept when they were already falling out of the sky. No, I think they were set up. The fact that the plane was shot down over the Caspian fits into this. They didn't want the locals to see that the fuselage was full of bullet holes. The tail just fell faster than expected. The SU-15's pilot just couldn't wait, bless his heart. If it wasn't for his itchy trigger finger we might have missed the whole thing.

"Another thing, it wasn't the two flap jockeys we monitored who were being fingered, but whoever they were ferrying in from Central Asia. The KGB, or whoever it was, wouldn't go to those lengths for a couple of low-ranking officers. For the same reason, I doubt it was two or three troublemakers they were after, because, again, you could simply arrange a car or elevator accident, and not get the Soviet Air Force involved. I'll push it a step further. I bet that group of people were of some notoriety, the kind of people you have to account for even in Soviet society, you know, with a clean little 'tragic crash with all of their colleagues.' It's more plausible than a lot of simultaneous fatal accidents. So in my view it was

34

a large group of people, related in some way, work or otherwise, whom somebody wanted to get rid of all at once. That somebody was high enough up to order the Soviet Air Force around, or at least a small part of it. And for all of these reasons I conclude that whatever is being hidden is significant, tremendously significant. The Soviets are merciless, but they have some sense of economy. They wouldn't go to this extreme to plug some leaks on an arms shipment or cover up local rioting.

"Do you know what it really reminds me of, Charlie?" continued O'Dwyer. "Do you remember in history class, about the building of the tombs of the pharoahs, King Tut and all that? Remember about how all the slaves who built those tombs were put to death as soon as they completed their work, and how the soldiers who killed them were also killed—all so no one would be able to say where the tomb was? If you ask me, Charlie, that's our situation. We know that the slaves were put to death after their work, but we just don't know what work they were doing. Now somehow, Charlie, we've got to find the tomb."

Admiral Evgenie Alexandrovich Komkov was perplexed by his new orders. He gazed from the deciphered communiqué out his office window in the East Wing of the Admiralty to the Red Fleet Quay, then over to Leningrad State University on the opposite bank of the Neva, and finally back at the transcribed order to see if he had in fact read it correctly. It had been received in the normal manner. The order had been hand carried to him from Moscow by a colonel in the GRU, the military intelligence service. The order itself was in cipher, so that even if it had been intercepted—for which of course the colonel would be shot—the message would be incomprehensible. The decrypting key had been sent to Komkov separately by a secure cable. It had taken him the better part of the morning to turn the nonsensical sequences of letters into a comprehensible message. Had it been a lower grade cipher he would have had his aide do the work, but when Komkov saw the white border on the gray envelope he knew that only he was to read the message. He received a "white" cable from the Kremlin only every few months, and usually they were just dummy messages to make sure he would not forget how to do his own deciphering. This was not a test. He had checked his transposition carefully, and there was no question about its accuracy.

One short year before, Evgenie, or Zhenya to his few friends, had become the youngest admiral to command one of the four great Soviet fleets. He had moved into the Fleet Admiral's offices at the sweeping Admiralty, built in its original form when Peter the Great had made Russia a naval power. He was, at forty-nine, the supreme military commander of Leningrad, the city of his birth. Only the party chief of Leningrad, a Politburo member, had more authority.

Zhenya lit a *papirosa*, a Russian cigarette consisting of a hollow roll of cardboard for a mouthpiece with a brutally strong plug of Georgian tobacco in the end, and walked to the window. He was a big man, his naval tunic unbuttoned to ease the press of a not inconsequential midriff bulge. The doctors insisted he get more exercise, but working to ten every night didn't make it easy. His prematurely gray, almost snow-white, hair was still full and thick. Already years ago in the naval academy, his unusual white hair and eyebrows, his size, sloppy appearance, and considerable strength had earned him the title *bely medved'*, the Polar Bear. He heard from his officers that the sailors still referred to him that way when they were certain, but nevertheless mistaken, that no officers were around.

Admiral Komkov looked out the window past the columns of the Admiralty to the bronze lions flanking the staircase down to the Neva. A brisk wind on the river snapped the red pennants on the Palace Bridge. He could see the white spray of the hydrofoils carrying the last of the season's tourists out to the summer palace of Peter the Great. Across the river the trees around the *strelka*, the spit of land where the former stock exchange stood, were already in autumnal colors. It was almost equinox now and the city of Pushkin was entering its brief fall radiance.

Zhenya truly loved the city, this Northern Venice, with its canals and Italian renaissance palaces from the days of the czars. Although he had facilities at Kronstadt, the fortified island naval base at the mouth of the Neva, he spent most of his time here. He had established an office for himself in the East Wing of the yellow Admiralty building, directly across from the pale-blue Winter Palace. It had become the fulfillment of all his dreams to be appointed to command the fleet at Leningrad. After four years in Vladivostok as vice admiral, and what seemed like five lifetimes on the Black Sea, he had finally come home. After all those years in the wilderness, he was doing exactly what he wanted to do in exactly the place he wanted to be. That realization made this new order even more disturbing.

Admiral Komkov was to plan for the eventuality of abandoning Leningrad to the sea. Conceivably, the former capital of the Russian Empire was to be evacuated and left to the tides. He was to prepare, in utmost urgency and secrecy, a comprehensive plan for a military response to massive flooding in the city of Leningrad and the other large coastal cities of the Baltic military region, Tallinn and Riga. He was to work out evacuation plans to inland areas for not only the population, but also for the city's key defense industries. He was to undertake a study of the feasibility of surrounding the base at Kronstadt, home of the Baltic Fleet, with a high dike and floating docks. While the Politburo awaited his report, there was to be no major construction in Leningrad or, for that matter, on the whole Baltic coastline as far as the Finnish border to the northwest and the Polish border to the southwest. There was no explanation as to why the Politburo wanted such a plan prepared, and Komkov knew he was not to ask—the order was signed by the General Secretary of the Communist Party of the Soviet Union.

The admiral's report was to show what he could do to respond to various specified maximum changes in the water level of the Neva River. The lower flood levels seemed to be just sensible planning for the periodic flooding of the Neva delta. After all, they didn't call Leningrad the "Northern Venice" for nothing. Komkov remembered reading his father's description of the spectacular flood of 1924. As a young student in the naval academy his father had gone in a long boat right up to the first floor windows of the Winter Palace. Fortunately, the waters had risen gradually enough that there had been time to remove both art and citizens to higher ground. There were still little plaques on the university buildings to show the high-water mark. While the experience proved that it made good sense to plan for some degree of rising water, the higher flood levels the Politburo contemplated in the cable were without historical precedent. What could the general secretary be thinking of, Komkov wondered. Such a flood would far exceed the highest water levels ever recorded.

The report the Politburo wanted him to prepare seemed more like war-planning than flood-planning. The lengthy cable was specific about what the Politburo wanted, rather demanded, to know. They required graphs estimating how many lives would be lost if during a major flood he was given only one day to evacuate, instead of a week or even two months. "Two months?" thought Zhenya. "No flood gives you two months' notice." They wanted to know what percentage of the Kirov works and other industrial facilities could be transported inland on short notice. His instructions specified a sort of resource triage. He was to take into account that he would not be able to save everything; sacrifices would have to be made. Priorities were to be established, and effected ruthlessly.

It was clear that the leadership intended that the top priority must be to retain the war-making capability of the armed forces, even in the event of a total disaster. If the art works of the Hermitage or a train full of children had to be sacrificed to achieve this, Komkov was not to flinch. It was almost as if the Politburo was convinced that in the middle of this great natural calamity some enemy would seize on this moment of weakness to attack the USSR. In fact, it was even more bizarre. As Komkov read on, it seemed it was not so much the defensive military capacity that was to be retained, but the offensive—as if in the middle of flood and evacuation, the Soviet Baltic Fleet was to launch a surprise attack.

When he finished the cable the admiral pushed it aside and spent a few minutes walking about his commodious office. He sat on the ornate Victorian sofa, but could not get comfortable. He began to pace again. There seemed to be only one experience in the city's history that was comparable to the kind of sudden crisis and mass evacuation that the Politburo had in mind, and the admiral trembled even to think about it. Komkov had been only five when in June of 1941, on the longest of the White Nights of Leningrad, his father, a captain in the Baltic Fleet, received a call to report immediately to his ship at Kronstadt. Zhenya should have been too young to remember that night; he had no recollection of specific events prior to that time. Nevertheless, he remembered that night clearly, as if it was just then that his memory began. That balmy summer evening in 1941 was the last time little Zhenya saw his father. With the summer solstice, his tranquil, well-fed life as the only child of loving parents came to an end. The walks in the Summer Garden, the swimming lessons at the officers' pool, sled rides in the Field of Mars, his happy childhood days were gone forever. Of course, it was only years later that he understood the political drama that extinguished those happy times.

The Soviet Union's ally in the 1939 conquest of Poland had reconsidered their nonaggression pact. Hitler had launched Operation Barbarossa, and the Wehrmacht was rolling through the border headed for Leningrad. In July and August as the Germans advanced, sweeping through the Baltic states, all industry vital to the defense of the Soviet Union was removed from Leningrad and carted east. The Hermitage art collection was crated and taken to the Ural Mountains. Voltaire's library, Pushkin's archives, the treasures of Catherine's Summer Palace, all trundled slowly out of the city. Little room was left on the trains for passengers. By August 30, 1941, it was too late for them anyway; the Germans had locked the city in a blockade that was to last 900 days.

Zhenya had hoped those blockade memories would dull with time, but they had not. It was in September, he recalled, exactly forty-four years ago, that the war had come to Leningrad. Zhenya remembered a few lines from a poem by Olga Berggolts:

Leningrad in September, Leningrad in September
Golden twilight, the regal fall of the leaves,
The crunch of the first bombs, the sob of the sirens,
The dark and rusty contour of the barricades . . .

On September 4, 1941, Zhenya heard his first incoming artillery shell. A few days later the complex of warehouses containing the city's food supply was destroyed by German incendiaries. The political authorities had centralized everything, and as a result, in one air raid 3,000 tons of flour and 2,500 tons of sugar were lost. As the city became desperate for food, the molten sugar was scooped up with the dirt from under the warehouses and passed out to the children as candy. Zhenya lived with his mother in their apartment on Gorky Prospect, across from the zoo. He was there so frequently that he knew the names of most of the animals. The day after the warehouses burnt, a bomb fell in the zoo killing Betty the elephant. All night long Zhenya clung to his mother listening to Betty's endless death agony.

By November the city of three million was beginning to starve. Little Zhenya's daily ration was just 400 grams: five slices of bread made from coarse, defective flour. By December, Zhenya's mother had boiled every bit of leather in the house, even his dead father's briefcase, to try and supplement the boy's diet. The two of them cut pine and fir bark in the Smolensk cemetery. Leningrad had no more fuel than it had food, so they would sit in the cold and darkness of the apartment slowly sucking out a few rosiny calories.

Zhenya did not know that his mother was also giving him food from her meager ration. One day in January she called to him. She was too weak to rise from her bed. She gave him an envelope with the address of the naval orphanage and told him to walk there, staying in the middle of the street. Cannibals had been known to grab little children, pulling them into dark doorways. She gave him both of their ration cards and half of a loaf of bread so he would have the strength to walk through the snow. Then she told him how much his father and she had loved him and how he was now their only hope; he must not fail them, he must not fail Leningrad. Then she kissed him good-bye.

Zhenya did not understand what was happening but, as always, did as he was told. He was happy to get the bread and chewed it slowly as he went down the stairs to the street. He had not been outside for two weeks. It was one of the coldest winters on record. Along the way he saw motionless people propped up against a wall or simply lying face down in the street. A shriveled old woman passed him pulling a bundle no bigger than he was, wrapped in white linen on a child's sled. He was tired, but was afraid to rest. On several benches he saw the vacant, frozen eyes of those who had stopped to rest only for a moment, only for eternity. At last he reached the orphanage and, because his father had been an officer killed in action, he was taken in. That night he asked to go home to his mother, but the administrator, sensing the situation, told Zhenya his mother wanted him to stay, but she would come for him soon.

Somehow he survived the next few weeks. Two bowls

of thin gruel a day were the only respite from constant hunger. Some of the children had swollen bellies; they looked fat but never ate. It was cold in the orphanage and it was quiet; rarely any talking, not even any crying. They all wanted to cry of course, they all wanted to bawl their eyes out, but they simply hadn't the strength. Crying took energy, energy took calories, calories meant food, and there was no food.

One night in February he was evacuated with the rest of the orphans over the ice of the frozen Lake Ladoga, the "Road of Life." That night too was almost the end of him, and if it hadn't been for one courageous young soldier, Komkov's little body would have been fish food at the bottom of a watery grave. But when the dirty dawn broke, little Komkov, no longer a child, was safe in the Karelian forest behind Russian lines. From then on the Red Fleet had been his only home. To this day he lived with the guilt of taking the last crust of bread from his starving mother, and with the neurotic inability to eat comfortably unless there were several extra and unnecessary loaves of bread piled up in front of him on the dinner table.

Now the Politburo was talking about another Leningrad evacuation, this time not from an advancing army but from an advancing sea. Komkov's orders said that he was to do nothing to alarm the population, and absolutely nothing that might come to the attention of the Western consulates in Leningrad. He was to cloak any necessary studies in the guise of routine civil defense planning, of mere "worst case" contingencies. The communiqué was explicit that none of his subordinates was to know that these orders had come from the general secretary, or had originated from anyone other than Komkov himself. If the preparations struck others as

43

farfetched, he was to cultivate the impression that it was owing simply to his overexuberance as the new commander of the Baltic Fleet. He should let his staff infer that he had independently come to the conclusion that Moscow would be pleased with his crisis-planning.

The admiral read the decoded message one last time and stared again along the embankment. The deep blue of the Neva lapped the buttresses of the Palace Bridge. Without lowering his eyes from the river, Komkov reached into his officer's tunic for his lighter and then, in accordance with standard procedure for a "white" cipher, quietly burnt the dispatch and his decoding diagram. They were both written on special coated paper that was consumed entirely by the flames. He called the communications room and told them to cable Moscow that their message had been received. He hung up, and then dialing again, summoned his adjutant to call a meeting of his staff for that afternoon.

Lee Carradine awoke to find himself upside down. Of course, he couldn't be sure he was upside down because in space one was always just as right-side up as he was upside down. But with the space shuttle at rest and the edge of the earth visible just past his toes outside the porthole window, he felt he was upside down. But then he always felt like that when he awoke in space. The microgravity was something you could live with but never really get used to.

Carradine had had rather a lot of time for sleeping the last few days. The space shuttle was docked next to an infant orbiting space station smaller than the shuttle itself. They floated in a steel embrace 184 miles above the earth's surface. The station was only one week old, the first unit of a modular system that would be expanded into a scientific-astronomic orbiting hotel in the stars. Carradine, a colonel in the Air Force, was proud that it belonged to the United States. When he reflected on its role in his secret mission, he was relieved as well. It wasn't something he wanted the Soviets to have first. As far as the public was concerned, the purpose of this extended flight for the interlocked station and shuttle was to assemble and test the operational systems of the station and to learn how the crew would function over time in the confines and peculiar environment of space.

There were six astronauts on this mission, and though there was plenty for the group's engineers and scientists to do, as shuttle commander, Carradine's role was rather limited. Both he and his ship, the *Constitution,* were, for the moment, just cosmic guinea pigs. Each day, armed with a battery of instruments, he was to study and evaluate the effect of space on his ship and on himself.

It was the Russians who had pioneered in all this space endurance stuff, Carradine reflected. Three cosmonauts had cruised 238 days back in 1984 in a *Salyut 7*— nothing more than an unmaneuverable tin can—just to prove it could be done. Of course, the Americans weren't going to take a Bolshevik's word for the long-term effect of living in space, thought Carradine, so here he was. Also the Russians hadn't had all this fancy diagnostic equipment draping out of every orifice of their bodies, the way he had. The dials and meters ticked away the slow but steady deterioration of his heart's muscle tone, the natural effect of prolonged weightlessness. Each day his bones were losing calcium. At the end of this mission they would be shrunken by almost twenty percent— skeletally, the equivalent of a 95 year-old man. Carradine's "antigravity" muscles, the everyday ones he used for standing and sitting instead of drifting and bobbing about the capsule, atrophied daily. As long as he remained in space, none of these physiological changes would be a problem, but when he returned to earth's gravity, he would be left an emaciated weakling. He had been through the long recuperation before, and wondered, only half-facetiously, if he could just put in with NASA to remain in space.

Brittle bones weren't the only medical problem of space. Half the astronauts NASA had sent up over the last twenty years had become motion sick, some of them so severely they could not function. NASA never said which astronauts had these problems, but one way to guess was to see which ones never went back on a mission. It was so unpredictable, thought Carradine. A man would go through all the tests, the accelerator, the rocket sled, aerobatics, without so much as a burp. Then he'd get to space and weightlessness for the first time and he'd be retching so hard you could barely cram a Dramamine down his throat.

Other astronauts developed no motion sickness symptoms at all, and Carradine was one of these. In fact, some of the tests he was to perform were designed to induce nausea in him, just to discover what might produce it in others. In these he had completely failed. No matter what he did—spinning himself at high speed, bouncing off the walls—he just couldn't manage to get sick. Bruised maybe, but not sick.

It wasn't all bone degeneration and space nausea, conceded Carradine; there were advantages in being an astronaut as well. NASA really took care of its people. Every day they gave him medical advice: what pills to take and where in the orbiter to find them. He figured the boys back in Houston could do remote-control open-heart surgery on him if they had to. He mused whether somewhere in the equipment locker they had tucked away one of those new, all-synthetic mechanical hearts. Sometimes it made him feel less like a pilot and more like a trained chimp. Carradine knew this had been the torment of the astronauts in the early space program. From the beginning there had been complaints about astronauts being treated as mere "Spam in the can." In the sixties, in the days of Project Mercury, this had been painfully accurate; there was little the 'pilot' could do to influence the deportment of his ship. For the original seven fighter-jocks turned astronauts, this had been humiliating.

None of that could be said of the space shuttle. From the *Columbia* onward, NASA had returned to real spaceships, not orbital projectiles. With the inauguration of the new Constitution-class shuttles, of which the *Constitution* itself was the first, there seemed to be little the orbiters could not do, except of course take off from the earth without their massive booster rockets and external tank. But once space borne, the ship was a dream, with almost twice the thrust and payload capacity of the *Columbia,* and able, once refueled, to achieve escape velocity and go beyond earth orbit.

There was another difference in the *Constitution,* one NASA didn't discuss. Carradine knew that this had been the element most responsible for the rapid development of the second generation of shuttle rockets. Beginning with the third shuttle voyage, the military had been a regular customer and increasingly generous bankroller of the space program. Almost one of every three shuttle flights was now a military flight, and kept secret. The Pentagon did not finance the missions out of a new-found fascination in pure science. The focus of their interest lay, in prototype form, in the forward cargo bay of the orbiting *Constitution*—a flourine laser cannon, able to burn with the energy of the sun and the speed of light.

Laser, *l*ight *a*mplification by *s*timulated *e*mission of *r*adiation, a simple idea whose time had come. Electricity generated by an onboard thermonuclear plant activated flourine gas stored in the shuttle to produce a beam of pure green light of a single wavelength, so-called coherent light. High-quality mirrors focused the beam on its distant target. This light did not diffuse the way normal "incoherent" light did, but stayed intact throughout its speed-of-light journey. The laser could generate a brief pulse of 200 billion watts, vaporizing metal and producing debilitating shock waves in the target area. They had named the laser "Shiva," for the Hindu god of destruction and regeneration. No one had figured out the regeneration part.

Lasers had become common in industry and everyday life. No decent cancer surgeon would be without his laser scalpel. Tumors were no longer removed, they were vaporized. Every modern American supermarket used a laser cash register that read a universal product code of black lines on each package. State-of-the-art stereo systems used audio compact disks played by a zero-distortion laser beam instead of a stylus. Most industrial cutting devices, from the steel industry to textiles, were now lasers—what metal blade had a margin of error of one wavelength of light?

On the battlefield, the first use of a laser had been as a homing device in the Falkland Islands war. In space the laser's potential was unlimited. Distance was no protection from a laser; sublunar space was traversed instantaneously. In 1983 President Reagan had launched the Strategic Defense Initiative, with his famous "Star

Wars" speech. The United States would move away from the offense-only strategy of Mutually Assured Destruction, to a defensive capability of knocking down incoming Soviet missiles. Soon space-borne lasers and particle-beam weapons would be part of an American antiballastic missile (ABM) system—a high-energy curtain of destruction for Soviet rockets. But for now, the initial application of Shiva would be that of satellite killer, able, once refined, to destroy the entire fleet of orbiting satellites on which Soviet missiles homed. For an intercontinental ballistic missile, an ICBM, the satellites were the bell buoys and signal lights guiding the deadly automatons into port. Without the satellites telling them where they were, Soviet missiles would lose their way on their short, lethal journey to their Western targets. The missiles would still land and still explode, but, it was hoped, well wide of their targets—whole cities might be spared. Once perfected, the laser could strike with a surgeon's precision, from a stationary orbit, any and all Soviet satellites on the laser's side of the earth. In its present state of development, however, the laser cannon could not assure first-shot accuracy on anything much smaller than the moon.

There was another problem. The Soviets were well aware of what a laser could do and were not likely to take its development by the United States as inconsequential. It did not take a Star Wars speech to let the Russians know the United States was hard at work on the military application of lasers. The Soviets had made progress in this direction themselves. They even had a prototype charged-particle beam weapon, but couldn't as yet do much with it. To date, the Russians could not be sure how successful the American program had been, but the firing of a laser immediately above the earth's atmosphere would change all that. The blinding strike would instantly be detected—Russia's worst fears would be realized. Once such a test was made, the Soviets might become so alarmed that they would force an immediate confrontation, rather than face the shift in the military balance of power that would come with the laser's perfection. The emasculation of the Soviet super arsenal of SS-20's would be a mortal blow to the prestige of the Soviet high command. The president of the United States had found this risk politically unacceptable and forbidden a sublunar test. Thus the United States military found itself in the awkward predicament of having spent $50 billion on a weapon system that had never been fired outside the laboratory. Nobody really knew what Shiva could do. That was where the space station came in.

It had not taken Washington's best and brightest to conclude that, if all the new laser could hit was the broadside of the moon, why not test it by firing it at the broadside of the moon. To escape detection all that was necessary was to make sure that the broadside was also the dark side. Hidden behind the lunar countenance, the shuttle could blithely blast away at cracks and craters and crags, and no one would be the wiser.

It was a long way to the moon, and the *Constitution* could not make the round trip on the fuel it could carry with it from an earth blast-off. As with an assault on Mount Everest, there had to be a base camp. Another shuttle would have to bring a liquid hydrogen and oxygen spare tank up to the orbiting *Constitution*. Already free of earth's gravity, the *Constitution* could depart from the station fully fueled and rendezvous with it after the test. For the folks back home the little station forecast the weather, reported on new galaxies invisible from earth's surface, and generally gave a credible scientific accounting of itself—but the station's secret mission, and the reason it had been rushed to completion at such enormous expense, was to serve as mother ship for the *Constitution*'s laser test.

Carradine was commander and principal pilot for the moon test-firing. He was the best NASA had: the best flyer, the expert on orbital maneuvering, the most instinctively knowledgeable about what the *Constitution* could and could not do. With Carradine at the controls there was little the new shuttle could not do. He lived in the ship and for the ship. Even now, while the other five were in the comfortable crew quarters of the station, he preferred to sleep alone on the shuttle's flight deck. He had done so many times. Carradine had no close friends and no other interests. An early childless marriage, following his graduation from the Air Force Academy, had ended abruptly long ago. Except for a gruff patriotism and a suppressed pride in his pilot's skill, he showed no emotion. You couldn't say Carradine was unfriendly, but no one had gotten to be his friend, either. Stuart Fisher, the *Constitution*'s jocular mission specialist, had probably come the closest. Everyone in NASA respected Carradine, yet no one felt he knew him.

If the Russians had maintained a strong presence in space, the United States would probably not be able to keep the laser test a secret. But the fact was, there hadn't been many cosmonauts around in the last few years. It was ironic that the country that put the first *Sputnik,* and then the first man, in space had seemed recently to lose interest in the subject altogether. "I guess they just ran out of rubles," said Carradine to himself. After some of the long orbital tests of the early eighties, the Soviets had recently stopped launching. Even some of their unmanned satellites had not been replaced. There had been that shot last July from outside the Baikonur space center in Kazakhstan, thought Carradine, but even that had seemed to go wrong. When NASA started tracking it they thought the large rocket was intended to put up a communications satellite, but instead of going into orbit it reached escape velocity and just continued out past Venus, headed for the sun. Carradine assumed it was a solar science probe or, possibly, the Russians had just thrusted it too hard and lost it altogether. He was a little surprised that the Soviets had launched from a site somewhat outside of Baikonur, instead of from the modern launcher right at the facility. But the Russians were always hard to figure. Even the name of the site, Baikonur, was intended as a code for the true name, Leninsk. How paranoid, thought Carradine.

This Soviet nonchalance was in total contrast to the beehive of space enthusiasm in the United States. The American psyche had gone space-happy. Every kid and his dad who shoved quarters into the video arcade games thought about space stations and trips to the next galaxy. Movies and TV sitcoms about fanciful extraterrestrial life dominated the popular culture. Astronauts were lionized and, increasingly, elected to Congress. NASA came to have a built-in bloc who would not only vote for but sponsor every new funding request for space-related research and development. The taxpayers would look up for a minute from a game of Galaxiana or the latest Lucas film, and say, "Fine, John, you know what you're talking about. Let's launch another probe." Following the man-on-the-moon *Apollo* missions of the sixties, the research and development years of the seventies had seemed to the public hopelessly dull. With the eighties the space shuttle arrived, and suddenly there were once again men blasting off. Satellite recoveries and space walks were on TV. Space was exciting again.

This reborn space enthusiasm had created a growing cult at NASA around Carradine. As the commander of the space station mission at a time when the country was enthralled with space, he received more attention than any astronaut since the original Mercury seven. Personally he found this embarrassing. All the years of test-piloting and astronaut training were for no other reason than his sincere devotion to space and the profession. The last thing he had wanted was fame. If anything, the constant isolation and separation of space appealed to Carradine. Ironically, and although he would never have intended it, his very deportment contributed to the public admiration. Diffident, indifferent, on the surface, to public notice, he was a man of few words— the central casting hero. To the American in the street he was a kind of technological Clint Eastwood, a modern-day Musashi, a lone warrior in the stars.

OCTOBER

Griffin toyed with the small flakes of scallops in the ceviche. His stomach reacted to unusual tastes, and raw seafood "cooked" only by leaving it overnight in lime juice was far too exotic for his palate. Leana, however, loved unusual food and Griffin would try anything if he thought it would please her. He had arrived in New York by Metroliner that Friday afternoon, looking forward to a beautiful early fall weekend with Leana. He hadn't been disappointed.

"Charles, just look at you, you're getting no exercise at all," Leana laughed. "How are you ever going to keep up with 'big, strong Russian woman,'" Leana joked, putting on an extra heavy accent.

"Prosti, prostite menya," Griffin responded ironically, begging forgiveness in Russian with a phrase suggesting extreme gravity. Leana laughed, recognizing it as the last line of the Czar Boris Gudonov to God before Boris'

dramatic death scene in the Russian opera bearing his name.

"But seriously, clever one," Leana continued, "you never know when you may need strength to fight or run away. The world is a dangerous place."

"But I have you to protect me." Despite his jokes, Griffin knew that Leana meant what she said. She ran every day and did gymnastics as well. She constantly seemed to be in training.

In that and other ways, Griffin supposed they were rather an odd pair. Leana was athletic with an almost military perception of the world, while Griffin didn't do much more than run for the bus. Griffin thought of himself as the last of the sixties liberals, even though he was only six when President Kennedy was shot. He felt guilty about everything; guilty about having well-to-do parents, guilty about being middle-class, guilty about being an old-line WASP in a city of immigrants and minorities. Griffin even felt guilty about not telling Leana things, as if it meant that he somehow didn't trust her. He told her everything, really. He loved to talk with her about Russia and about his job. The only thing he hadn't discussed with her was the meeting with O'Dwyer about the Ilyushin crash. He had really wanted to tell her, but O'Dwyer had specifically admonished him not even to tell his supervisor, and Griffin respected and maybe even feared O'Dwyer a little. Griffin had said nothing, but now he felt that by keeping secrets from Leana he was cheapening their trusting relationship; it was in a way like cheating on her.

Leana was different; she felt guilty about nothing. While they were rarely visible through her external exuberance, control and retribution were the dark elements of her soul. Although Leana was four years younger than Griffin, they increasingly slipped into a parent-and-child caricature with Leana cast as the stern father and Griffin as the recalcitrant adolescent.

Griffin sensed that his physical condition was a subject in need of a change, and commented on a necklace Leana had begun to wear when they were out together. It was a half circle of elongated, waxy-looking yellow beads. In the center was a tiny blue amulet in the shape of a bell, no bigger than a gum chiclet.

"Is that amber?" he asked.

"Yes, it's from Riga in Latvia. Do you like it?"

"Sure. You've been wearing it a lot."

"Silly, you know I don't have much jewelry, and it's one of the very few things I still have from my student days in Moscow."

"What is the little bell?" Griffin said, reaching over to feel it. Leana pulled away a bit, placing her hand over the amulet.

"Oh, it's just a children's toy my father gave me. I wear it in remembrance of him. It's supposed to be the Czar Kolokol. You know, the bell at the Kremlin, the biggest bell in the world—the one with the crack."

"Sure, I know it. Every tourist in Moscow goes to see the pair: the Czar Bell and the Czar Cannon."

"Yes," Leana rejoined. "They reflect of course the typical state of high technology in my former motherland, a giant cannon that couldn't shoot and a giant bell that was cracked in the foundry and never rang. Funny, how they've become hallmarks of Russia—big and broken."

"Yes, but your old comrades say that that's all changed under socialism. The waste and stupidity of czarist times is all behind you," said Griffin, playing devil's advocate.

"Ha," said Leana. "Now it's worse. The inefficient, corrupt state has taken over all aspects of daily life and yielded our people an inefficient, corrupt economy. If it weren't for Western technology and American grain, the people would starve. Your silliest former professors at Columbia couldn't do a worse job."

Griffin chuckled and shook his head. The surest way to fire up Leana was to say something positive about the Soviet government. The next surest way was to say anything negative about prerevolutionary Russian culture or the indefinable soul of the Russian people.

"By the way, speaking about my former government's ability to mess up anything it touches, how is that little inland fish cannery getting along?"

"Oh that," said Griffin. "Well, you know it's the damndest thing. The construction along the Arctic littoral seems to have pretty much dried up. You know, big harbor projects and all I was following. They've just ground to a halt. The crews have been assigned elsewhere to higher priority projects, mostly inland or out of my area altogether. I've been thinking of doing up a report on it, but I figure that it's just because Central Asia and Eastern Siberia have more possibilities to develop export industries, you know, oil and strategic metals. I've been meaning to touch base with the guys who follow those regions to see if that's where the Sovs have moved their crews. It's hard to get the big picture when you do just one area."

"But you've not heard anything about it on the intercept?"

"Not really. I mean, the normal bitching about stopping a project, explanations about state planning orders from Gosplan. Some crews seemed to have been moved out of Murmansk and Archangel, the only big cities on the Arctic, but they themselves don't know where they're going or why. Jesus, can you imagine doing that to an American worker? You know, 'Your construction crew is being transferred to a new project, and naturally you're coming along, and by the way it may be on the other side of the country, but we can't tell you where, because frankly we don't know ourselves, so have a little vodka and try not to think about it.' "

"Yes, that sounds like life in the worker's paradise, all right," said Leana.

"There was one strange thing, though. It was during the visit of a candidate member of the Politburo to Archangel. There was a phone conversation between him and the commissioner for harbor development, a heavyweight named Sokolov. I've run across Sokolov several times and he's a real go-getter for his region. You know, a *tolkach,* a pusher, able to get materials when no one else can. He's always scraping for resources and improved allocations. I love to get him on intercept because he'll promise or threaten anything if he thinks it'll get his projects a higher priority. It wasn't on a safe line and started out with the normal provincial-versus-capital banter. 'How's life in the big city?' 'You're cold here? No wonder, you're from Moscow, for us that's the tropics! Ha ha.'

"It sounded like they knew each other fairly well," Griffin continued. "They talked for a while about an arctic seal coat that Sokolov had presented to this fellow's wife. Then Sokolov, after sweetening this guy up for awhile, started pumping him for information about all the slowdowns and cutbacks in the region. He's really a genius about turning on the charm and wheedling around to get what he wants. Sokolov whined that even his repair budget had been eliminated, not to mention the monies for projects begun but not completed. Meanwhile the candidate member was backpedaling and giving Sokolov the normal gradeschool hogwash, or eyewash, as the Russians would say. You know what I mean, all sorts of eloquence about difficult choices and national priorities, and the strain of competing with the Americans, defense needs, the whole litany. Anyway, after a few minutes of this Sokolov was furious.

"Sokolov just blew up at him. The intercept was great and every word was audible. It was eavesdropping at its finest." Griffin continued, cradling a glass of wine. "Sokolov said that for years he had exceeded his plan requirements and built Archangel into a modern port, and the whole time he'd never forgotten his friends. If they needed something, presents for their wives or someone else, they only had to call. A lot of interesting merchandise from all over the world came through the port. But now, when his whole operation was being hung out to dry and his crews sent off to other places, God knows for what, he was getting pious homilies about national priorities. 'Since when was the development of the Arctic coast not a national priority?' he yelled into the phone. He didn't even have enough men left to unload the ships. Finally at this point the Moscow man got a word in edgewise. He sounded really apologetic. He said he had done all he could for Sokolov. He had always stood up for him. But just now, temporarily, nothing could be done. It was a decision at the highest level. He emphasized that, 'at the highest level,' and remember, this guy is himself a candidate member of the Politburo.

"Even this didn't appease Sokolov," said Griffin, draining the rest of the wine in his glass. "He is after all one of the most powerful guys in the region, and I guess he thought he was entitled to some answers. He started asking directly: why was Archangel being cut off? In exasperation, the other guy said it wasn't just him and it wasn't just Archangel. It was across the board—the whole coast. This only seemed to make Sokolov madder, so then he said, 'What the hell is going on? What are you keeping from me?' Then the Politburo man started yelling for Sokolov to shut up; nothing was going on and he might be overheard. No dummy that Politburo man. But instead Sokolov blurts out, 'It's got to do with catastrophe, doesn't it, catastrophe.' He used the Russian word *bedá*. He said it—rather he yelled it—twice. And then the strangest thing; the Politburo man said *'chto,'* you know, just 'what' and the line went dead." Griffin looked down for a minute and rubbed his forehead. Then he poured himself another glass of wine.

"Maybe he didn't understand him and then the connection broke," Leana volunteered. "The phone system isn't all that dependable."

"Yeah, that's what my genius of a supervisor concluded," said Griffin sarcastically, "but I wonder. It really depends on your interpretation of the final *chto* and of what Sokolov meant by *bedá*. As you know *chto* in Russian has the same scientific field as 'what' in English. It's an interrogatory, but it's also an exclamation. It can be the question 'what?' like 'what did you say?' or it can be an expression of shock and disbelief, like 'what are you trying to suggest' or 'what, you dare to say that!' It's not the word so much as the intonation contour, but linguistic concepts like that are pretty much lost on my supervisor. I heard the guy say it and I don't think he was asking Sokolov to repeat himself. Which leads me to believe that just maybe *bedá* had a bigger meaning here than just 'the situation is calamitous, a real mess.' For that reason the use of the term over a public telephone freaked out the Moscow man, and not knowing what better to do, he just hung up."

"It sounds like you're reading an awful lot into it," Leana responded slowly.

"I guess so."

"And the higher-ups didn't think it was anything special?"

"No. Oh, everybody agrees there's a slowdown on Arctic projects—but that's happened before. The brass at NSA are just pleased the Sovs aren't building rocket gantries. Anything less bores them."

"So it's pretty much been forgotten."

"Yes, it has." Griffin paused. "But you know, there's one funny thing. I haven't told anybody at NSA about this because my supervisor would get wind of it and think I was trying to make him look bad—I mean about his decision that the Sokolov conversation was insignificant. He's jealous of my language ability as it is, and I don't need any more problems. Anyway, here it is. I used to get something mentioning Sokolov practically every day. Either something in the trade papers, or some intercept talking about him, 'Sokolov this, Sokolov that.' A lot of times I'd get Sokolov himself yammering away. The man was omnipresent. But since that conversation with the Politburo man, I haven't heard his name once. I mean the guy's just dropped out of sight."

When the receptionist alerted Admiral Komkov to the arrival of a certain colonel of military intelligence, the head of the Baltic Fleet knew what to expect. Ten seconds later the GRU colonel was in Komkov's office arranging an American Polaroid camera on a desktop tripod. The camera had a shutter delay so the colonel could himself be in the picture. Both men took their places in front of the camera with the clock in Admiral Komkov's office visible above their heads. The colonel checked the clock's accuracy against his own wristwatch, then gave Komkov a gray envelope with a white border. The admiral held the envelope up to his chest with the outer markings visible to the camera. The colonel held up a copy of that morning's *Pravda*. Only one picture was taken. Komkov signed the back and handed it to the colonel. It was a grim snapshot of a grim exchange. Both men knew their roles, and both men knew their lives depended on precise execution. Throughout the ceremony neither spoke. The colonel left immediately to return to the Kremlin.

Komkov assumed that this "white" cable was not an order to steam out of Leningrad and attack the NATO forces in the Baltic. Such an order would come in the same way, but Komkov supposed that in that case he would receive the decrypting key in advance, so that no time would be lost. He opened the envelope and studied the contents, several thin cellophane sheets bearing huge grids of Russian letters in no apparent sequence. In a few minutes a clerk arrived with a cable from Moscow— the new key. To his dismay Komkov saw that the Politburo had added yet another layer to the onion of Russian security. The new cipher was in double transposition. Once he had followed the keyed columnar pattern to rearrange and transpose all the letter groups, instead of having a coherent message in plain Russian, he would be left with just another incomprehensible scramble. A second cable, which arrived a few minutes later by a second, discrete system of transmission, revealed how he was to manipulate that new scramble before he could get something he could read. Komkov did not object to security but felt it had become a mania. This KGB obsession slowed everything down so, he reflected; what used to take the morning would now cost him the afternoon as well. Komkov called his secretary to cancel all his appointments and got down to work. It irritated him that the operations of an entire fleet were to come to a halt while he played code clerk to the Politburo. The hours passed as he slowly unraveled the well-concealed message.

A month earlier Komkov had outlined to his staff the evacuation feasibility study he needed. They had all agreed to start work right away, but then did nothing, hoping the whole idea was the result of a bit of undigested kolbasa from the admiral's breakfast, to be quickly forgotten. Komkov was forbidden to explain that the orders had come from the Politburo, nor could he give a plausible explanation why the studies were necessary. His staff, serious men, many of whom were older than he, could only conclude that the new admiral had concocted some wild fantasy about a great flood coming to swallow up Leningrad.

In order to get the report finished and submitted on time to the Kremlin, Komkov was forced into the unwanted role of petty tyrant. Relations with his staff, normally warm and cooperative, had soured over the project. Just as the general secretary had suggested, the whole matter was perceived as Komkov's attempt to curry favor with Moscow by dreaming up ridiculous assignments for his junior officers. The admiral's reputation as a stern but reasonable, no-nonsense commander had been strained by the whole affair. Still, at the time, Komkov had taken comfort that it was only a study. He had fully expected that, having delivered what the Politburo wanted, they would file it somewhere and leave him alone. The partly deciphered "white" cable he now held proved otherwise.

The cable reviewed the evacuation plan that Komkov had submitted. It complimented the job he had done under such brutal time constraints, but went on to make many suggestions. In each case the proposed modification indicated that Komkov had not gone far enough: he had not planned for a serious enough flood, he had counted on having too much warning prior to evacuation, his emergency facilities were not far enough from the seacoast, his food reserves were insufficient.

As the admiral continued decoding, it became clear that this was not, after all, a theoretical exercise. He was instructed to incorporate the Politburo's remarks into his evacuation plan and begin immediately to construct the necessary support facilities. However, he was to perform virtually no work in Leningrad itself or in those areas within 30 kilometers of Leningrad where resident foreigners were permitted to travel without visas. Certain unavoidable construction in Leningrad, reinforcing the main Neva bridges, for example, must be disguised as routine maintenance. Similar construction must begin immediately on the high ground inland from Tallinn and Riga. These preparations were to take precedence over all other fleet operations, and weekly progress reports were required. The cable sanctimoniously added that the Politburo anticipated the same total dedication to this delicate endeavor that they had witnessed in their young admiral so often in the past. Once again Komkov was to tell no one where these orders had originated and, as always, the cable itself was to be destroyed.

To Komkov, a loyal Leningrader, a blockade survivor, the thought that the city might actually be abandoned, that the Politburo seriously believed that such a natural disaster was not only possible, but imminent, left him reeling. He stared in bewilderment out his window and across the Neva to the University Embankment. What could possibly cause the short, broad river to so overrun its banks? The whole Neva was only forty-six miles long, running from Lake Ladoga, Europe's biggest lake, to the Gulf of Finland. How could it be that this lake and the Karelian forests that fed it would take on so much excess water? The great Russian rivers of the region, the Onega, the Ilmen, the Svir, and the Volkhov would have to be awash with torrents. Was it to rain every day for a year? And even if it were, why not put his efforts into dams and drainage canals, instead of pulling out of the city and transplanting the Kirov works. Had the Politburo gone mad?

As an experienced Soviet officer, certain other dark possibilities could not be ignored. Slowly visions of cloudbursts, melting ice flows, and nature gone mad gave way in his imagination to another plausible explanation as to why the Politburo had assigned this task to him. He was particularly troubled that he could not reveal the source of his orders, and in fact was not even to retain the one scrap of evidence that proved he had not simply taken leave of his senses. Komkov had received some foolish orders in his long military career, some of them with horrible, unintended consequences. But just so long as he had been given a direct command, it wasn't Komkov who had borne the blame. He had only to prove that he had been acting on orders; orders that he had scrupulously obeyed. The more he thought the command misguided, the more insistent he had been on having evidence. It was part of the universal military procedure of protecting your rear. He had seen many a fine young officer scapegoated, demoted, or packed off to a post on the Chinese frontier, because some senior officer's plan had gone awry. He reflected again on his own position. Did it not have all the warning signs he had learned as he climbed the ranks? He had been given the most bizarre order of his career, he could get no explanation from above, his staff was already grumbling, and he was not to say where the instructions had originated but instead to create the impression he was acting unilaterally. Massaging the cable between his thumb and fingers, the old Polar Bear wondered if he smelled a plot.

Komkov thought he had managed as well as any senior officer to stay in the graces of the Party and of the security police, the KGB. This was essential to an officer's survival. The Party, the military, and the KGB were the three points of the triangle of Soviet power. Soviet politics had no other contestants. Being the only players in a three-handed game, they eyed each other carefully. In particular, the KGB and the military were wary of each other. They were, after all, the only two armed groups in the Soviet Union. Having no other mission beyond espionage and counterespionage, the KGB was an exceedingly adroit opponent. Komkov had so far succeeded in staying clear of the secret police plots and intrigues, but other officers had not been so lucky. It didn't take much—a false report here, a mysterious incident there—and a promising career would be broken. They had their ways.

The admiral knew the vicious secret war the KGB's predecessor, the NKVD, had waged on the great military leaders of the Second World War. They were stories that would never be read in Soviet history books, but were kept alive nonetheless by generations of cadets at the military academies. They were passed along from upperclassmen to lowerclassmen, always with the solemn warning that much of military school could be forgotten, but this was a lesson to be learned by heart.

Marshal Konstantin Konstantinovich Rokossovsky's experience was a lesson hard for any aspiring officer to forget. He was perhaps the greatest Russian field commander of the Second World War. Rokossovsky was the only Soviet commander to successfully counterattack the German army in the earliest days of Operation Barbarossa. At Smolensk and at the gates of Moscow, it was the Sixteenth Soviet Army led by Rokossovsky that proved the Wehrmacht could be defeated. Later it was again Rokossovsky who, commanding the Don front at the Battle of Stalingrad, encircled the main German battle group and broke the back of Hitler's army. It was the turning point of the war on the eastern front. Victory followed victory for the brave commander, and when Berlin was captured and the war was at an end, it was Rokossovsky who deservedly commanded the victory parade on Red Square. But where was this brilliant general when the Germans were planning their invasion? Was he training the Russian army and preparing for the defense of the motherland? No, he was instead busy being tortured by the secret police. Rokossovsky was in prison awaiting execution.

The theory for his arrest was that he had been a drafted private in the czarist army. His desertion to join the Bolsheviks and his brilliant career as a corps commander of the Red forces in the civil war notwithstanding, he was caught in the Great Purge. Komkov had a cynical enough view of secret police politics to believe that the real reason Rokossovsky had gotten into trouble with the NKVD was precisely because he had been a brilliant and popular Red Army commander. In prison, Rokossovsky was beaten methodically and brutally. His toes were smashed, his ribs were broken, his teeth were knocked out. Under sentence of death he was more than once awakened for execution. While other former Soviet generals were shot dead at his side, he would be "shot" with a blank bullet in a macabre NKVD game of cat and mouse. He would not have escaped for long. In only one year during the Great Purge, 33,000 senior Soviet officers of the rank of brigade commander or above were liquidated by the security police.

Then things changed. With the German attack impending, the secret police were in a delicate position. They had had their fun and liquidated most of the experienced general staff of the Soviet army; but now they found that Hitler had assembled the largest invading force of all time on their border and they had no one left to lead their country's soldiers. Naturally they themselves did not wish to be exposed to enemy fire. So they dusted off poor Rokossovsky and gave him the rank of major general with a mechanized army corps to command—but they never lifted the death sentence. The commander of the victory parade on Red Square was subject to execution by his grateful country's secret police at any time.

Over the years the struggle between the military and the KGB had been refined somewhat. It had certainly lost the mass execution quality that it had under Stalin. But the insecurity remained; on one day in February 1960, 500 generals were peremptorily dismissed from the Soviet army. The rivalry, the loathing, and the fear were still there. Reluctantly, Admiral Komkov had to admit that since Brezhnev's death the KGB had been in the ascendant. The loss of Marshal Ustinov, the military's principal defender for forty years, was the crowning blow. The KGB had immediately tightened their control of the economy and the populace. They lost no opportunity to embarrass the military and keep it in its place. As always, anyone who had power or recognition independent of them was viewed as a threat. Studying the decoded order again, the admiral asked himself: Could it be that he, the rising star of the Soviet navy, was to be set up, ridiculed, and then perhaps removed?

For the first time in his long career, Admiral Komkov began seriously to consider disobeying a direct order; an order from no less an authority than the General Secretary of the Communist Party of the Soviet Union. The general secretary also held the title of Chairman of the Defense Council, and in that post was supreme commander of the Soviet armed forces. Still, it appeared to Komkov that perhaps this "white" cable should not be destroyed. He knew he could not prevent the KGB from purging him if they wanted, but at least he could prevent them from making him look incompetent. That, for Komkov, was the greater fear. If his fears were justified, by showing the cable to a few senior officers, he could at least preserve his reputation. Stories would circulate in the military academies about him the way they did about old Rokossovsky.

Yes, perhaps this cable should be quietly filed away, thought Komkov. And, in the planning and exercise of the evacuation procedure, there might be other things he could do to help Leningrad and its citizens, even if it meant "reinterpreting" his instructions from the Politburo. After all, if everyone thought preparing for a flood was his idea, none of his subordinates would realize he wasn't carrying it out in the manner he was told. Still, he would have to be careful. There might be *stukachi,*

informers, sent to keep an eye on him. If it was suspected he was resisting, it would be the end.

The admiral carefully reviewed the entire cable. At
the end there were some general cautionary remarks,
emphasizing the importance and sensitivity of undertaking his orders without question. In time he would be
told more, but it was impossible to do so now. Komkov
appreciated the vote of confidence. There was a final
point. The project had acquired a code name known
only to a handful of men in the top Soviet leadership.
The code name itself was to be treated as top secret and
should never be spoken first by the admiral; when he
heard it from another he would recognize its significance. The word in Russian was *bedá*.

NOVEMBER

"According to Dean Swift, 'old men and comets are reverenced for the same reason; their long beards and pretenses to foretell future events.' The author of Gulliver's Travels *knew the derivation of his words, in Greek,* kometes *meant 'long-haired.' "*

Charles and Leana leaned back in two of the plush chairs that circled the rotating, steel-black Zeiss-Ikon projector. Overhead, the stars of the Northern Hemisphere in November were brilliantly displayed on the hemispherical ceiling of New York's Hayden Planetarium. A furtive pointing arrow played along the ceiling and came to rest near the constellation Taurus low in the darkening sky, less than twenty degrees above the horizon. The low omnipresent voice of the narrator continued his monologue.

"The appearance of a comet is known as an apparition, and it is in this area of the sky that you can now

*dimly see the apparition of the most famous comet
known to man, the great Halley's comet."*

On the ceiling the dim outline of a comet came into
view and then grew brighter and brighter as the projected "night" grew darker. It had a long tail that played
out behind it across the sky. Griffin turned to Leana and
whispered, "Isn't it pitiful that, since the City throws off
so much light, we have to come to the planetarium to
see what is going on above us in the sky right now."

*"It is hard to imagine the trepidation with which our
ancestors greeted a new comet crossing their sky. In
1528, the French doctor Ambroise Pare wrote, 'This
comet was so horrible, so frightful, and it produced
such great terror that some died of fear and others
fell sick. It appeared to be of extreme length, and
was of the color of blood. At the summit of it was
seen the figure of a bent arm, holding in its hand a
great sword as if about to strike. At the end of the
point there were three stars. On both sides of the ray
of this comet were seen a great number of axes,
knives, and blood-colored swords, among which were
a large number of hideous human faces, with beards
and bristling hair.'*

*"This apparition of Halley's will not be so dra-
matic as that of the comet the good doctor described.
In fact, it will be disappointing compared to the two
most recent passes seen by our ancestors. The closest
Halley's will come to the earth this time will be next
April 11th when it will be 39 million miles away. In
1910 the comet came within 13 million miles, and in
the spectacular apparition of 1835, Halley's was only*

5 million miles from the earth. To make matters worse, when the comet is at perihelion, meaning its closest point to the sun, the earth will be on exactly the opposite side. So just when the comet will be at its most glowing, we won't be able to see it from the earth at all. For those of us in the Northern Hemisphere, the best view will be this month, about November 27th. Naturally, one has to get away from the lights of the city to see the comet, and clear viewing can be obtained only with binoculars or a telescope. But don't worry, if you aren't satisfied, Halley's will be back in just seventy-six years, in 2061."

"Very funny," Griffin muttered under his breath, "biggest non-event of the twentieth century."

"There have been twenty-nine previously recorded apparitions of Halley's comet. It is the first to be recognized as periodic, and it is named of course for the man who predicted its return, the English astronomer, Edmund Halley. It is coming to earth from the outer reaches of the solar system beyond Neptune, where it turned back toward the sun in 1948, from 3.2 billion miles away. Halley's comet is basically a dirty snowball of dust and frozen gases five miles or more in diameter barreling through the solar system. When it is far from the sun it is inert and has no tail and no 'coma.' A comet's coma is the spherical cloud of dust and gas that surrounds the nucleus. The coma is millions of times larger than the comet's nucleus. When the comet gets close to the sun, approximately within the orbit of Jupiter, its frozen nucleus begins to warm up and its gases start to

evaporate, or as astronomers say, to sublimate. It is these gases, and the dust blown off with them, that create the coma and tail and turn the comet into the 'chariot of fire' we can now see in the heavens. This continuous erosion of dust and frozen gas makes the comet smaller each time it orbits the sun. As much as one percent of the total mass can be burnt off during each perihelion passage. Halley's is big enough, however, that there should be plenty of comet left for many more generations."

When the show ended, Charles and Leana walked through the small park on 81st Street to Columbus Avenue. "It's still an amazing thing," said Griffin, "even if we can barely see it. Do you know who Mark Twain was?"

"Of course, silly. We read more nineteenth-century American literature in Russia than you do here in America."

"I suppose that's true. We tend to talk more about our writers than read them. Anyway, Mark Twain was born in 1835, when Halley's was in the sky. And he always said that he would die when it returned. And he did; in bed, in 1910." They walked on. "Do you want to go to Zabar's?"

Sure, if you buy me some *ikra*," Leana said coyly.

"*Ikra, ikra.* Russians don't consider it a meal without their caviar."

"Well, I'm not talking Beluga. The red, salmon caviar is only twenty dollars a pound."

"No problem for us well-paid government bureaucrats. Sure, I'll get you some black bread and caviar. Anyway, it's supposed to be a good aphrodisiac."

"Really? Are you afraid you may be needing one?"

They kissed. Griffin hugged Leana close and then

said slowly, "Lucky me. But I'll get you your caviar anyway."

Carradine placed the high-density polyethylene pouch of freeze-dried shrimp creole on a small rack and dialed in the number six. He then pushed the rack down against a large-gauge needle, which punctured the pack's seals and injected six ounces of water into it. The pack was then slipped into a tiny convection oven where it was heated to 180 degrees, rehydrating the food. He then took a package of Tang and squeezed water into it from a tube. He shook it but it did not reconstitute well in space. Carradine was to eat 3000 calories a day. Snacking was fine; he was encouraged to nibble on such high-tech delicacies as intermediate moisture apricots, or thermostabilized Vienna sausages, but he was not to miss a meal. There was a whole pantry of items to choose from. In the first week of the mission the crew had even had fresh bread and fruit, but by now most foods were irradiated or freeze-dried.

Before Carradine's time, in the earliest days of space flight, all solid food had to be low-residue; the body had to digest almost everything consumed because there was no place to dump the remainder. Those "urine only" days were past, and since the shuttle had started flying, the menu had been upgraded almost to gourmet level. There was turkey tetrazzini, peach ambrosia, and beef almondine. Some foods were in natural form, like Life Savers, cashew nuts, and raisin granola bars. There were even condiments like taco sauce and mustard in little fast-food cellophane packets. Each pouch and retort had been carefully packed in a surgically clean room to reduce the possibility of what Carradine called space trots. The food was even flushed with nitrogen to displace decay-causing oxygen. Happily, water was plentiful. The *Constitution*'s fuel cells produced water as a by-product of combining hydrogen and oxygen to generate electricity. Carradine ate his shrimp with a normal fork and cleaned it afterward with a little ammonia-soaked towelette.

As Carradine finished cleaning up, Stuart Fisher, the mission specialist in charge of Shiva floated down onto the orbiter's middeck. Fisher was in his late thirties, a decade younger than Carradine. He was shorter, darker, and heavier-set than his tall, ascetic commander.

"Afternoon, Colonel," beamed Fisher.

"Good evening, Major," corrected Carradine. "It's already dinnertime. The scientists will be eating in the space station again so you should fix yourself something."

"Oh, yeah," responded Fisher. *"Tempus fugit."*

"What?"

"Time flies. How can we be expected to keep track of time anyway," said Fisher rhetorically. He reached into the pantry for a retort pouch of almonds. "Any beer in the refrigerator?" he added teasingly.

"Unfortunately, there's no refrigerator and there's no beer, unless you've been trailing a six pack since blast off, in which case it should be pretty cool now, unless it's on the sun side. If it is, the cans have already exploded, and the beer has vaporized into the microatmosphere. As for keeping track of the time, you might try your watch."

"Watch? That's right! I knew there was a reason they'd issued me one of those."

Fisher's temperament was completely different from that of the no-nonsense Carradine, but Carradine agreed that space could get pretty dreary; a few laughs couldn't hurt. Fisher opened the pantry, pulled out an irradiated roast beef, and started to prepare it. It was the end of another long, quiet day, and even the taciturn Carradine felt like talking.

"I wonder if the taxpayers know that among the grave dangers of a long-term space mission is the grave danger of going out of your mind from boredom," said Fisher. "Do they realize what's the worst privation up here? There're no damn honeys. I looked everywhere. I looked in the pantry, I looked in the storage locker. Not one honey. I can't believe we've been up here for two months. Jesus, what this is doing to my average."

"Some flights have women astronauts," said Carradine.

"Oh, sure. Grab one of those amazons in the airlock and you'd be lucky to come out breathing. Besides, all they're interested in is science." He smiled at Carradine, "And I get all the science lectures I need from you, Colonel."

Carradine chuckled, "What made you decide to put in for astronaut in the first place?"

"Fame and sex, of course, but not necessarily in that order. Hey, you can't have a better ticket with the girls now than to be a space jockey. But don't worry, that's not the whole story. Seriously, I guess it's, you know, we're on the cutting edge. If there's one thing that in a thousand years the history books are going to say our generation accomplished, it's space exploration. Hell, Colonel, it's like being on the damn *Santa Maria*."

"Nobody in the program thinks he's wasting his time. But why this flight? You could easily have stayed with the one-weekers. You didn't have to volunteer for an endurance mission."

"Oh, that, well, mostly it's Shiva. I just wanted to be

the first one to fire her, and then too I wanted to be in on the first days of the space station, and I guess I just wanted to get the hell out of Dodge for awhile."

"Girl trouble?"

"Yeah, you could call it that. In the old days I didn't have to worry much about getting attached. I grew up in San Diego, but then after college the Navy moved me every year or so. That changed when I joined NASA. I've been stationed back in San Diego for almost five years, and I guess the rolling stone gathered a little moss."

"What's the moss's name?"

"Diane."

"Pretty?"

"Yeah. And smart too. That's a first for me."

"So, what's the problem?"

"Oh, I just don't know if I want to give up the life-style. She's the right woman all right, if I wanted to get married, but I don't know if I ever want to get married. Why should I?

"So, you're up here mulling it over?"

"Yeah, drying out after a real bender, you could say. It's funny. Even though we're in nearly constant communication with Mission Control, and on national television every few days, from a personal point of view we're completely cut off. We might as well be camped out in the Hindu Kush.

"I guess that kind of appeals to me."

"What about you, Colonel? Now that I've spilled my guts out all over my flight suit. You were married once, weren't you?"

"For about three years. It was a long time ago, twenty years or more. We got married when I graduated from Colorado Springs. It was the thing to do at the time. Probably half my class got married."

"You didn't love her?"

"Oh, I loved her all right. That wasn't the problem."

"Then, what happened?"

"Flight test at Edwards."

"God, I've heard that before. She just couldn't take the pressure?"

"We had a real bad string out there one autumn. Several guys in my flight group, guys we knew personally, well, they just . . . augured in. Margo was left to console the widows and wonder if I'd be next. During the worst of it we were going to more funerals than movies. Margo was a nervous wreck. She kept trying to get me to quit. Then one day I was out doing some performance maneuvers in the desert. There were two planes, and a guy named Wolf Thomas was in the other one. It so happened we shared a duplex with the Thomases in the base officers' quarters. The wives were close. Anyway, Wolfy got himself into a corner and flamed out. Ground control saw him and radioed. They asked if he wanted to declare an emergency. Wolfy tried to get the damn thing fired again, but he was losing altitude. I radioed to him to eject, but the last words he said were, 'Negative, negative, I am not declaring an emergency.' Five seconds later he hit the desert floor. Bad news travels fast; Margo was already gone by the time I got home."

"You couldn't get her to come back?"

"Oh sure, in a minute, but there was one condition: give up flying."

"And she held firm?"

"She sure did. Margo was tough. I guess I respected that in her. She said she wasn't just doing it for herself. We'd been thinking about children. She said she owed it to them, even before they were born, to get me to stop. She said she didn't want to explain to them how

79

I'd been, she used to say 'burnt beyond recognition.' She said she knew that if I kept it up, sooner or later I'd end up like Wolfy—I'd crash and burn."

"But you wouldn't give it up?"

"No. So I lost her. She remarried a guy back East and had kids."

"And you never found anybody else? I mean a lot of women can deal with that problem."

"Oh, I know, I know. It's not that I couldn't get over Margo. There've been other women in my life, but I just couldn't make the commitment, because somehow deep down I agreed with what Margo said, that if I kept at it, sooner or later, I'd crash and burn. Hell, if even I was beginning to think that way, I couldn't in good conscience start a family."

"But here it is twenty years later, and you're still at it. You're at the top of the profession."

"Yeah, if I'd known that then, I'd have grown kids now. The problem is you don't know if, and you don't know when. And meanwhile, I haven't changed, I'm still trying to push the envelope, I'm still piloting the experimental aircraft, and now spacecraft. I'm still at it, and I could still crash and burn."

Kolya Voroshilov, Deputy Chief of Station of the Soviet Mission to the United Nations in New York City, walked for almost an hour in Manhattan's Fort Tryon Park. It was a bleak Tuesday morning in late November, and Kolya was quite cold. Still, he was a cautious man and wanted to be absolutely certain he was not being followed. Finally, after a number of switchbacks and retraced steps, Kolya climbed the steep path, crossed the drive and, at the top of the hill, entered the squat fortress museum known as the Cloisters. The Cloisters, high above the Hudson on the northern tip of Manhattan, housed the principal medieval collection of New York City's Metropolitan Museum of Art. It was fitting, thought Kolya, that this little castle, the donation of the great capitalist family, the Rockefellers, should be so useful for his work. He had not however chosen it out of any sense of ironic social justice, but because it was ideal for brief, clandestine meetings. During the weekdays it was almost deserted. Only the most intrepid and informed tourist had the energy to take bus number 4 all the way up through Harlem when, after all, there was so much else to see. Furthermore, since the Cloisters was built to resemble a fortress abbey of the middle ages, there were plenty of ramparts, windswept terraces, and quiet court-yards; you could easily see if anyone was on your trail before you slipped into a thick-walled chapel for a fur-tive meeting. Then too, if you did by chance run into a UN colleague or FBI counterintelligence officer, what could be less suspicious than your interest in one of the great medieval collections of the world—outside Russia of course.

Kolya paid for his little metal MMA button—the color was pale blue today—then fastened it to his lapel. He climbed the steps of the circular, stone entrance, taking his time to absorb the architecture. He went straight, through the arch of the Romanesque Hall, and then began a slow, clockwise circuit of the carved capitals and art treasures. He was absolutely silent as he did this, lis-tening attentively over the piped-in music of medieval horns and lutes for the click of shoes rising on the stairs from the ticket booth to the entrance hall. He passed the door leading to the bright Cuxa Cloister, and spent a few minutes studying the statute of Clovis, the first

Christian French king. Looking through a twelfth-century portal into the Saint Guilhem Cloister, Kolya noticed a young woman sitting at the far side of that sky-lit room, reading a thin, green Michelin guide. She looked up at him without expression. Kolya continued his transit to the next portal and went through, entering the Fuentiduena Chapel. Here he spent less time, barely glancing at the portrayal of Christ in the Romanesque style, the Tuscan holy-water font, or the Carrara marble doorway. He paused just long enough to ascertain that no one was in the immediate vicinity of this group of rooms, and then strolled nonchalantly into the Saint Guilhem Cloister.

Kolya walked to the northwest corner of this cloister, near where the young woman was sitting with her Michelin guide, and studied the skylight overhead. There were only three doors to this room: one from the Romanesque Room, from which he had first seen the girl, and two from the Fuentiduena Chapel, from which he had just come. There were also two windows onto the cold, overlook terrace. No other visitors were visible; they were quite alone.

Kolya said in English, "The original abbey is near Montpellier, France, isn't it?"

The young woman responded coolly, "Benedictine, founded 804."

Kolya smiled faintly and begán slowly in Russian, "Were there any troubles, Leana."

Leana did not smile, but said only, "No troubles, Comrade Voroshilov. If there were, I wouldn't have come."

"Of course, Leana, of course. It's just that . . . it must be hard, cut off from your people . . . carrying on an affair for so long with someone you care nothing about."

Leana resented Kolya's avuncular tone, knowing full well that his motivation was not at all well-meaning. She knew by reputation, confirmed by observation, that Kolya was a vicious opportunist and not to be trusted. "I never expected the life of a spy to be easy."

"No," said Kolya. "I suppose not." After a pause he continued. "I asked you to meet me because there is a message for you from Moscow. Our friends on Dzerzhinsky Square wish me to say they are very pleased with your work. Your socialist motherland thanks you."

"To what do I owe this honor?" said Leana, not fully disguising the suspicion in her voice.

"They believe that your report for October on the NSA translator Charles Griffin's observations as to the postponement of Arctic projects is of interest. In particular, they are interested to know if he again intercepts the word *bedá* used as a code word or for any reason has further suspicions about the time he heard it before."

"Are we privileged to know more precisely about our government's concern, or perhaps what special meaning *bedá* has?"

"No," said Kolya with a sigh, "we are not. But I can say this: the KGB is very concerned. They insisted that I meet with you, even though you are under deep cover, and there is always some risk in a meeting. I believe that whatever this Arctic slowdown or *bedá* business is, knowing how much the Americans know is of great importance. In fact, if you should at any time feel that your personal charm is insufficient to worm out of Charles Griffin everything he may know about these matters, you should know I am authorized to use less pleasant means."

Leana glared at him. "You mean you would kidnap an employee of the NSA. The Americans would know immediately that the Soviet Union was behind it."

"The KGB is mindful of the risk, Leana, but sometimes even extreme risk is justified. I am telling you that
this is one of those times. Remember, your naive, young
paramour is a rather insignificant junior employee of a
very large federal agency. They would investigate, find
nothing, and then forget all about him."

"So you would have to kill him," said Leana slowly.

"It wouldn't make much sense to have him tell on us,
would it?" responded Voroshilov coolly. He paused, again
listening for footsteps. "Leana, I have told you before.
You are not to get involved with this American. He is a
source, a tool, a leaking faucet of vital information,
nothing more. I know it is hard because you have been
with him for so long. Normally these 'honey traps' are
short: a night, a lost weekend, a business trip to Moscow,
that kind of thing. Given the length of your relationship, it is perhaps inevitable that you become a little
attached. You have been on this case a long time, too
long perhaps, but clearly I cannot take you off it now.
We are under orders from Moscow to pursue this source
of intelligence. You must see Charles Griffin as often as
possible and, up to the limits of his suspicion, learn
everything you can. So long as he continues to confide
in you, we need do nothing further, but if you think that
he is holding back, tell me and I will handle things from
that point on. Is that clear, Leana?"

Leana glared silently for a moment, and then said,
"Yes, Comrade Voroshilov, perfectly clear."

"In the meantime, do nothing suspicious. No weapons or signals. If you need to talk to me, call the emergency number and ask for John, then when Ivan comes
on the phone, ask if there is a sale on vacuum cleaners.
The answerback is, 'Toasters, only toasters.' I will let you
know where to meet me. And Leana, remember: the

KGB will look out for your best interests."

"I will remember," said Leana, unconvinced.

"Good. Now give me ten minutes." Voroshilov walked out of the Saint Guilhem Cloister and back into the Romanesque Hall. Seeing nothing suspicious, he turned left and headed toward the door.

Leana stared down at her Michelin guide and slowly reviewed the conversation. She was troubled by Moscow's sudden interest in Charles Griffin. She had surprised herself at how protective she was of Griffin when Kolya had threatened him. Perhaps Kolya was right; she was becoming involved. Leana knew though that it was more than just Griffin. She had grown fond of her whole new life. When Leana had been recruited in Moscow to work for the KGB she had known nothing about the United States beyond the trite denunciations in *Pravda*. Becoming an agent in New York had seemed patriotic, even glamorous. Now, however, Moscow was a fading memory. The Americans she knew at Columbia were gullible, naive, even foolish, but they had been good to her. The very lack of suspicion that permitted her to operate so effectively was in its own way disarming. Somehow, in the delis, bars, and bookstores of the Upper West Side her ideological purity had simply melted away. It wasn't that she had forgotten her motherland or suddenly felt remorse; she just didn't want to change the status quo. She didn't want to lose her freedom, or give up the excitement of New York for the drab tediousness of Moscow. She was happy. As a result she had grown wary of her KGB superiors. Voroshilov, in particular, reminded her of a cold vulture circling and waiting to tear her to bits at the first sign of weakness. He was a dark shadow over the new life she had made.

That was why Leana was troubled by *bedá*. What could

this code, the Russian word for "calamity," possibly mean? Kolya had said that Griffin was just an insignificant junior employee to the NSA. Well, Leana supposed that also she was rather junior and insignificant to the KGB. It occurred to her that if anything happened to Griffin, the suspicion of the American authorities would immediately fall on her. She would probably be questioned, arrested. Had the KGB planned for this problem, or did they care? All in all, Leana feared the effect of major discoveries on minor agents. She was worried about Griffin and she was worried about herself.

DECEMBER

Captain Mikhail Murov bent over a large, square table covered by a giant map of the city of Leningrad. The map was almost ten feet on each side, so even a tall, thin man like Murov had to lean out over the table with his pointer to show items toward the middle. The map was centered on Leningrad's Palace Square and went to the city's outskirts. Not only every street and canal, but even every building and outside door were clearly marked. As he talked, Captain Murov walked around the table, here pointing out something in the northern, island districts of the city, there mentioning a railhead or truck depot in the south. He spoke with the assurance for detail that only a native Leningrader could have. One man walked with him, asking an occasional question, muttering periodically in agreement; that man was Admiral Evgenie Alexandrovich Komkov.

"So Admiral, this is our physical city. Now I will start with the overlays to show you the total plan for evacua-

tion to the vicinities of the surrounding towns of Gatch-
ina, Tosno, and Volkhov. These towns are all in the
required range of at least eighteen miles from the Gulf
of Finland and no more than sixty miles from Leningrad. They all have infrastructures, at the present time,
for supporting between fifty and one hundred thousand residents. Hardly enough to feed and shelter the
one million Leningrad refugees that each will have to
hold, but at least it gives us a base to work with. I shall
now, with your permission, Admiral, begin the overlays
to show the procedure and timetable for evacuating the
city."

"Please proceed," said Komkov.

The captain took from a large portmanteau a series
of clear plastic sheets, each about a yard square. These
were all numbered to be placed on a certain section of
the larger map. Each of the overlays had multicolored
arrows and numbers. Once in place, the overlay showed
where the inhabitants of each building in the city were
to go to be transported away from Leningrad. Total
population figures were indicated, the number and type
of transport available, and approximately how long it
would take to evacuate 50, 90, and 100 percent of the
inhabitants of each section. After almost two hours of
studying each of the many overlays, Komkov asked, "I
notice that your estimates for getting from 90 percent
to 100 percent evacuation are as long as getting from
plan initiation to 90 percent. Why does it take so long to
get the stragglers?"

"Evgenie Alexandrovich, a total evacuation this large
has never been attempted before, but it is our assump-
tion, that despite our warnings and threats, there will be
some people, the older ones perhaps, who will just not
be willing to leave the city. This is, after all, Leningrad."

"So you mean you have factored into your estimate that the last 10 percent you will have to take against their will?"

"Yes, Admiral, a house-to-house search. Frightened babushkas, sobbing poets, the whole mess."

A wry smile passed Komkov's lips. "How much easier if I'd asked you to prepare for the evacuation of Moscow."

"Oh, yes," retorted the younger Leningrader. "I'd only have to shout, 'You're free to go,' and we'd be trampled in the stampede." The two men laughed out loud.

Komkov was pleased with Captain Murov's work. It was only sensible to have a Leningrader prepare the plan; the admiral needed someone thoroughly familiar with the city, its every pothole and cul-de-sac. In addition, he had chosen a rather junior officer. This too was by design and represented an old command technique: when you needed to have someone carry out a scheme generally considered preposterous, your senior staff officers were hopeless. They would find a million undetectable ways to derail your plan, all the while telling you what a thorough job they were doing. A young, ambitious officer, by contrast, would work night and day for the chance to impress a commander several levels above him. Komkov had given Captain Murov full power to carry out this assignment. He had squashed any attempt to undermine Murov's authority, and in the end, the admiral had his detailed plan, just as the general secretary had demanded. As ordered, Admiral Komkov had never divulged that he himself was not the initial author of the entire evacuation concept.

"How is construction at the resettlement camps proceeding?" asked Komkov.

"On schedule. Today, we could perhaps house a total of one million individuals, but under the most cramped, barracks-like conditions. Construction is at a crawl now because of the frozen ground and drifting snow. If the evacuation took place in the spring, we would have tent space for another million, but without heat and with primitive sanitation. We expect that another million will prefer to stay with friends or relatives in inland cities. We will encourage this and make transportation available. As you instructed, I have told everyone that the facilities are for new infantry recruits. When I later gave orders for them to put in women's toilets and movable partitions for families, I'm sure all my superior officers thought I was mad or incompetent or both, but in any case they did as I said."

"Do you have any thoughts on how the plan would work in practice?"

"The only experience we have is with our civil defense drills, where, in practices for limited groups like a school or a factory, we've had acceptable performance. But there are important differences. We aren't sending people out of the city in those drills, simply into the subway tunnels. It's not a big inconvenience for the participants. Also, because of the blockade during the Great Patriotic War, the older people are all convinced of the necessity for bomb shelters and give us their full support. They scold the children who treat the drills without sufficient seriousness. A *total* evacuation by train and truck would be a vastly different undertaking. However, if the flooding were obvious to the people, they would of course be glad to flee to high ground. A practice drill on the other hand, without a rain cloud in sight, would be very hard to enforce."

"Yes, of course, the question of the people's will."

Komkov studied the overlays to the east of the city. "Tell me, Captain, the site at Volkhov, how far is it from the shore of Lake Ladoga?"

Murov put a chart on the table and measured off a scale with his pointer. "About twelve miles, sir. Is this a problem?"

"I was just thinking that it is the biggest lake in Europe, 125 miles long and 80 wide. If there were going to be flooding . . ." Komkov's voice trailed off.

"Our historical record shows nothing that would affect more than a mile from the coastline. The resettlement camp is on high ground well above the Volkhov River itself."

"Very well. Forgive me Captain if my concern seems extreme. I have my reasons." They were interrupted by a call from the admiral's receptionist. Returning, the admiral said, "There is a phone call I must take, can we resume tomorrow after lunch? That will give me a chance to get through these briefing books you've prepared."

"Of course, Admiral."

As Murov neared the door, Komkov said, "By the way Captain, this is an excellent piece of work."

"Thank you, Admiral." Murov beamed and departed. Admiral Komkov retired to his office and asked that the call be put through. His desk phone rang.

"Hello, Komkov here, is that you Joseph?"

"Admiral, please forgive a call from this old relic. I know you have so many demands on your time."

"Joseph, please. You are embarrassing me. I always have time for you, you know that. Are you well?"

"Can't complain, can't complain, at least not too loudly—it's not permitted." Joseph laughed.

"How are things with your trading company, Len—Finn Torg?"

"Not bad. I make the round-trip to Helsinki two or three times a week. Mostly these days it's eggs for the city. Oh, Evgenie Alexandrovich, you should see those Finnish girls. The styles they wear."

"Please Joseph, it's Zhenya to you, I'm embarrassed when you use my formal title."

"OK, OK, but you're a lot bigger pine cone today than when we first met."

"Well, a better-fed pine cone at least," laughed Komkov, reflecting for just a moment on that first meeting on the ice of Lake Ladoga over forty years before.

Zhenya was six on that cold morning in February 1942, when he was told he would be taken out of Leningrad with some of the other orphans over the "Road of Life," the only land route out of Leningrad during the 900-day Nazi blockade of the city. The Road of Life began in the city and went thirty-five miles by rail or road to the shores of the giant Lake Ladoga, to the northeast of Leningrad. It was then a thirty-mile run across the frozen lake to the eastern shore at Novaya Ladoga, safely behind Red Army lines.

Military Automobile Highway No. 101, as the Lake Ladoga ice road was officially known, was treacherous. The ice was thin in places, and a truck with a ton of freight needed a full eight inches. In one of the worst weeks, forty trucks went through the ice to a watery repose 100 feet below, their cabs instantly converted to chill sepulchers for their unfortunate drivers. The winter was one of record-breaking cold, sometimes forty below zero, and on the ice there was no place to hide from the wind, no place to build a fire. As if nature were not cruel enough, there was the Luftwaffe. The Germans knew that Leningrad was starving. Russian soldiers too weak to lift their guns were no threat to the

Wehrmacht. It occurred to the German General Staff that perhaps Leningrad could be taken without a fight. If this supply route could be closed, the city would surely starve. The road was therefore bombed and strafed incessantly. Even at night the dark trucks against the moonlit ice were easy targets. The "Road of Life" was for many the "Road of Death."

Little Zhenya had been loaded into a small one-and-a-half ton GAZ-AA Red Army truck. The older, bigger boys had taken the warmer seats near the truck's cab, and poor Zhenya had to sit at the very end of the bench next to the flapping canvas tarp. They were waiting for dark, but did not have to wait long; in early February Leningrad is dark by three in the afternoon. Zhenya's truck pulled out of the orphanage, followed by a second truck full of starving children. As Zhenya was in the very back, he could see the driver in the cab of the following truck. The driver saw Zhenya looking, and smiled and waved at the sad little boy. This was about the first smile Zhenya had seen since the blockade began. Somehow he managed to move his cadaverous face to smile and weakly waved back. The driver of the second truck was Joseph, at that time a young private in a Leningrad transport regiment.

It took a full five hours of traffic-swollen, shell-pocked roads to reach the shore of Lake Ladoga and pull out onto the ice. Leaving the protection of the forest, the frigid wind of the Arctic came at once upon them and tore at the canvas canopy of the little truck. Next to the flapping tarp, Zhenya had the most exposed seat of all. The cold tore at his heart, but Zhenya consoled himself with the thought of the hot meal that awaited him when the truck reached Novaya Ladoga on the other side of the lake. There was no conversation. The children were too hungry and too frightened to do anything but shiver. The two trucks carrying the orphans were attached to a loose convoy and then began the slow creep across the frozen lake. On both sides the road was strewn with the carcasses of wrecked cars and trucks. At every kilometer there was a traffic station and an antiaircraft battery, surrounded by a half-igloo of icy fortifications. The moon was bright, the night too clear. The drivers were anxious.

At kilometer number nine, Zhenya heard the growing whine of airplanes above the truck engines and felt his truck begin to pick up speed. They started to swerve and zigzag. The following truck dropped back and also began evasive patterns. In the distance Zhenya heard the repeating thump of an antiaircraft gun. Then with a scream the Nazi dive bombers were upon them. The explosion of nearby bombs was deafening. Coming in low from the rear, a squadron of German planes swooped over them. To the side of the truck a bomb blew a hole in the road, tearing the tarpaulin with razors of flying ice. They raced on as the dive bombers banked in the distant sky, circling for another pass. The high-pitched buzz grew fainter and then louder again.

The bomber squadron had circled behind the convoy and was coming in again, machine guns blazing. Through the torn canvas covering, Zhenya could see bursts of staccato lightning from the tiny planes. At a distance, they looked like fireflies hanging above them in the winter air. As the planes again roared over the convoy, the driver of Zhenya's truck tried to dodge the bullets and bombs. The ice road made quick movement impossible, and at every twist and turn the wheels lost traction and the truck lost precious momentum. The clear sky made the lumbering trucks easy targets. A German

plane dove immediately above them, its wing bombs
tumbling forward. Released a second too late, one bomb
just missed the truck. The bomb exploded directly before
them, rending a swimming pool-sized hole in the ice.
The truck driver was lacerated by shrapnel and bits of
shattering windshield. He screamed and tried to brake
the speeding truck, but it was too late. The wheels locked
and the truck slid sideways over the edge, disappearing
into the inky water.

For a few seconds, all was silence. Joseph, in the truck
behind, skidded to a stop and ran to the hole. At first,
air bubbles alone broke the surface, then up popped a
tiny, swaddled figure, struggling for air. Joseph spun
around, searching for something to extend to the small
child. On the ice there was nothing. The little boy struggled, splashing the freezing water to stay up, but his boots
and heavy clothing were too much for his emaciated body
to support. He disappeared under the surface. Joseph
cursed, threw off his greatcoat, unsheathed his combat
knife, and dove into the frigid darkness. The icicles of
death were forming on Zhenya's weakened heart when
he felt a strong hand snag him and yank him once more
to the water's surface. Joseph screamed as the freezing
water penetrated his clothing. He pulled like a bear for
the side and swam the few yards with Zhenya in one
hand, the knife in the other. Then, with one hand, Joseph
flung Zhenya over the edge onto the ice, where he slid
like an otter. The counterforce pushed Joseph under
the water, but he broke the surface again with a piercing
cry. Reaching the edge, he kicked as hard as he could,
throwing his upper torso out of the water. He slammed
the knife into the ice to stop from slipping back into the
black hole. He kicked the water, but its near freezing
temperature sapped his strength. The ferocity of his

struggle was ebbing. Little Zhenya skittered back to him, grabbed Joseph's collar, and pulled like a grown man. Joseph roared and kicked harder, got a knee on the slippery edge, and suddenly they were both, strong soldier and starving child, rolling over the ice. By now the air attack had broken off and other trucks were pulling up; men were racing to their aid. Zhenya could feel his soaked clothing begin instantly to freeze in the thirty-below darkness. Joseph and Zhenya were bundled into the warm cab of a larger truck. Rough, friendly hands pulled off their clothing, wrapping their naked bodies together in army blankets and Joseph's dry greatcoat. Zhenya was handed a mug of hot water from a thermos. Huddled knees-up on Joseph's lap under the blankets, Zhenya's shivering eventually stopped. He suddenly realized that the other orphans had not gotten clear of the sinking truck. His seat in the back by the torn tarp, his father's swimming lessons, and perhaps his will to live had made him the sole survivor. He wanted to cry, but instead fell asleep in Joseph's arms.

Joseph's transportation regiment was stationed at Novaya Ladoga, the eastern terminus of the Road of Life. As the brutal winter wore on, Zhenya became their mascot. There were a thousand little errands that Zhenya could run, freeing the men for more important work. Until the ice became too thin for the trucks, there were convoys out on the lake every night. Between January and April 1942, over a half a million Leningraders were evacuated on the Road of Life. On April 24 the last food supplies, 65 tons of onions, were unloaded in Leningrad. The Road had made survival possible for some, but the blockade of Leningrad would remain the greatest single catastrophe ever to befall a city. A million and a half of her citizens did not live through that one terrible winter.

When the Road closed it was time for Joseph's regiment to move on. There was a war to fight and they were needed at the front. Zhenya was sent to the safety of the Urals, where he would be a ward of the Soviet navy. Though three thousand miles and a war separated them, Zhenya and Joseph never lost touch. Zhenya wrote Joseph regularly from the Urals orphanage and then from cadet camp when the war was over. Joseph became a second father to Zhenya, and for Joseph, Zhenya was the child he and his wife failed to have. When Ensign Komkov graduated from the naval academy, the only one he knew to invite was Joseph. The camaraderie and trust born of that freezing night on Lake Ladoga was to last.

"Zhenya, we have a little difficulty and I need your advice," said Joseph.

Zhenya's thoughts returned to the present. "My advice is to tell me what I can do to help," he responded. The problem was that Joseph's nephew, a top student with excellent marks on his entrance exams, had been denied a place at Leningrad State University. Joseph did not have to explain further to Komkov. Joseph and his nephew, like other Leningraders, had Soviet internal passports. In these passports was a place for nationality; but even though Joseph and his nephew were Leningrad-born, their passports did not say "Russian"; instead they said "Jewish." This distinction was not of their choosing, but was forced upon them.

"Tell me Joseph, have any of your relatives petitioned to emigrate?"

"You know I have no children, and since my wife

died I have lost contact with her relations. Perhaps a distant second cousin, I don't know, but no one in the immediate family, my sister and her children. Since Brezhnev's death it has become very difficult to have an emigration petition approved, so most people don't even apply for them."

Zhenya reflected for a moment and then said, "Maybe I can try something. Can you get me your nephew's exact scores on the entrance exams, his grades in school, everything you have. Pull it all together in a way that even I can understand it, and get it over to me right away."

"Oh course, Zhenya, it's as good as done. You know I appreciate this. I wouldn't ask if it were me, but he's such a good boy."

"Don't thank me until we see what I can do. These are delicate matters. I'm not as big a pine cone as you think." They rang off and Komkov called his commandant of personnel to see what he could find out about the rector of Leningrad State University.

By the next morning Admiral Komkov had Joseph's nephew's grades, and a file on the rector. He was pleased to see that the rector had numerous children, and one of the younger ones was just beginning his required military service. Komkov ordered his call, waited for his secretary to get the rector on the line, and then kept the man hanging. Finally, Komkov picked up the phone.

"Rector Andrei Andreiovich Minakov, this is Admiral Evgenie Alexandrovich Komkov, Admiral of the Baltic Fleet."

"Well, yes Admiral, of course I know who you are.

This is an honor, indeed. To what do I owe the pleasure?"

The two men discussed the situation for some time. Komkov carefully described the young man's grades and test results. The rector admitted that under normal circumstances they would be more than adequate, but the boy's "background" made things rather difficult.

"It's the policy, Admiral, the policy of the Soviet Ministry of Higher Education. There's really nothing I can do. I appreciate that he's bright, the devil take me, all of those people are bright. But if I let him in, I'll be in trouble with the ministry. Last year my colleague the rector of Moscow State University was able to report that not one Jew would be enrolled in that year's class at Moscow State. You should have seen how pleased the minister was. Admiral, I do want to help, but this is absolutely beyond my control. If there is anything else I can do for you, just name it."

"Well, Rector Minakov, I suppose that what you tell the minister is your business. I assume you control your records and what information goes to Moscow. Naturally, I would not presume to tell you how to run a university. I myself know nothing about running a university, but I do know something about running a navy. And I always say that the right man in the right place is the key to it. Wouldn't you agree, Rector?"

The rector knew he was being led like a lamb to slaughter. He did not want to hear what the admiral had to say, but had no alternative. The admiral of the Baltic Fleet was, on the iconostasis of Soviet power, many tiers closer to the altar than a mere academic like himself. The rector could not afford to offend him. He said only, "Yes, yes, of course, Admiral."

"Why, just today I was looking at a file on a young man who will be coming to us soon. What was his name? Oh yes, Pavel Andreiovich Minakov. Know him, Rector?"

There was a pause, then with a sigh of resignation, the rector said, "My son, Admiral."

"Ah, yes, your first name is Andrei. Really I should have guessed. Now naturally I have already asked that as soon as young Pavel is inducted, he will come to the Red Fleet. As a Leningrader, I'm sure that that is what you intended. The only question then is his assignment. I have two openings in mind. One here in Leningrad. A desk job, no weekend work. A cushy berth really, good for making contacts. It's right in the Admiralty; he could practically wave across the Neva at you over there on University Embankment. The other spot is a bit further away. Have you ever heard of the Svalbard Archipelago, Rector?"

"Yes, Admiral," moaned the rector.

"It makes Leningrad look equatorial by comparison, way up there on the 78th parallel. The Soviet Union has a little coal mining operation. Two thousand miners, mostly drunkards and ex-convicts. Since the Norwegians have formal sovereignty, we station a few men there to keep the miners out of trouble. You know, break up knife fights and that sort of thing. He'd come home once a year for two weeks' leave, of course. We could let your boy know that you'd had a hand in his assignment."

After a lengthy and profound silence on the other end of the phone, the rector began to speak faintly. "There is a special program of admission for our very brightest students. It is by invitation and provides intensive instruction that actually shortens the time to a candidate's degree. Since the program is exclusive and separate, I might not even learn the details of a student's ethnic background."

"Of course. No one could expect you to keep track of so many people," said Komkov exuberantly. "I knew you were a resourceful man, Rector. That sounds perfect. And, you know, come to think of it, I might have another candidate for that post up in Svalbard. When young Pavel comes aboard, call me up and the three of us will get together. The navy is an excellent career, but it helps to have someone looking out for you."

"Thank you, Admiral. What you say is true, and I look forward to having Pavel meet such a skilled diplomat-soldier. In the meantime, I will call your young protégé and make all the arrangements. He will start his program immediately."

The rector rang off, and Komkov passed the news on to Joseph, who was elated. "It's really so embarrassing," the old man said. "I want to return the favor, but with your position, there's not much a nobody like me can do."

"Joseph, my violin is on my shoulder. What will it be, a melancholy gypsy ballad, with plenty of sobbing?" Komkov laughed and continued, "I must remind you that you've already done plenty, and who knows, maybe in the future you'll be able to help me again."

When they hung up, Komkov felt pleased that he'd been able to do something for his old friend. He reflected, though, that if the Politburo was correct, and Leningrad was in peril of inundation, there might not be any Leningrad State University left for Joseph's nephew to attend. This thought troubled Komkov. As he mulled it over in his mind, he decided to have another look at the "white" cable he had received from the Politburo in October, the only document he had that indicated this whole evacuation plan was prepared pursuant to direct order. He had hidden the cable in the one place he knew it would never be discovered, in one of his large steel file cabinets full of ten-year-old long-range planning studies he should have thrown out as soon as they were written. He had not looked at the cable since he had hidden it. Knowing it was safe might give him some sense of security, at least for his reputation. In the middle drawer of the five-drawer file he found a binder called Strategic Plan Linkage, dash 2 Forecast. He pulled out the looseleaf and flipped to the back. When he reached the hiding place he froze. "*Sukin syn,*" he said under his breath. "Son of a bitch. I should have known." The cable's charred remains were crumbled between the pages of the binder. It had completely oxidized, burnt up from contact with the air as surely as if it had been lit with a match. He couldn't read any of it. He couldn't even tell the scorched fragment had once been a cable. Komkov sat down heavily. Finally he said, "Maybe they're too clever for you, old man." He stared wide-eyed out the window at the Neva for quite some time, then narrowed his gaze and said, "No, they're not." Komkov rose and replaced the old binder. He closed the file cabinet and returned to his desk, then pulled out another of Captain Murov's thick briefing books and continued his review of the plan to evacuate the city.

The Metroliner from D.C. was late again, and Charles Griffin had to battle the Christmas crowds at Penn Station to get the Broadway local. He considered going upstairs and hailing a Checker, the strong lumbering cabs that were disappearing like dinosaurs from the New York scene. But if he did he knew he'd have to deal with the young black boys who made a business of hailing cabs in front of the station and then demanding a tip, as if they'd performed some indispensable service. Anyway, ninety cents for the IRT was still the best deal in New York.

He was ravenous as he squeezed out of the train at the 79th Street stop and walked to 80th and Amsterdam. It was cold enough to force the Puerto Rican families who spent their evenings on the stoops near La Minita grocery to retreat to warmer locales. Griffin continued east and then climbed the gray stairs of the 1890s townhouse at 120 West 80th, anticipating a crackling fire and ice cold Zybrowka vodka. The doorbell buzzed, the outside door popped open, and in a moment Leana was in his arms.

The apartment had been the back parlor of a grand turn-of-the-century residence for a family of property. Now the five floors were divided into ten apartments with tiny kitchens and bathrooms stuck in like a belch after a banquet. On the one hand, Leana's ceiling was fourteen feet high and the fireplace was delicately carved; on the other, her toilet leaked, and the cockroaches were barely at bay. It was just the balance of elegance and decay that Griffin loved about New York. On the table was what the Russians called *zakuski,* the smorgasbord of cold cuts, pickles, smoked fish, cheese, and dark bread, that constituted the principal course of a Russian banquet. As expected, there was a silver-plated bucket with an ice-bedecked half-liter of 80 proof Polish vodka. Gooey, red berries of salmon caviar completed the ensemble.

"Somebody's been shopping," said Griffin after their long embrace.

"Nothing but the best for refugees from the provinces," Leana responded.

She hung up his puffy down jacket and poured them

both a shot of vodka. He took a slice of the bread, gave a toast to New York, and then, Russian-style, they drank the vodka at a gulp and inhaled through the rich, porous pumpernickel. A few of these warmed Griffin right up, and in minutes he had forgotten his tiring journey. They sat down to Leana's *zakuski,* the vodka and dark bread passed frequently back and forth. Griffin became quite talkative after a few drinks and he started to reflect on their visit to the planetarium the month before.

"From Fort Meade you can see it, not very well of course. It's just a little patch of glow low on the horizon. Once you get to the outskirts of Washington, it gets lost in the city lights. I've been reading all sorts of things about its history. The really fascinating part, is the effect it's had on people as a kind of omen. For example, they say that Halley's comet foretold the revolt of the Jews against Rome and the burning of the temple of Jerusalem. Then the Nuremburg Chronicles tell about the comet's appearance in 684, and say they had three months of rain, all the grain and livestock died, and there was a plague. Simply spectacular, but then came the biggest one of all. In 1066, Harold was King of England. Right before William the Conqueror invaded, Halley's comet appeared. Harold's men took it as a bad omen, and at the Battle of Hastings, William won and Harold was killed. There's a famous tapestry at Bayeux in France showing the comet, with Harold's men looking up at it. It says, 'They are in awe of the star.' "

"It sounds like you are in awe of the star," said Leana, offering him a section of matjes herring.

"And then there was the 'Eadwine Psalter,' made after the appearance of Halley's comet in 1145. It has a picture of the comet, which it calls a 'hairy star,' and then the monk who copied the psalter says that, comets appear rarely 'and then as a portent.' Even Shakespeare got into this messenger-of-calamity thing when he wrote somewhere, 'when beggars die there are no comets seen; the heavens themselves blaze forth the death of princes.' "

"Bravo," said Leana, "you have been studying."

"But here's the best one," Griffin continued. "In 1456 the Turks were laying seige to Belgrade when Halley's appeared, so the Pope, Calixtus III, decided it was an agent of the devil and excommunicated the comet! In fact, our ancestors were so upset about comets, that it even shows up in our language. The prefix *dis-* denotes something negative or bad, like ability and disability. Well, our word *star* derives from the Latin *astrum*. You see its forms and derivations in all sorts of English words, like *astro* in *astrology*, or *aster* in *asteroid*. Since a comet was an evil star, you just put the negative prefix *dis* in front of *aster* and get *disaster*. It's an obsolete usage, but *disaster* literally means 'the evil influence of a heavenly body.' You still hear the anglicized version of *disaster* in the old-fashioned phrase 'ill-starred.' "

"So a comet is a disaster, an evil star."

"That's sure how people used to feel," said Griffin, laying a slice of smoked trout on some rye bread.

"There's no similar linguistic connection in Russian," Leana continued. "I suppose the most common translation of the English word *disaster* would be *bedá*."

As Leana said this, they both stopped eating and stared at each other. They both wondered, silently but simultaneously, if the code word Griffin had once intercepted, and which Leana knew to be significant, could somehow be tied to this curious astrological etymology and hence to Halley's comet itself. Leana immediately wished she had not made this connection. Then she reflected that if it was linked, it was accomplishing the opposite of what code words were intended to accomplish. A code word was designed to disguise a plan by substituting a meaningless word for a significant one. If however there was a connection between the plan code-named *bedá* and disaster, evil star and Halley's comet, then the code word was not disguising the plan, but actually providing a clue to it. This, thought Leana, was impossible. Still, for some reason, she wished she had not made the observation. She waited for Griffin to speak.

"You don't think it could have anything to do with that conversation in Archangel?" said Griffin. "You remember. I told you about a guy I intercepted who used *bedá* like a code word?"

"But really Charles, are code words supposed to be like riddles and provide little hints about what people are planning?" she said, a little too defensively.

"No, I suppose not," Griffin said. "I guess that would be pretty foolish."

Leana poured Griffin another vodka and got up to change the record. Charles finished his musings and drank it, forgetting for the moment about evil stars. When she sat back down Leana changed the subject, and brought Griffin up to date on all of his former colleagues at Columbia. She painted their futures in the grayest of colors: little hope for jobs, less for tenure. She reinforced for Griffin that he had done the right thing to leave academia when he had. "You jumped just in time," she told him. "The poor rats are going down with the ship." After a while, when the entire half liter of vodka was upended in the ice bucket, Leana gingerly returned to the subject of the Arctic slowdown, taking care, however, not to mention the word *bedá*.

"Oh yeah," said Griffin, slightly slurring his words. "I wanted to tell you about that. It's really funny. There's nothing going on in the Arctic coastal cities themselves, but I'm getting all sorts of tidbits about activity going on behind them, anywhere from thirty to sixty miles inland. South of Murmansk, there seems to be some kind of 'tent city' going up in the town of Olenegorsk. It seems that it's supposed to accommodate tens of thousands of people and have hospitals and power plants. Every construction worker on the Kola Peninsula has been pressed into service, but progress is painfully slow. As you know, it's dark twenty-two hours a day there at this time of year. The Russians I hear talking about it are confused as hell about why they're building it. They say they've been told it's to house an army division, but they themselves are skeptical. It's the same thing on the White Sea at Archangel. In the middle of the Arctic winter, they've started to build a jet runway at Kholmogorie, almost fifty miles from the city. What, I wonder, is wrong with their new one on Dvina Bay?"

"Were you able to convince your boss that this is important?"

"Oh, I think that at last they're concerned. You see, scuttlebutt is that it's not just the Arctic Ocean seaports, but that there's all sorts of weird construction starting inland along the Pacific and around Leningrad. It's almost like some crazy science fiction thriller, where the Politburo thinks the polar ice cap is going to melt, or something crazy, and wants to be prepared. I'm considering reminding my supervisor about the disappearance of that harbor commissioner. And, maybe while I'm at it, I should get the word *bedá* put on the list of words the computers watch for. If my supervisor won't listen, I might just go to Big Stan O'Dwyer himself."

Leana did not respond. They both sat pensively for a time, lost in thought. Finally, Leana got up to put away the uneaten food, and Griffin, realizing how tired he was, retired to Leana's small bedroom. In a few minutes she joined him and they made love. Griffin sensed that Leana was distracted, upset somehow. He wanted to say something, but knew from experience that Leana would insist that nothing was the matter. She never talked about her feelings. This was mysterious to Griffin, who thought people should open up to each other. Griffin was always talking about his feelings and emotions, sometimes to near strangers. Still, he told himself, Leana's upbringing was very different, and educated people shouldn't make cross-cultural judgments. As he fell asleep, Griffin thought to himself how lucky he was to have such a beautiful girl love him.

JANUARY

As Griffin ambled out of Le Zinc carrying his overcoat, he was pleased to see a large Checker cab a short stroll down the curb. He was feeling the effects of the house wine and was glad that in New York, even more so than in D.C., you could drink all you wanted and never had to worry about driving home.

The night was crisp but not cold for January. It was past one o'clock and he had had a great evening. The girls at the long, metal-topped bar that gave the restaurant its name were all pretty enough to be models. This being New York City, they probably were all models. Just sitting there over his pâté de maison was like watching a fashion parade of New York's beautiful people. He couldn't believe he hadn't gone out more when he lived here. The dinner had been excellent as usual. His steak with mustard sauce was done in the French style, still almost blue. Leana had a special salad of lettuce and chicken livers. It never ceased to amaze him that, given

109

the opportunity, an Eastern European almost invariably ordered herring or internal organs.

They had spoken about their work, and as always, he had done most of the talking. Leana had seemed exceedingly curious whether he had heard anything further about *bedá* and had returned to the subject several times. He had in fact encountered the term, and although no one usage had been significant, Griffin was sure by now that it had some encrypted meaning. It was coming up too frequently not to. But he didn't want to go to O'Dwyer with just some unconnected examples; he wanted to decode *bedá* and present them with the solution. That would show them he was more than just a translator. In describing the seemingly unrelated intercepts to Leana, he thought that he could sense a frightening pattern, but he was too tired and tipsy to think it through right then. He had been so caught up in his relationship with Leana—they saw each other every weekend now—that he never had the time to do the research that might put the pieces together. He made a mental note to himself that it was really high time he put the word on the watch list—he probably should have done so long ago. However, he didn't torture himself over it; Leana looked ravishing, and the main thing on Griffin's mind was getting back to West Eightieth for some serious romance.

Griffin saw to his disappointment that the big Checker had its Off Duty sign on and thought that he would have to catch a regular cab that, with the small back seat and the metal grate between him and the driver, always made Griffin feel like he was being escorted to the dog pound. But when the Checker's black driver saw them, he clicked off the sign and flipped the release unlocking the back door. Griffin smiled, thinking the man took him for a big tipper, and pulled open the door for Leana to get in. Instead, Leana drew back and stood as if frozen on the curb.

Seeing Leana hesitate, the driver barked at Griffin, "Come on man, you want a cab or don't ya?"

Griffin, the great liberal, always hating to anger minorities, said "Okay, okay" and got in the car, motioning for Leana to follow.

Leana looked furtively from side to side. She started to call to him in Russian "Charles, nyet . . . ," but then her breath was knocked out by the sharp jab of something metal thrust into her kidney from behind. Leana was thrown headlong through the open door of the cab by a bull of a black man. She hit the floor of the Checker at Griffin's feet with the big man on all fours on top of her. The cab ripped away from the curb, throwing Griffin back against the seat in total panic and confusion. Making the yellow light at Duane and Church Streets, the cab swung north and started to accelerate. No sooner had Griffin recovered his balance than he saw a flash of lightning from the gorilla's hand and was thrown back across the seat, his head smashing into the glass of the side window. Seized by pain and terror he pitched forward and lost consciousness.

Without moving his knee from Leana's back, the gunman peered out the back window to see if they had been observed or if anyone had heard the muffled blast from his silencer. There was no one behind them. The cab veered left onto Canal Street and headed for the West Side Highway.

"Is it cool?" he yelled to the driver. The front of the cab was separated from the back by a protective metal guard with plexiglas windows behind the driver's head, making it difficult to communicate.

"Yeah, man, but for Crissake finish it, and let's dump 'em."

"Just drive, Blood, I tol' you I know'd my business."

The gunman rolled Leana over, still straddling her on the floor of the taxi. For the first time she got a look at him. He was more brown-skinned than black, but from his accent definitely an American black and not a West Indian. He wore wraparound dark glasses and a black knit ski cap that had "Skiing Means Fun" stitched around the brim. In his left ear was a thin gold earring. He was strong; his muscles rippled with the adrenalin of the capture. At over 200 he outweighed Leana by seventy pounds.

The gunman held his right hand tight around Leana's throat. In his left was an automatic pistol ending in a three-inch silencer. He slowly brought the barrel to within inches of her forehead, his face contorted by the immediacy of his next kill. But as he looked down at Leana's face in the intermittent glow of the passing streetlights, he was amazed to see she showed no fear. He had just shot her boyfriend in the chest, and she herself was within seconds of death, and yet she just stared impassively right into his eyes. He had never had a victim quite like this. Sensing she would not scream, and knowing there was no one to hear her if she did, he released the near stranglehold he had on her throat and sat back a little, his rump on her pelvis, to look at her.

The driver sped to catch the light onto the West Side Highway. The route had been well rehearsed; they had not had to stop once. Heading north along the Hudson, they spaced themselves from the other cars in the thin traffic. It was eerily quiet in the back of the cab as they raced along the wharves on the West Side of Manhattan. The huge ships loomed above them, and every few seconds the quick flash of headlights from a southbound car passed above the gunman's head. Griffin's body was slouched in the right hand corner of the back seat, his head cocked against the window. His eyes were closed and his mouth hung open. He looked like a typical drunk trying to get uptown from an evening in Soho or the Village. As the minutes went by the gunman started to relax. He was safe. They had gotten away, now they were just another nondescript yellow cab rolling down the desolate highway. He was in control.

As he sat looking down on Leana's supine body, the cab's front wheel hit one of the many chuckholes that pocked the West Side Highway. The car jumped, and Griffin slid off the seat on top of them. Out of cruelty, the gunman leaned forward and bashed his pistol down hard on Griffin's unfeeling head, then shoved his body back on the seat. But at the moment the assassin shifted his weight forward to swing the pistol, Leana momentarily freed her left hand and, pulling her necklace up to her mouth, bit off the tiny blue amulet that hung from its center. Her lizard-length tongue pushed the small object up under the gum at the front of her mouth. As the gunman turned back to Leana, he saw she was almost smiling at him. He thought to himself that the sucker on the seat couldn't have meant much to her. "What a bitch!" he muttered, almost in admiration. He wondered if she might like to try a real man, as a kind of going-away present.

Still on his knees astraddle her stomach he shifted his position, freeing Leana's arms. Her legs were twisted behind him in the small floor space. Clutching the automatic, he bunched up the lower part of her wool sweater with his right hand and, watching her expression, pulled it slowly up over her head. Leana made no move to resist.

113

When the sweater came off she pulled back her shoulders and left her arms at her sides on the dirty carpet of the cab's floor.

"Wha' da hell you doing back there, Nicky. You tol' me dis was a quick hit. We almost to fuckin' Forty-Second," whined the driver through the plexiglas.

"I tol' you befo' t' shut yo' ass, Willy." Leaning over her, the gunman's face broke into a grin, and Leana could see the gold teeth of his twisted mouth. "We jus' gonna' have us a little fun first, ain't we."

Methodically, Nick picked up Leana's handbag, her sweater, and anything else she might grab, and sliding both panels of plexiglas screening over to the driver's side, stuffed everything through the opening in the grate on to the front seat. Satisfied that Leana was powerless and that Griffin's battered body was no longer a threat, Nick dropped the automatic through the grate on to the front seat. When Willy saw the gun fall on the seat next to him, he whirled around to see what was happening on the floor behind him.

"Jesus," he cried, seeing Nick's hand on Leana's exposed bosom. He pushed the two plates of plexiglas back across the guard to the passenger's side to get a better look. With this move the big taxi ran off onto the shoulder a bit and skidded. Willy jerked back around to gain control of the car.

"You asshole!" screamed Nick. "I'm gonna bust yo' black ass. You drive dis car. Dis ain't fo' you. Don't look back here agin!"

Pushing Leana forward on the small floor until her head and shoulders were pushed up against the right-hand door, Nick had enough room to reach under her skirt and pull her underwear down below her knees. Then unzipping his fly he eased out his penis and, his

legs bent at the knees, lowered himself down on top of
her. As an added precaution he put his arms around
her a few inches above her elbows, pinning her arms
securely to her sides. During all this Leana had done
nothing to resist him, staring impassively right into his
eyes. Nick thought that she must either be dazed with
fear, or stupid enough to think that afterward he would
let her go. To him it was all the same what she felt. He
had a job to do and this was just a momentary diversion.
He kept his eyes riveted on her as their chests met. Then
as he started moving up and down she seemed to relax.
Leana closed her eyes and brought her lips up to his.

"What a crazy bitch," thought Nick to himself, "she
loves it." He brought his lips to meet hers and immediately Leana's long tongue slithered so far back into his
throat that he gagged. It seemed as if he might even
have swallowed something small, her chewing gum perhaps. He pulled his head away and saw Leana's bright
red tongue circle her lips and smile at him knowingly.

For the next three minutes Nick had slow, grinding
sex with Leana on the floor of the racing Checker. Their
bodies were contorted by the physical constraints of
intercourse in a two-and-a-half by five foot space
bounding down the highway. The back of Leana's head
was smashed up against the door, her back and rump
bruised by the folded jump seats and small floor hump
of the gas line. Nick was not gentle. Leana did not kiss
him again, but tucked her head down tight against her
breast and shoulder, like a sleeping sparrow. She listened carefully to the heavy throb of the assassin's heart.

Nick held her in a vice-like embrace, totally absorbed
in the building sexual tension of his body. He did not
notice the accumulating taste in his mouth until it was
overpowering. Some kind of nuts, Nick thought to him-

self, but he couldn't recall eating any that day. In fact, he hadn't eaten much that day at all, but his mouth was burning as if from hot spices. His throat felt numb. Leana smelled his heavy breath as he slowly exhaled above her. *"Mindal'*," she thought, remembering the smell of almonds from the groves of Uzbekistan in Soviet Central Asia. Her hands were free below the elbow, and she forcefully pulled Nick's waist in towards her. Keeping her chin tucked firmly down between them, Leana began to exhale slowly, in a low murmur. She did not do so from stimulation but, with the acrid vapor of Nick's breath filling the small floor of the Checker, she was afraid to inhale.

Feeling Leana pull him close, hearing her begin to moan, Nick thought she was near orgasm, and this excited him all the more. Ignoring the strange taste in his mouth, he began to push himself harder and quicker into Leana's warm body. But in his exertion, as he tried to pull in more air, it seemed his chest was resisting his attempts to do so. Nick's inhalations seemed short and choppy, but his exhalations took a long time. His chest felt constricted, as if unseen hands were squeezing his lungs.

Each breath grew more difficult. His lower jaw stiffened and his heart throbbed. He felt a little groggy, almost dizzy, but he didn't want to stop. He was close now, close to orgasm. He didn't know what he was feeling, nausea perhaps, car sickness. He pulled Leana tight against him. All he could taste was almonds, bitter almonds. His stomach seemed to be full of them.

Suddenly Nick's whole body was ripped by a powerful convulsion. He groaned, he whimpered, he tried to catch his breath, and then a seizure sent him into violent writhing. He seemed to be all over the floor of the cab, shaking like a dervish. Leana clung to his powerful body

116

with all her strength, his thick penis still inside her. She was bashed repeatedly into the folded jump seats in the front of the compartment, but she did not let go. Leana kept her neck pressed against the gunman's chest, the muscles taut, her chin down on her collarbone, with her shoulders high. She prayed that he would not, in a final moment of realization, have the strength to snap her neck. She wrapped one leg around his and clung like a spider monkey; her only protection, to stay tight against him in that final instant.

Leana felt Nick's arms uncoil and release her; she braced for the attack. But instead of grasping her neck, the gunman's muscular biceps flopped uncontrollably about the floor of the cab, as if in an epileptic seizure. His arms and legs flayed the seat and doors like a pinned cockroach. Nick made a barely audible, guttural sound and belched up red foam and a cloud of the almond-scented vapor. Then suddenly, the twisted, gyrating limbs all froze. The seizure stopped; the convulsions ended. Nick's now-flaccid penis, deprived of its last orgasm, fell from Leana's body.

Leana immediately rolled the paralyzed bulk off her, toward the wall of the passenger compartment, out of the driver's line of sight. The heavy black body was covered with sweat. As the head rolled forward, Leana saw that the assassin's eyes were still open, with the eyeballs bugged out from their sockets, like those of a huge insect. Bloody foam bubbled from between the thick lips.

How long had the little pill taken—five minutes? Peristaltic action would have whisked the amulet down Nick's esophagus to his stomach in a second. Once there, the blue coating, impervious to saliva, quickly dissolved in the gastric acidity of the stomach. When the coating was penetrated, clouds of hydrogen cyanide billowed out

117

of Nick's stomach. Respiratory collapse inexorably followed. Nick was literally gassed to death from inside. The bell tolled.

Leana was halfway there, and had only a moment to plan her next move. Still lying on the floor of the cab, face to face with her foaming rapist, Leana started frantically rifling his pockets. She prayed for a knife—Nick must have one—a razor-sharp stiletto, a dagger, a switchblade, anything. But all she could find was a 39-cent Bic pen.

Willy called back over the seat, still too afraid of Nick to look around, "Shit, Nicky, you okay? I ain't never heard such a commotion. You mussa' fucked her cunt off back there. Nicky?"

In a second Willy would look back. He was no muscle man like Nick, but was sure to have a gun in his belt. Anyway, Nick's automatic was still on the seat at Willy's side, out of Leana's reach on the other side of the plexiglas. Both sliding pieces of plexiglas were pushed over to the passenger's side, leaving nothing between Leana and the back of Willy's head. In most cabs the plexiglas behind the driver's head was immovable. Leana guessed that this had been altered to give the driver a clear shot into the passenger compartment. She could wait no longer.

Leana reared up on her knees behind Willy's head. With her left hand she grabbed the hair at the crown of his head and jerked it back exposing the length of the beardless neck. Willy was just able to shriek before Leana's right hand circled his ear and brought the cheap pen down point-first right below his bulbous Adam's apple. Willy's shriek became a snake hiss as the wind from his lungs escaped out the new hole in his trachea. Before

Willy's hands could get from the steering wheel to his punctured throat, Leana brought the back end of the pen up under his chin and, with all her strength, shoved the entire shaft down through the hole into Willy's windpipe. Blood and ink from the shattered pen tip drained into Willy's bronchial tubes. Abandoning the wheel of the speeding cab, Willy struggled in a mute frenzy to wrench the pen from his throat.

Leana dropped to the floor of the big car and braced herself against Nick's body for the crash. Willy went off the highway at fifty, still grasping for the pen lodged in his trachea. The car went down a small embankment, stayed upright, crashed through some leafless underbrush, and smacked into a tree. Willy's foot never quite reached the brake. When the car hit the tree, Griffin's body came forward off the back seat like a dummy on a rocket sled. Leana heard the bones snap as he hit the steel barrier that divided the passenger's compartment from the driver. Leana's breath was knocked out as she was bounced around on the floor and then slammed into Nick's corpse. Griffin's limp body collapsed on top of her. She was breathless in a pile of mayhem. All was finally still. Leana knew she had survived.

She fought off the desire to pass out; the car could burst into flames at any moment. Leana pushed the bodies off of her and struggled to the right rear door. It was jammed. Leana was shaking all over and could not focus her strength on the door handle. She sat down on the car seat and tried to compose herself. She looked to her side and saw that Nick's head was twisted toward her in the wreckage. The enormous black pupils stared at her, the mouth open and still salivating. Suppressing panic, Leana braced herself against the door and pulled back on the handle with all her might. It gave with a pop, springing Leana out of the cab on to the frozen ground.

Struggling to her feet, she ached all over. She was naked except for her crumpled skirt. Around her was a sparse woods, and apparently no one had heard the crash. This surprised her, as she knew they must still be in Manhattan; they had not crossed a bridge. Leana thought they must be in one of the parks north of Harlem, Inwood Hill or Fort Tryon perhaps. The front door on the passenger's side had been snapped open by the crash. On the floor Leana found Nick's discarded weapon. A glance over to the driver's side told her she would not need it against Willy. The steering shaft had taken the full impact of the crash against the tree and had rammed backward through Willy's chest. He slumped there, an impaled cadaver.

Leana returned to the passenger compartment and setting down the gun, pulled on her sweater and coat. Then she grabbed Griffin by the feet and pulled him out of the cab onto the frozen ground. She knelt down next to him in the darkness and the cold feeling for his pulse—but it was of no use. As she had suspected all along, Griffin was dead, killed by a shot through the heart from Nick's automatic.

For a minute Leana did not move, remaining quietly at Griffin's side. Then with an earsplitting cry, she scooped up Nick's automatic and snapping her wrist, blew out one of Nick's horrible bug eyes. No sooner had the half head stopped bouncing, then she slammed a second shot through the remaining eye, leaving virtually nothing of Nick's cranium. Then Leana started to cry.

FEBRUARY

Miguel slowly regained consciousness to find himself lying facedown, spread-eagle on a cold stone floor. His cheek had gone white and numb from his granite pillow. Around him Indians chanted an undulating, twangy prayer. He could smell incense, pine needles, and candle smoke. Still, he knew he was not dead. How could he be so sure, he asked himself. It was the pain. Yes, it was the pain, and the feeling that what, if anything, he had eaten in the last few days would soon take leave of him. Surely the dead were not concerned with such matters. A few meters away two Indians rolled on the floor drooling and giggling, and a minute passed while he groggily tried to place himself. Although Miguel could not reconstruct the prior evening, he slowly concluded that he had ended up at the Church of Juan Bautista in the village of San Juan Chamula.

His wife had warned him about drinking with the Indians, and she was from Chiapas and should know.

Like most of the local mestizos, Isabella found the Indians pitiful and boring. Miguel, though, had not grown up with the different tribes the way his wife had; he was intrigued with their culture. He had even learned a bit of Tzotzil, the local Indian language. He had been talking up a storm with a couple of the Chamulan elders the night before when they offered him a glass of their liquor. They were all drinking it—how could he refuse? The Indians name for the potent moonshine was "posh." Well, they didn't serve posh at the astronomy faculty in Mexico City. Tequila he thought he could handle, even mescal, with its stubby agave worm, but this had really taken him from behind. He pulled his arms in toward his body and slowly rolled over on his side to see the interior of the church. He had never had such a hangover. Against the walls were a couple of rough wooden tables and groups of icons, carved statues of religious figures with Indian features. Along the back wall of the church stood one large group of scorched and blackened religious statues. Miguel had been told that these icons had come from an earlier church, which had burned down. As they had failed in their duty to protect the old church they now had to stand in penitence at the very back of the new one.

The damn thing was that it was a sacrament. Posh was actually part of the Eucharist—and that wasn't the worst of it. If his old priest in Mexico City ever saw the service at San Juan Chamula, thought Miguel, the poor man would leave the religion. There were no chairs in the Church of San Juan Bautista, just a stone floor with pine needles strewn about. Although it was Saturday there was, as always, a tremendous amount of activity. There were many priests, but they did not wear the vestments of the Catholic clergy. Despite the fact that the

church considered itself devoutly Catholic, services were
conducted by village elders, who wore the normal garb
of the Chamulas, a kind of belted, sleeveless tunic over
a white cotton shirt. The only difference was that the
religious leaders wore black woolen tunics, while the
younger men wore white ones. Villagers would come to
pray, and be assisted by one of these lay priests. A family
would choose a kneeling place near the back door if it
was their first prayer on a particular subject. If their
prayers went unanswered, the next day they would
return, creeping up a little closer to the altar.

The family would bring the basic elements of the
Eucharist, including a jar of posh. Posh was pure alco-
hol, sugar-cane-distilled, white lightning at about 192
proof. The men in the family, and especially the priest,
would drink down a big glass of posh to begin the service. The priest then repeated a modulating, rhythmic
chant with a distinct nasal twang. As many little services
were being performed simultaneously, the whole church
reverberated with the chorus of these odd harmonic
sounds. The other sacraments of the service were as
bizarre to Miguel as the posh. They consisted of a hard-
boiled egg and a bottle of Coca-cola. These were carefully arranged on the floor with pine needles and burning candles, in a kind of private altar. During the service
the priest would pass the sacraments in a circle over the
faces of the petitioners. When the service was all over,
the head of the family drank the Coca-cola and ate the
egg for lunch.

To Miguel, though, the weirdest thing about Chamulan Catholicism, and he supposed the most heretical,
was that they had replaced the central role of Christ with
that of John the Baptist, or Juan Bautista as he was known
in Spanish. Christ's importance was principally that he

could put a good word in for you with John. In a peti-
tioner's progress from the back door to the altar, he first
commissioned prayers to local deities, then to luminar-
ies such as the Virgin Mary, and only in the last instance
to John the Baptist himself.

With all the chanting, candles, and incense, and the
continual throwing-back of *vasos* of posh, the atmosphere in the church got pretty riotous. Men rolled about
on the floor talking in tongues, some were seized with
hysterical movements, others had done as he had and
simply passed out stone drunk on the floor. Everyone
was particularly uninhibited now because the Mardi Gras
celebrations had started. Everyone had four days of
Carnival to get out of his system before the coming
Wednesday, Ash Wednesday, the beginning of Lent. To
keep a vague lid on things, several two-man squads of
Chamulas, with armbands and yard-long billy clubs,
strolled among the faithful. The Chamulas took their
unusual rituals very seriously, and did not care to adver-
tise them to the outside world. The occasional tourist
who wandered in from the nearest town, San Cristobal
de las Casas, was warned not to photograph what he
would see. Just the day before, Miguel had seen two *nor-
teamericanos* surrounded by a crowd of angry Chamulas
when they took a picture of an icon being paraded
through the market. They had been forced to surren-
der the film to a tourist department official. They were
lucky; some years before two photographers had been
beaten to death by drunken Chamulas for taking a picture inside the church.

Miguel respected the bizarre piety of the Indians who
lived in these mountains. It was so different from the
smug, upper-class society of Mexico City. His parents
had thought him crazy, first for marrying a girl from

the provinces, and then for accepting a job in the mountains of Chiapas to run the government's astronomical observatory. He had explained to them that it was the best observatory Mexico had, with a full sixty-inch mirror telescope, at a station a mile-and-a-half high in the cold, clear mountain air. He had a small American computer left over from Mexico's oil-boom days and no particular constraints on the type of research he did.

Although it was certainly not like the mammoth 106-inch telescopes the Americans had, Miguel had a better vantage point than most of them because he was in the high mountains and nearer the equator. Also, many of the big American telescopes had problems with light from cities. Even the biggest telescope of them all, the giant 200-incher at Mount Palomar, was left half-blind by the high-pressure sodium street lights of San Diego. By contrast, the village at Nagun Chuac, where Miguel's observatory was, had no electricity except for the observatory generator; the worst air pollution was a smoky campfire.

Miguel knew there was much worth observing in the skies over Mexico. The Mayas, distant ancestors of the Chamulas, had known that a thousand years ago when they built their great observatory at Chichen Itza in the Yucatan. Miguel's father, predictably, was unconvinced. He couldn't imagine leaving the comfortable life in the capital to mix with a bunch of primitive Indians down on the Guatemalan border. Miguel, by contrast, found the Indians—all the different tribes with their bright clothing and ancient traditions—more interesting than anything he had experienced over margaritas with Mexico City's young gentry at the Hacienda de los Morales or the San Angel Inn.

As Miguel dragged himself to his feet and lurched

out into the daylight, he cursed the old Indian who had gotten him to drink that posh. He frowned at the boxy church, covered all over with cheap, green paint. He saw that Monday was mostly gone and twilight was coming. It would soon be time for him to begin his observations, and he had a splitting headache. But tonight was one night he could not miss, even though it was Carnival time. As luck would have it, Carnival had coincided with the return to view, from its swing behind the sun, of the great Halley's comet.

Yesterday, Sunday, February 9, was the day of the so-called perihelion; after seventy-six years the comet had again looped round the sun and was heading back out by earth to distant space. It would return only when Miguel's little children were old men. The world had briefly lost sight of the comet as it swung behind the sun, but this coming morning, just before dawn, it might be visible again with a strong telescope. Since it was winter, the Northern Hemisphere was tilted away from the sun, making it difficult for the telescopes in the United States to see the comet. However, because of Nagun Chuac's position in the lower latitudes, Miguel might be able to make the first post-perihelion sighting of the 65-billion-ton "dirty snowball" rounding the sun 144 million miles away.

Miguel drove his jeep the seven miles back through the sparse pine forest to San Cristobal. It was one of the few paved roads in the area, and given the state of his head, Miguel was thankful. Still, he took it slow; the Indians used the road for their walkway and it was getting dark. He passed a group of pink-robed Zinacantans with their goats. They were the most colorful of the tribes; all the men wore long pink sarapes and flat straw hats with long bright ribbons down the back. The married

126

men put a knot in their ribbons, the single men let theirs dance in the breeze.

Approaching San Cristobal, he decided not to stop by his home. Isabella would be as snappy as a Chihuahua; he would have to apologize and could not simply walk out again. It would then be pitch dark for the drive to Nagun Chuac. He would call her from the observatory, of course. The connection would be bad—it always was—so they wouldn't talk long and he could start his calculations. Satisfied with this, he reached the outskirts of San Cristobal, turned right on the Pan American Highway, passed the Pemex station, and drove on through the mountains to the observatory. It was getting cold. It would probably freeze again; he would have to check the generator. His assistant had gone down to Tuxtla Gutierrez, the state capital, for supplies, so Miguel would be alone tonight at the telescope. This didn't bother him in the slightest. He liked Manuel well enough, and appreciated his help, but there was something irresistible about being alone on the mountain with the heavens. The sky was clear. Nagun Chuac's one meteorological blemish was the dense mountain fog, but tonight there would be none before morning.

After a shower and a cup of coffee, Miguel called Isabella to assure her that he had not been kidnapped by the primitive Lacandon-Maya Indians. He was too embarrassed to admit that he had passed out drunk in a church, and told her instead that he had gone down to Tuxtla to help Manuel. He had tried to call but there was trouble with the phone, as it was the rainy season. Having placated Isabella for the moment, Miguel began to plot the position at which he would first be able to see the comet's return. He studied the computer diagram of Halley's ephemeris, its plotted track through the heavens. American astronomers had calculated this even before the comet was first resighted in October of 1982; they had been right on target. It was only a question then of setting the telescope's computerized tracking device to follow the ephemeris. The comet was just emerging from beyond the sun, slightly to the north of it. It was night now, the Western Hemisphere was turned away from the sun, so the comet was, of course, not visible. By dawn it would be too bright to see the little spot of light far across the solar system. But Miguel had calculated that he could get the briefest of views of the comet in the few seconds right before dawn, and right before everything faded into the brilliant sunlight.

Miguel did some routine observations and prepared a report on the week's activities. It occurred to him that he should be able to see the lights of the American space shuttle and the infant space station. After consulting his charts, he found them in geocentric orbit high overhead. He watched for quite a while and wondered what it would be like to see space from inside. Miguel again calculated the position of the telescope in relation to the comet's appearance. He didn't expect to see anything himself, but with luck he could take two pre-dawn pictures for later analysis. His work done, and with the light of the moon warming the floor of the observatory, Miguel lay down for a nap.

The few minutes before dawn found Miguel studying shots of the normal sky at the spot where he would take his pictures. He would compare these control shots to the new pictures to see what was different—the difference would be Halley's comet. At the appointed moment the telescope's camera began clicking its exposures. For thoroughness, Miguel was bracketing his calculated shots with several others both before and after

the expected appearance. He kept shooting until a spectacular dawn broke across the mountains of Guatemala
to the east. Although normally he would leave develop-
ing and printing to Manuel, he went immediately to the
darkroom and began working. One hour and a pot of
café con leche later, he began analyzing the two principal pictures, comparing each one to the normal-sky
model. He was soon disappointed. He was sure these
shots would reveal the comet, but he found nothing out
of the ordinary. No matter how long he stared through
his magnifying glass, the exposures were indistinguish-
able from his control pictures. Miguel cursed himself;
he had obviously made a mess of the delicate computations.

The phone rang and it was Isabella. She was worried
about him. He was normally home by now and he hadn't
come home yesterday at all. What was the matter? By
her tone he knew it would be a long call. Miguel tucked
the phone between his shoulder and chin so he could
have his hands free. While he listened to her, and apol-
ogized again for yesterday, he idly fingered the earliest
shot of the series he had taken. Although there was no
chance it contained the comet, it was the clearest of the
group and the easiest to study. He tried to concentrate
on where his calculations had gone astray. At just the
moment Isabella was explaining how difficult it was to
raise the children without him, Miguel saw a small flaw
in the corner of the enlargement, a speck of light surrounded by a diffuse glow. He knew Mexico's morning
sky well enough to know there was no star there.
Explaining to Isabella that he had no intention of shirk-
ing his responsibilities, he fingered the second expo-
sure. It had the same corner flaw, the same diffuse glow,
and Miguel wondered if the whole batch of film was

defective. At about the time Isabella was asking if they would see each other at all during Carnival, and he had shrunk to his, "Yes dear . . . of course dear," defense, Miguel verified that the flaw was in the third picture as well, the same speck, the same diffusion, almost like the tail of . . . Miguel jumped up, letting the telephone receiver crash to the floor. He grabbed the first picture and compared it to the third. *"Madre Dios, Madre Dios,* the flaw is moving, the flaw is moving!" Miguel scooped up the receiver, yelled, "Isabella, that flaw is Halley's comet, and it's got no business being there!" and hung up the phone.

It couldn't be there, it just couldn't be there! It was way out of position, tens of thousands of miles out of position. The place was wrong, the time was wrong, everything was wrong—but the pictures were right. Miguel grabbed his ephemeris and rolled it out on the floor. He pulled out his star charts and got down on his hands and knees with his photos. On his star chart, Miguel tracked the changing position of the comet as it was shown moving through his pictures. He then took the mathematical coordinates of the charted path and compared it to the ephemeris. The path of the comet was not only changed, its divergence was increasing. It didn't even appear to be in the same plane anymore. So drastic was the course change that in the fourth picture he had taken, the one he thought would first show the comet, the comet had in fact left that portion of the sky altogether; it didn't even appear on the photo. If he had enlarged the shots any further, or started with a more powerful telescope, he wouldn't have seen the speck in the corner at all. Miguel gasped at what this might mean. Given the winter tilt of the earth, the big telescopes in the United States were too far north to pick up anything before dawn. They wouldn't even try to sight Halley's for another day or two. Unless somebody, in Brazil perhaps, had happened to photograph that little section of the sky right before dawn, it could just be that he, Miguel Vega Galindo, was the only man in the world who knew that something had happened at perihelion and that Halley's comet would never be the same again.

The phone rang again and Miguel knew that it must be Isabella. How could he answer? What was he going to tell her—that the most dramatic event in a thousand years of astronomy had taken place, and he was possibly the only man that knew about it? He let the phone ring. All right, perhaps Isabella would not understand, but whom could he tell? All he had were three dim specks of light where none should be—according to him at least. Perhaps he had overlooked something basic, some fundamental that any good astronomer would catch in a second. Perhaps his method had gotten rusty down here in the provinces. Perhaps the posh had clouded his brain. He had to be cautious. With Manuel out of town there was no one nearby who would even comprehend what he was talking about, much less be able to check his work. How embarrassing if he had completely misinterpreted the situation. He could almost hear the laughter back in Mexico City: "Miguel just called up from Chiapas to tell us that Halley's comet was way off its course, and I had to explain that he was just seeing interference from a new communications satellite. Oh, that Miguel! *Estupido! Perfectamente estupido!*"

No, he must start from the beginning and review everything. But he couldn't verify anything in broad daylight. That would have to wait until night, to be precise, early the next morning before dawn, when the same portion of the sky came into view. Meanwhile, the phone had stopped ringing and started again. Miguel needed time to think, but he couldn't simply ignore Isabella. She would soon come looking for him.

"Yes, Isabella . . . Yes I know it's you, I'm sorry . . . Yes I'm all right . . . It's just . . . something's come up at the station, and you know Manuel's not here. I've got to do it myself . . . I know the children are having a piñata party . . . It's true I promised . . . No I don't want them to hate me. I . . . Listen, Isabella, I'll meet you later. Yes, for the big parade this evening. Seven o'clock. In front of the Palacio Municipal. We'll have dinner at the Ciudad Real . . . No I won't be late . . . Of course, it's the biggest occasion of the year. Carnival, I know, no meat 'til Easter. I'll be there . . . Yes my sweet . . . *Hasta luego.*"

For many hours Miguel checked everything: star quadrants, parallax, interference. He examined every possible cause for error, from such trivial ones as typos in the ephemeris to grand Einsteinian ones like distortions of light rays caused by the sun's gravitational field. He even went back to the basic texts he had used in his doctoral program at the University of Mexico to review his research procedures. Miguel studied his photographs and developed them again in the darkroom; he shrank them, enlarged them, turned them upside down.

By the end of the whole process, night had fallen, and he was more convinced than ever that what he had seen was Halley's comet—hopelessly and irreversibly off course. This struck the exhausted Miguel as sad. Since Halley had first seen the comet in 1682, and since its first predicted reappearance on Christmas Day in 1758, the comet had been one of nature's great timepieces, coming back from seventy-five to seventy-nine years later, as if to count off another human lifetime. Now, one way or another, that would never be the same again.

It was at this point that it dawned on Miguel that he could in fact determine, on a rough basis, just where the new path of the comet would be. After all, he had three plots, and knew exactly when each had been taken. This would give him the direction and the speed. If the distance the comet had moved from picture one to picture two was less than the distance moved between pictures two and three, he could get some idea of the acceleration.

Miguel sat down to do some rough calculations. He carefully plotted the tiny portion of a giant ellipse shown by his pictures. He was intrigued to see that the new plane of the comet in three-dimensional space was not far from the plane on which the earth orbited the sun. Miguel drew the line of the comet's path out further from the sun, and then checked the coordinates of Mercury and Venus. Since the comet's plane was now closer to that of earth's orbit, he thought that earth might get a better look at it than the 39-million-mile fly-by dictated by the original path. His grandparents' generation had had a much better look in 1910, and if this were to be the last time, it seemed only fair that Halley's should soar by in one last blaze of glory. He continued to plot the arc of the comet and then, when he had extrapolated the path out to the earth's orbit, he tried to calculate how long the comet would take to reach that point. He figured that his margin of error on the comet's speed was greater than his margin of error on the comet's path, but the exercise was all fairly theoretical at this point anyway.

He arrived at an approximation of the date the comet would intersect earth's orbit—April 18, 1986, just over two months away. The last thing to do was to see exactly where the earth would be on April 18th, so he could then calculate how far away the comet would pass. He checked a standard reference to ascertain the earth's position on April 18, 1986—and suddenly the exercise became anything but theoretical. The path of the comet would pass within a quarter of a million miles of the earth.

Miguel immediately gathered up his data and went to the computer room. He booted a five-and-a-quarter-inch disk that showed the precise orbits of the planets around the sun. He then began to feed in quadrants with associated margins of error for the movement of another object, the comet. He instructed the computer to plot the comet's possible paths based on combinations of all the maximum errors, a Monte Carlo variation.

The computer generated a form that looked like a long, skinny cornucopia, starting with a point at the present position of the comet and spreading outward to a large disk as it reached the orbit of the earth 144 million miles away. The comet could pass the earth anywhere within the large circle at the end of this conical-shaped flight path. The earth itself was not, however, in the circle, but just beyond its perimeter; there was no possibility of collision. Miguel sat back in his chair a little and some of his tension abated, but he was far from relieved. What would be the effect of such a close pass? And what if his margins had been too conservative? There might after all be some chance of an actual impact, and that, Miguel knew, would make World War III look like a cap-gun contest. Earlier Miguel had not been worried in the slightest about a collision. The odds of such a thing, given the magnitude of space, and the relatively puny size of the objects, were remote in the extreme. After all, Halley's comet had been rocketing about the cosmos for millennia and had never had a mishap. But now here it was, an actual near miss, and it would occur in less than ten weeks.

He turned again to his computer and requested the flight path, assuming each of his calculations—trajectory, spin, speed, and acceleration—was perfectly accurate. The diagram pictured on the computer's liquid crystal display changed from an expanding cone to a straight line. The distance from that line to the earth at its nearest pass was 240,000 miles—an astronomer's whisker.

Miguel twisted his head from side to side to stretch his neck. He had been hunched over calculations or crawling around on all fours over diagrams since before dawn that morning. He had had nothing to eat since his 9 A.M. café con leche. He looked at his watch and saw that it was almost midnight. He put his head back, slowly closed his eyes, let his body relax, and then lurched forward and shot out of the chair. "*Dispenseme Dios,* I completely forgot about Isabella." Miguel grabbed his jacket and ran out of the observatory. As he locked the door he realized that he would have to be back in five hours to begin the preparations for his pre-dawn verification pictures. The day just would not end.

Driving into San Cristobal, it seemed to Miguel that every resident of the sleepy little town was drunk on the street. He drove up Diego de Mazariegos until the crowds of revelers prevented him from going any further. Turning left, he parked the jeep in the municipal lot off Guadalupe Victoria and set out to walk across the Plaza Mayor to the Hotel Ciudad Real.

In the square, Indians danced and hollered. Loudspeakers hanging from the street lights blared the local hit parade. No sooner had Miguel set foot on the plaza when a local merchant tried to embrace him and press some tequila upon him. No sooner had he pried himself away, than a drunken man in the dress of the Tenejapa tribe slipped on some spoiled fruit and splashed posh all over Miguel's jacket. A wave of nausea passed over Miguel as he recalled the day before in San Juan Chamula. Many of the Indians were in elaborate costumes. In accordance with tradition, a number of "evil monkeys," with tall conical hats of monkey fur, tormented other participants dressed all in white, symbolizing Christ's Passion. In the middle of the square he was kissed by someone in the costume of an old witch, while Father Time looked on with a smile. After a half dozen drunken collisions he made the edge of the plaza, crossed the street and walked through the entrance and beyond to the courtyard of the Hotel Ciudad Real.

There were no Indians here, but the tourists and local mestizo shopkeepers were having a grand old time. A big green parrot swung on a little perch next to the bar, and three guitarists, accompanied by a boy pounding on a wooden box, played a discordant "Guantanamara."

Miguel pushed his way up to the bar and called out, "Juan, have you seen Señora de Vega?"

"Si, Señor, she was here a long time waiting for you, but she left a few hours ago. I think some *estúpido* told her that he saw you yesterday up at San Juan Chamula, and forgive me for saying so Señor, but when my Rosalita is in a mood like that, I'm afraid to go home at all." The parrot spun around on his swing and said, *"Borracho, fundadamente borracho,"* then winked at Miguel.

Driving homeward on Avenida Cristobal Colón, Miguel resigned himself to the irony of his position. The fate of the world was hanging by a quarter-million-mile thread, and he was the only person who knew it. They may all be dead in two months, but now he was going to catch hell for missing a party. It was not that Isabella was unreasonable; she was eminently reasonable. She didn't know what he knew; he hadn't told her. How could he expect her to feel? It was the biggest holiday of the year in a fairly boring provincial town, and he had spent Mardi Gras with a telescope and computer, and the day before that passed out on the floor in some pagan ritual with a bunch of near savages.

He couldn't recall ever having been more tired. He was hungry too, famished, but too nervous and upset to eat. As he parked the jeep, Miguel resolved that the only honorable thing to do, and coincidentally the only thing that might placate Isabella, was to explain the whole business just as it was. When she saw the gravity of the astronomical situation, his peccadillo with the Chamulas and the missed Mardi Gras would pale into insignificance. She would forgive him and urge him onward in his research. There was no question that she would be greatly worried by what he would tell her, but within a few days the whole world would be worried, and he couldn't protect her from that. Better that she hear it first from him. And what he must certainly do is sit with her calmly and lay out the situation dispassionately. He had to stop this pattern of screaming some remnant of an incomprehensible discovery at her and then running out on the conversation. That he must never do again. She had married a scientist, not a hyena.

Despite the cold, he found Isabella sitting outside in the interior courtyard. It was one-thirty in the morning, but she was still waiting up for him. Miguel sat down across from her.

"Isabella, I know you are angry, and I know I've hurt your feelings. But there is a reason, a very good reason, one I was not sure of when we spoke before, but now I am sure. Something very important has happened today, certainly the most important thing in my career and perhaps the most important thing in our lives, and I want you to know the whole story."

When she heard the seriousness in his voice, Isabella straightened her shoulders and didn't say a word, waiting for him to continue. Miguel gazed at her silently for a moment, sitting there in the cold, clear mountain air. She looked so beautiful with the light from the pale moon reflected in her dark eyes.

"The moon, the moon!" bellowed Miguel, jumping to his feet. "How could I have missed it! *Madre Dios*, it's true! The moon is 240,000 miles from the earth! 240,000 miles!" Miguel yelped, ran back out to his Jeep, and roared away.

MARCH

Major Stuart Fisher eased himself down onto the *Constitution*'s waste collection system. He was by this time used to it, but nevertheless it was quite a contraption. He hooked his toes underneath two little flanges to prevent himself from simply floating around the orbiter's mid-deck. But even this didn't give him enough leverage to keep himself on the seat, so he fastened a harness around himself and adjusted the spring pull to take up the slack. Not much of a tug was necessary, certainly no more than the snugness of a trouser belt on earth. With no gravity, even a slight force is sufficient to move or hold a large mass. The first problem of going to the bathroom in space was to keep yourself on the seat; the second, to form a seal of some sort between the waste collector and the flesh around one's excretory orifices. With that seal in mind, the seat assembly was separated into a urinal portion and a so-called bio-waste portion. They could not be used simultaneously. You had to make a choice.

The reason for the great concern over a good skin-to-seat seal was that in a microgravity environment, there was no reason for your excretions to fall. A piece of feces would simply bounce along your fanny, break free, and then float by you in the cockpit. On a long trip, the shuttle's flight deck would begin to look like an asteroid belt.

To avoid this scatological unpleasantness, in compensation for gravity, a high-velocity airstream whooshed past your buttocks and blew any excrement down into a chamber, where, as if it were some precious essence of the immortals, it was vacuum dried, chemically treated, and stored to await removal on earth.

Fisher contemplated all the freeze-dried little packets he and Colonel Carradine must have built up in the last six months. Then, kicking the vacuum shutoff control, and pushing back the two Nomex privacy curtains, he removed the waist restraint, pulled up his flight suit, and floated up through the interdeck access hatch to find Carradine studying the TV console monitors.

"Any more instructions from Houston?" asked Stuart.

"Nothing."

"You'd really think that with all the best physicists in the world working on the project, they'd have figured out some way to stop this thing."

Carradine considered the matter for a moment and said, "Well, it's not like they've had a lot of experience with this sort of thing. It's really quite a challenge, a 65-billion-ton comet speeding through space."

"I see that the Russians are falling all over themselves to help out," said Stuart. "Asking for all sorts of data on the *Constitution* and its capabilities. I'm sure their interest is only motivated by the purest scientific spirit, a deep-felt desire to help mankind in its hour of need," he said sarcastically. "Jesus, it's almost like they were prepared for this."

"The thought had crossed my mind," said Carradine.

"Another thing, I can't understand why it was that some beaner with a puny, sixty-inch telescope on the Guatemalan border was the first one to figure out what was happening. What was Palomar doing with their 200-inch soup bowl? Looking at us, I suppose?"

"That one's easier to explain," said Carradine. "It's winter down there in the Northern Hemisphere, and the United States, Japan, Europe, the Russians, everybody's tilted away from the sun. There aren't any big dishes around the equator, but this guy in southern Mexico was just far enough south to pick it up. The Aussies would have spotted it pretty soon. The Mexican did some fancy figuring to put the whole thing together. I can imagine the look on NASA's collective smug face when the president calls to announce that he has just spoken to the president of Mexico who tells him that Halley's comet is on a collision course with the moon, could they please look into it, and don't they think it's important to let him know about such things."

"Well, it may be all politics, but I guess NASA figures this Mexican knows something. Apparently they've brought him up to White Sands to work at the tracking station."

"It can't hurt. Honestly, the guy's figures were right on the money, and he did the whole thing with a 64-byte computer—practically a toy."

After a silence, Fisher turned to Carradine. "Lee, if we're wrong about a nuclear rocket launch to try and displace Halley's, if they decide against it, do you think they'll try and use Shiva?"

141

"Shiva? You're the mission specialist. You tell me."

"I've got my doubts. I mean we can hit it all right, even at those speeds. But destroy it? I don't see how. This isn't some little satellite we're talking about. The thing is huge. And it takes so much energy and flourine that we'd only get about a three-minute burst. Even if we could break it up, with what result? We don't even know for sure what Halley's is made of. And the risk is always there that we'd simply slice it into big chunks, one of which might hit the earth. I mean, right now the situation is bad. God knows what will happen when it hits the moon. But better the moon than the earth. Just look at the impact craters on that old man up there. What's one more, more or less. It's been hit before. It can take it, roll with the punches, you know. I think it may be better to just do nothing. Just sit back and watch it come."

"Maybe, but I don't think it would be just a kiss and a wave," said Carradine. "Even the early readouts show a tremendous impact on the moon, a million-megaton slam. I don't think it can just take it. I think we may get a whole new lunar orbit or maybe a set of Saturn's rings. The climatic effect on earth could be devastating. But you're right that anything's better than having the earth itself take the impact."

"Well, anyway, we're safe here, and that's the main thing," said Fisher, turning away to examine the hydraulic indicators.

Carradine shot Fisher a hard look, then seeing he had turned away, he thought for a moment and said, "Yeah, Major, real safe."

After a few minutes, Carradine continued. "Stuart, do you know what happened to the dinosaurs?"

"No, Lee, I must have missed that class in aerospace

142

engineering," said Fisher good-naturedly. "They didn't talk about it much in flight school either."

"Under the circumstances it may be useful for you to know."

"You're the skipper."

"It's just a theory; one of many. But it's a new one and it explains so much. The amazing phenomenon, that none of the other theories could really account for, is that most of the animals alive at that time, not just the brontosaurus and the big dinosaurs, but most everything down to microscopic plankton died all at once, within maybe a few thousand years at the outside, or maybe even in just a couple of years. Since this all took place 65 million years ago, it's hard to know the time span exactly. But in any case, in geological terms, in evolutionary terms, it was the blink of an eye. The other theories, like loss of habitat and climatic changes, don't explain how fast everything died out, or why the changes affected life from one cell to the biggest creatures ever living. The theory that mammals just took over, you know, the rats-eating-dinosaur-eggs stuff, doesn't jibe with the fact that mammals coexisted with dinosaurs for three-quarters of the time the dinosaurs were around, and that was for a hundred million years."

"What about the theory that the dinosaurs were too big to fit in Noah's ark?"

As usual, Carradine ignored Fisher's sarcasm. "Now to bring in a little something closer to home, Stuart, what do you know about iridium and the cosmic rain?"

"Okay, now you're giving me the easy ones. Every year about 100,000 tons of cosmic dust falls on the earth. The dust is rich in several elements that are rare in the earth's crust—elements like iridium, osmium, and, so dear to my heart, platinum."

143

"So as a result, when these rare elements are found in sedimentary layers of the earth's crust, it's taken for granted that they arrived as cosmic dust, raining down from space upon the earth's surface."

"You got it, commander."

"Well, as it happens, in sediment deposited just at the time that all these big changes were taking place in the earth's population 65 million years ago, there is an incidence of iridium anywhere from thirty to almost 500 times normal. In Italy, a thin deposit of iridium-rich clay less than a centimeter thick was found sandwiched between the limestone layers from the Cretaceous era when the dinosaurs lived, and the Tertiary era when they had all died out. What could have caused it?"

"Well, normally I'd say the communists, but considering it was 65 million years ago, I guess we'll have to let them off the hook ... Seriously, that much iridium, it would have to be extraterrestrial. I mean, it sounds like millions of tons of meteor dust were raining on earth all at once. But I don't see how; the stuff is fairly constant."

"How many millions of tons of dust do you think a comet's impact would make?" said Carradine.

"I think I'm beginning to get the point," said Fisher slowly.

"Let's just suppose that a comet, or maybe an apollo object or asteroid, say about six miles across, hit the earth. What would be the result?"

"Let me crunch some numbers," said Fisher. "The energy would be equal to one-half of the mass of the comet times the square of the velocity of impact. At the kind of velocities we're talking about, each ton of comet would be like about a hundred tons of TNT." He pulled out his pocket engineering computer and, after inputting a few numbers continued, "So, Jesus, something that big would be equivalent to a 100-million-megaton blast."

"The biggest volcanic eruption in recent memory was when Krakatoa blew up in 1883. They say people all around the world talked about brilliant sunsets for the next two years. Krakatoa's dust caused that. But an impact like this," Carradine continued, "would dig out a hole over a hundred miles across. That much dust, earth, and comet combined in the stratosphere would block out the sun altogether, worldwide, for several years."

"So anything that needed light to live was in for a hell of a time."

"Exactly," said Carradine. "The tiny photosynthesizing sea plants went immediately, and in fact there's an exact geological line, called the 'plankton line,' where the remains of this die-off can be detected."

"Cosmic genocide," mused Fisher.

"And then of course it went right up the food chain: land plants, herbivores, carnivores. The dinosaurs that didn't get killed outright in the blast just staggered around in pitch blackness looking for something to eat; but all of their food was dying."

"It sounds pretty grim," Fisher responded, "but obviously some animals survived. Why didn't it just kill off life altogether?"

"Presumably the darkness just didn't last long enough to kill everything. Some of the plants had seeds that could lie dormant for a few years; some of the smaller animals must have lived on the carcasses of the big dinosaurs. A brontosaurus could make quite a feed for a small mammal—it could last for years, and maybe by then the skies were starting to clear. The birds could eat seeds and nuts. The crocodiles were the only big reptiles to make it; possibly because they could swim open-mouthed through the water, scooping up all the decaying plant and animal matter washing downstream. Otherwise, everything bigger than fifty pounds just became extinct. When the dust finally settled, the few survivors looked around and found the big reptilian predators all gone. From that time on, the mammals were in control."

"So our ancestors were the ones who were content to sit in the dark and chew decaying dinosaur hide for a few years. What a lineage! I guess the meek really did inherit the earth," reflected Fisher, setting the radio frequency for the next scheduled conference with the capsule communicator at NASA. "Maybe I shouldn't be surprised. With all the comets, and a couple of thousand apollo asteroids with orbits near Earth's, collisions must happen from time to time. I suppose that now it's time."

"To quantify that a bit," said Carradine, "based on the existing craters in the earth's surface, about every 250,000 years some comet or asteroid about a half-mile wide hits the earth. Maybe once in a hundred million years or so something the size of Halley's comet collides with us. The moon is smaller and so far has been lucky: the last big asteroid hit it about four billion years ago."

"I marvel at our good fortune. Imagine, a grandstand seat; it doesn't happen every day, you know," said Fisher, his voice thick with irony. "But wait, Lee, you said a blast like that would make a hundred-mile crater. Where is it?"

"It must have hit at sea, or some part of the world that has become sea. There is a kind of giant submerged ring off the north coast of Australia that is a possible candidate. Naturally the ocean floor has weathered a good bit in the last 65 million years."

"Yeah, time heals all wounds."

"Another possibility is Iceland."

"Iceland?" said Fisher. "Iceland's a volcano, not an impact crater."

"True enough, but Iceland is situated right on the mid-ocean ridge, right where two of the great continental plates come together," Carradine responded. "Now what if, to make the odds even wilder, the comet hit close to that ridge?"

"It could possibly punch its way right through the earth's crust."

"Right."

"And that would result in a tremendous volcano spewing up a mountain of lava, right out of the ocean floor. Needless to say, Iceland is a volcanic island."

"Right again."

"And one more thing, Lee. I'm almost afraid to ask, but let me guess. How old is the volcanic rock in Iceland, about 60 to 65 million years?"

"You got it," said Carradine.

"Jesus, it all fits," said Fisher, stretching his back. After a minute he added, "Well, I just hope Halley's doesn't become our coffin the way the last big one finished the dinosaurs."

"Precisely why I thought you should know their fate, Stuart. You see, it's happened before."

"Damn, just our luck to be around when the moon's number came up."

"Somehow, I think this one was more than luck."

"It was just a figure of speech, Skipper. I . . . "

"I know, Stuart," interrupted Carradine, "but there's a whole side to this problem that we haven't explored, and if we do, we may conclude that there is a pattern of comets raining down on us, there even may be a pattern of extinction, but that this incident doesn't necessarily fit the pattern." Carradine paused, "I'm sorry, Stuart, forgive my rambling monologue. I know you've got work to do."

"Wait a minute, Skipper. You can't just leave me hanging here. What kind of pattern of extinction? For God's sake, Lee, go ahead and ramble, it's more than you've said to me in six months!"

An electronic beep and the blue liquid-crystal display on the Orbiter's control panel announced an incoming television transmission from the Mission Control Center at the Johnson Space Center in Houston.

"Looks like we're within range now. The tracking satellites will get us a television signal," said Carradine. "We'll finish this discussion later."

Fisher set the frequency monitor to the Ku band and set the communications computer. Within seconds the receiver locked in on the transmission from NASA. Both men turned to the small monochrome screen to receive their orders and the latest news from home. With a crackle, they saw the familiar visage of General George Lockhart, the military head of NASA.

"Colonel Carradine, Major Fisher, how are you boys feeling?"

"Just fine sir," replied Carradine.

"I'll be brief," said the General. "Before you go over the hill and we lose contact, you will receive your new orders by encrypted facsimile, on the cyfax receiver. Please use the cyfax for your response. As you know, we cannot prevent interception of televised signals. However, I wanted to let you know the results of the latest studies on Halley's impact on the moon. As you know, this is just about the only thing anyone down here on earth is thinking about. I suppose it could be worse, but things look very bad indeed.

148

"It now appears that the comet's impact will be a glancing blow on the far side of the moon, which we believe the moon will be able to survive. However, the collision will force the moon down into a much lower and faster orbit. The only good news is that we believe that this new orbit will be stable. The new orbit will still be outside the Roche limit—the point at which the gravitational forces of a planet are more powerful than the internal cohesiveness of its satellite. Therefore the moon will not disintegrate, and we won't get rings like Saturn. In addition, the moon will revolve around the earth faster than its present speed of .64 miles per second, so the increased centrifugal force will balance the increased gravitational pull of the earth. This increased centrifugal force means that the new orbit will not further decay, and the moon will not eventually fall into the earth's surface.

"Ironically, the astronomers tell me that when the earth was formed the moon was in fact much closer. So this in a way is like a return to old times. The only hitch is that in those times there was no life on earth, and therein lies our problem. The ecological effect of a 'near' moon is devastating. We're only guessing at most of the problems. But the one we'll have to deal with right away is the tides.

"Now, I'm going to say a few things that I'm sure you boys already know, and know a lot better than I do. Still, in the interest of setting it all out, let me bore you with some basic physics. As you know, the tides on earth result from the moon's gravitational pull on the surface. This differential creates stress and twisting, known as tidal forces, on all parts of the earth. But since the air is invisible and the earth is solid, you really notice the effect of tidal forces on only one part of the earth's surface—the sea. The closer objects are to each other, the greater their gravitational attraction, and the greater the tidal forces. The power of these tidal forces, given the moon's new orbit, will be roughly ten times what it is today. We don't know what that will do exactly, but it may well make the coastal area of much of the world uninhabitable. Just imagine what it will be like: every beach will have tides like the Bay of Fundy, and those tides will change direction several times a day. Tidal waves of enormous power will become daily occurrences in what are now the most populated coastal areas of the world.

"Right now, it may be routine up there in space, but down here it's anything but. Congress is meeting in continuous session and the president has ordered evacuation plans for all seaboard cities. The military reserves have been called up, and whole Quonset cities are being built back from the coast. The stock market has collapsed and gold is at $2,000 an ounce. Real estate values have swung to astronomical highs in inland cities like Cincinnati and are in a free-fall in New York City and Los Angeles. There's even discussion of moving the capital to Atlanta. We've had some panic, emotional hysteria, and such, but by and large, citizens are preparing themselves, physically and, most of all, psychologically. People are responding and trying to make the best of it, which is surprising, because frankly, short of a general thermonuclear exchange, it is hard to imagine anything that could be more devastating for this country.

"Well, I hate to be the bearer of such bad tidings, but that's the way it is. You men will have the best vantage point for the collision, and naturally the scientists will want you to document the whole event. We will be in frequent contact, but for now, this is Mission Control, signing off."

No sooner had the televised signal faded than the S band receiver started to beep, indicating an incoming message on cyfax, or encrypted facsimile. Fisher switched on the communications computer to begin decoding. Within minutes a message in plain text appeared, which both men read in silence.

> The *Constitution* will be used in an attempt to deflect or destroy Halley's Comet. Given weight restrictions and the grave dangers this mission will impose, crew is to be kept to the minimum necessary. Therefore, only Colonel Carradine and Major Fisher will crew the *Constitution*. The rest of the men will remain with the Space Operations Center (SOC). The *Discovery* has been readied for blast-off from Vandenberg Air Force Base and will rendezvous with SOC and *Constitution* at 2100 this Friday. Colonel Carradine and Major Fisher should be in the SOC wardroom at 2200 to receive new orders. Prepare *Constitution* to receive cislunar external tank to be carried into orbit by *Discovery*.

Carradine finished reading first and sat back silently in his pilot's seat.

"It's gotta be Shiva, Lee, otherwise they wouldn't have asked for me," said Fisher, serious for once. "But it won't work, I just know it won't work."

"The others will be disappointed that they can't come," replied Carradine.

"I really hadn't bargained for this," said Fisher. "One shot to save the world."

The produce looked good at Fairway that day: there was a high mound of green peppers, the broccoli had thin stems with no yellowing at the tips, the acorn squash

151

was firm and forest-green with flecks of orange at the crown. Horst must have been delayed, but no matter, this was a fine place to browse and squeeze the vegetables. The morning air was chill, but not cold enough for the store to put up the plastic canopy around the outside fruit bins. Kolya Voroshilov could survey the street as he moved among the outside carts of neatly piled vegetables; he would be able to watch the big East German as he approached. Kolya had plenty of time to study the other customers in the crowded Broadway market. When Horst arrived, the two men could exchange a few quiet words in English at the tomato stall, or wherever in the aisles it seemed most discreet. In the hubbub of clattering carts, with the constant "Watch your back, watch your back" as the Puerto Rican boys brought more produce, it would be impossible to focus the cone of a listening device on them. Kolya would put the worn, brown document protector in his empty basket on the floor, and when he walked away, Horst would simply take the basket and continue shopping. At the checkout counter, the cardboard folder would fit neatly into the doubled plastic Fairway bags, along with Horst's grapefruit and apple juice. Kolya would queue up in the cheese line in the back of the store and watch Horst leave, walking south to 72nd Street to take the West Side IRT back to Chelsea.

Voroshilov was a cautious man; in his twenty years of service abroad for the KGB he had seen even the simplest things go awry—agents going to the wrong restaurants, forgetting the password, mistaking warning signals for safety signs, or leaving their confidential papers in taxis. There had been that absolute fiasco in Buenos Aires, when his man had taken the documents, put them in his shoulder pouch with his groceries and then walked out of the store, forgetting to pay. The swarthy little Argentine shopkeeper ran right after the idiot. Instead of apologizing and offering to pay double, Kolya's operative panicked and started to run, with the Argentine right on his heels, yelping like a terrier. The hapless spy hadn't gotten 200 meters when another shopkeeper along the crowded sidewalk tripped him up. Kolya watched helplessly as an army of the native petite bourgeoisie swarmed over his man like locusts, pinning him to the ground. The police arrived, and when the contents of the shoulder pouch were fully examined, what at first seemed a routine shoplifting matured into a case of Soviet espionage. The foolish agent was given life imprisonment for treason. He was lucky; if he ever got out, he was to be liquidated immediately by his former comrades. These were Kolya's final instructions before he himself fled Argentina the very night of the man's arrest.

Unfortunately the bungler had not just dragged down himself. The captured documents compromised two of the Cuban "illegals" whom Kolya had spent so long establishing in Buenos Aires. Like all so-called illegal operatives, the Cubans were not operating under diplomatic cover; rather they had assumed false identities as Argentine citizens. They had insignificant jobs, and for the present, lived the life of law-abiding, rather dull tradesmen. If, on the other hand, in a time of crisis, diplomatic relations between the Soviet bloc countries and Argentina were broken, and all of the Eastern European diplomats and businessmen were sent home, the illegals would become the Kremlin's only eyes and ears in the country. If relations deteriorated further and Argentina became particularly offensive to Soviet interests, there were a host of prearranged sabotage missions that the illegals were to carry out. The Cubans were part

of a larger network of "Spetsnaz" diversionary agents—
trained cutthroats who carried out long-range reconnaissance and terrorist operations. It was amazing what
a blown power station, a few key assassinations, and some
poison in the reservoir could do to bring a big city to a
terrified standstill.

Kolya had not been blamed for the Buenos Aires
fiasco. He had not recruited the man, and, in any case,
the Argentinians were regarded by the KGB as hopeless
bunglers. Kolya had stayed cautious and risen to one of
the top foreign posts in the KGB, head of operations in
New York City, the financial vortex of the Western World.

Voroshilov was troubled this day, but it was not about
the competence of the man he had come to meet. Kolya
knew he would not see any dumb mistakes from Horst
Enders, head of the "Spetsnaz" diversionary company
in the New York metropolitan area. Horst was method-
ical, emotionless, and brutal. He had first visited the
United States, under a different name, many years ago
as a member of an East German wrestling team. Like
many of the less distinguished members of touring Soviet-
bloc sports clubs, his mission was not to win amateur
trophies but to observe the cities to which he might return
in time of war as a professional—a professional killer.
Under an illegal identity of a West-German-born U.S.
citizen, he held a job as a shipping clerk for the New
York Port Authority. He worked on the wharves of
Manhattan's lower west side and lived in a two-bedroom
apartment on Ninth Avenue in Chelsea.

Horst lived a simple life; he belonged to a target-
shooting club and worked out at the West Side YMCA,
but if the Soviet diplomats were for any reason sent home,
Horst would be in charge of all KGB activity in New
York and the rest of the northeastern United States. It

would be his responsibility to activate the "Spetsnaz" forces, the dozens of Russian illegals and other terrorists in the pay of the Soviet Union. It was Horst who would see that Moscow's orders were carried out. Voroshilov knew that Enders had an additional reason for care at their rare meetings, one that did not apply to him. If they were apprehended, Enders would be in a federal penitentiary for a very long time, whereas he, Voroshilov, would simply be returned to Moscow. Under his cover as deputy chief of station at the Soviet Union's Mission to the United Nations, he was entitled to diplomatic immunity.

Voroshilov respected Enders, but he also hated him. In Voroshilov's opinion, Enders was as arrogant an East German as he had ever met, and they were all arrogant. Enders considered himself a super spy, the Richard Sorge of the 1980s. He was so haughty that he constantly contradicted Voroshilov and tried to order him around, despite the Russian's higher rank. To make matters more humiliating, Enders was tall and muscular, with a nearly bald, bullet-shaped head. He physically dominated the smaller Russian, who was thin and had a chronic cough. Kolya knew that Enders did not fear him, did not respect him. Kolya could not forgive Enders for this. It was because he did not want to admit any mistakes to the overbearing East German, that Voroshilov had avoided telling Enders anything about the problem that dominated his thoughts as he fingered the radishes that cold day in March.

The problem was Leana. Since she had escaped from the double execution Voroshilov had arranged in January, there had been incidents. Kolya did not know for certain if she had been involved, he didn't even know for sure if she was still alive, but he had long ago learned that if something unfortunate happens once, it's coincidence, but if it happens twice, it's enemy action. There had been the incident on the Tappan Zee bridge. Two of his best spies—a husband and wife team—had been knocked clean off the bridge by a semitrailer. The local paper said that when the police booked the driver, he told them an incredible story about picking up a beautiful hitchhiker with a foreign accent. The raven-haired girl had pretended to want to make love to him, but then, when his guard (and his pants) were down, she had knocked him unconscious. According to the driver, the next thing he knew the police were pulling him from the cab of his semitrailer saying he'd hit and killed two people in a sedan.

That wasn't all. There was that botched blackmail / bribe to a key member of the U.N. delegation of a certain mineral-rich African state. The Soviets had first "burned" the diplomat by photographing him in an embarrassing situation with another man, and then "turned" him by agreeing not to reveal the pictures if the African cooperated with Soviet goals. To add a carrot to the stick, there was also to be a small pourboire to seal their "friendship." The African was simply awaiting delivery of the agreed payment, designed to ease his conscience about taking his future orders, not from his country's capital, but from Moscow. One of the junior officers at the Soviet mission was carrying the compromising photographs and a small packet of large-denomination U.S. dollars. They had anticipated no problems. The Soviet was not a trained agent, he didn't even know what he was delivering. He stopped in the men's room, entered a stall, hung his coat on the hook and sat down on the toilet. Just as he started to strain, a hand shot over the top of the stall and whisked away his jacket.

Blackmail pictures and money disappeared out the door
before the startled diplomat could pull up his trousers.
As a result of this bungle, the African diplomat had
apparently been turned again, and seemed of late to be
most supportive of the arguments in the U.N. General
Assembly of the delegation from the United States.
Curiously, even though the theft occurred in a men's
room, the young Soviet swore that the hand that grabbed
his jacket was that of a young woman.

Finally, and worst of all, was the loss of Professor
Fielding, perhaps the best source of U.S. intelligence
secrets since the Rosenbergs. He had jumped, fallen, or
been pushed in front of a subway train on his way to
deliver a mother lode of top secret defense documents
to Kolya. Kolya feared that Leana was behind all of these
incidents.

Kolya still found it hard to believe that the termina-
tion had not succeeded; it had been planned so well,
and the killers were said to be the best. How could a girl,
whom he himself had ordered to carry no weapons, have
dispatched the two professional assassins? Voroshilov had
not of course contacted the hit men himself; that had
been done through a chain of two intermediaries. The
murderers never knew who their true client was; not
even the man who hired them knew who the true client
was. Had the gunmen been caught, if they had talked,
the only name they would have known was that of another
hoodlum. As soon as it was learned that the mission had
failed, this other hoodlum had himself been executed
by the KGB. This, to a certain extent, was punishment
for hiring incompetent killers, but more importantly it
was done to break the chain before it led upward to the
Soviet Embassy. Thus the bungle could be contained
before it became a diplomatic fiasco. Still, all in all, it had

been a bleak winter for the KGB in New York.

Now it seemed that the whole Soviet delegation would be sent packing. The month before, the world had learned of the diversion of Halley's comet and its collision course with the moon. Western scientists were unanimous in their opinion that a collision would play havoc with the world's tides and therefore cause massive flooding in coastal areas. Evacuation plans were already prepared for New York City residents to move to the Catskills and the Poconos. Many of those with relatives inland had already left.

The City was still functioning, but the disorientation was severe. The best business to be in was furniture moving, because all the people wanted to get their possessions to high ground. The northern bridges and western tunnels out of the City were choked with vans and semis 24 hours a day. Small businessmen were desperately trying to get their inventories to Westchester, but the biggest concern for the Wall Street banks and corporate headquarters was not their buildings or equipment, but retaining their records. Those employees who came to work spent their days entering data into massive IBM memory banks for electronic transfer to inland branches.

Renters were the new kings of the Big Apple. They strolled about window shopping for distress merchandise, while owners and insurers glumly contemplated bankruptcy. For the first time that anyone could remember, there were apartment-to-let signs in the windows of every residential building. A two-bedroom cooperative apartment in the Dakota was going for $50,000, down from fifteen times that amount the month before. Many of the big grocery stores were still open; there were still millions of people to feed. Admittedly, food prices had tripled. Every store in Manhattan was having a going-out-of-business sale and, for once, most of them really were. Still, New Yorkers were used to inconvenience, and the majority of them stayed put and kept going in to work, stoically convinced that something would deliver them. In any case, the collision, if it came, was over a month away.

In this time of national crisis, the United States government saw no particular advantage in being responsible for the evacuation and protection of hundreds of Soviet diplomats. The vulnerability of the nation to espionage was also a consideration. Congress therefore appeared very close to a resolution demanding the temporary return of all individuals holding Soviet and Eastern European passports to their homelands.

It was precisely for this reason that Voroshilov had called a rare personal meeting with Horst Enders. If and when the Soviet delegation left, Horst and his Spetsnaz regiment would be the sole source of intelligence information for Soviet power. In addition, the opportunities for sabotage and disruption during the evacuation were unparalleled. The worn Redweld document protector held at Kolya's side contained explicit instructions to the Spetsnaz regiment on the terrorist activity they were to undertake. Specific assassination targets were identified, as were plans for generators, nuclear power plants, food storage areas, and all the key elements of U.S. survival in a national emergency that were to be attacked. There were volumes of information, most of it on microfiche. It represented the culmination of all Soviet intelligence work on the northeastern United States since the beginning of the Cold War. It would be ruinous if this information were to reach the FBI. The entire structure of KGB intelligence would be revealed; the cover of most of the agents in the Spetsnaz regiment would be blown. Normally, such a rich nugget of intelligence would not be turned over to one man, and certainly not all at one time, but these were not normal times. An opportunity like this was worth the risk. In any case, Kolya reflected smugly, both he and Enders were armed and, more importantly, were experienced and careful; no one could get to close to them, there was no possibility of an interception.

The telephone on the southeast corner of Broadway and 74th Street was out of its cradle, hanging by its knotted cord. There was a torn piece of notebook paper saying "out of order" taped across the change drop. Nevertheless, a woman's hand in a ripped, fingerless, gardener's glove held down the cradle for a few seconds and then reached behind the sign and dropped in a quarter. At her feet were three large shopping bags, filled to the brim with pieces of paper, junkyard finds, and the scavengings of an urban derelict. She was hunched over, a wool stocking cap pulled over her forehead to eyebrow level. A dense clump of matted gray hair fell over her cheeks to her shoulders; little of her face was visible. Not that anyone would want to look at her; like the thousands of homeless people in New York City, she was tattered and filthy, and smelled of garbage and stale urine. However, she attracted no attention in this neighborhood of stumblebums and winos. They sat on stoops, leaned against doorways and congregated on the benches in the median strip of plantings and scraggly trees that divided northbound and southbound upper Broadway.

As a large bald man on the far side of Broadway turned into Fairway, the baglady punched in a seven-digit number from memory. The phone rang once and was answered, "NSA, Special Investigations."

"I want to speak to O'Dwyer. Tell him it is Leana, the Russian. I have phoned him before."

"We know," came the reply. "Where are you?"

"Get me O'Dwyer."

After the briefest of pauses, the call was transferred and another man's voice answered. "This is O'Dwyer. Where are you?"

"You want to get the man who had Charles Griffin killed?"

"Of course I do."

"Are your men ready as I asked?"

"Yes Leana, we can be anywhere between 59th and 110th streets in Manhattan within five minutes. But you've got to stop this one-woman show and turn yourself in. You are not in charge of counterespionage in the United States."

"Really, well, maybe I should be. I'm doing a damn good job."

"Look, I knew Charles too, and I want to get those responsible. Maybe personally I sympathize with what you're doing, but damn it, it's criminal. I told you I can get you a pardon, a new identity. The president himself will authorize it, but you're jeopardizing the whole thing with this damn reign of terror."

"What I'm doing is what you should be doing. Did you pick up the briefcase I left for you?"

"Yes, we did. Full of secrets on our high-energy beam research at Lawrence Livermore. You were right. Professor Fielding, Nobel laureate, was selling documents—to the Russians I suppose."

"You suppose! Did you see the minicamera, the code system? You think he was working for Liechtenstein?"

"OK, OK, but you didn't have to kill him."

"You really don't understand what you're dealing
with, do you? Listen O'Dwyer, catch me if you can. You
want to know who killed your prize translator? His name
is Kolya Voroshilov. He is deputy chief of station at the
Soviet Embassy to the U.N. and undercover head of the
KGB. You may come and get him now. He will wait for
you quietly. I'm at the Fairway, Broadway and 74th, and
don't let Horst Enders get away. He's an East German
illegal in charge of the Spetsnaz regiment in Manhattan.
They'll be passing documents. See that you get them."

"Horst who? What do you mean 'regiment?' Leana,
you've got to . . . " O'Dwyer was cut off midsentence by
the click of the receiver.

Leana undid her old woolen overcoat and reached
inside to adjust her shoulder holster. Then, assembling
her bags, she slowly ambled across Broadway. She passed
the bench in the tree-lined median; even with the cold
it was standing room only as the derelicts passed the bottle of Night Train. She waited for the light to cross
southbound Broadway, but did not yet hear a siren. She
passed the pharmacy and the dress store on the southwest corner and came dead even with Fairway. Voroshilov and Enders were at the avocados, squeezing and
choosing, studying the color and firmness, exchanging
a few muffled words. The document protector was in
an empty wire basket at their feet. Voroshilov had put it
there; Enders would pick it up. Leana heard the distant
wail of a siren and begán to cross the sidewalk to the
outside fruit stalls. She was not fifteen feet from the two
agents, and she was closing. Switching the bags to one
hand, she reached inside her tattered overcoat.

Out of the corner of his eye Voroshilov had seen the
baglady coming. Had it been someone dressed differ-
ently, a housewife or businessman, he would have stopped

playing with the avocados and critically observed the individual. Kolya was careful, especially careful on a mission like this. But like so many other comfortable, jaded New Yorkers, inured to urban poverty, Kolya not only ignored the old baglady, but actually turned his gaze away, so as not to have to see and smell this bit of down-trodden urban flotsam. Horst Enders did the same, muttering something about "rounding them all up." Leana had counted on this small human frailty to buy her another ten feet, and perhaps a moment's inattention from the two armed and alert spies.

By the time the woman was too close to ignore, was in fact only five feet away from him across the mound of avocados, Kolya looked up and straight at her. What he saw was not a baglady, but a young woman dressed as one. Moreover, the young woman had a gun, the gun was pointed at him, and, as a final observation, he realized that the young woman was Leana. Voroshilov's terror was total. He tried to speak but no words came; he began to urinate, and then a slug from a large caliber automatic hit him so hard in the forehead that he was transported backward, taking an entire stand of canta-loupes with him. Pieces of Kolya's brain were splattered in a ten-foot arc from the tomatoes to the butternut squash. Enders looked once at what was left of the head of his former boss. Leana dropped her pistol to fire at Horst's abdomen, but rather than going for his gun as she expected, he pushed the table over, scooped up the document protector, and ran south. Leana dodged the crashing table and took off after him. The fruit stand erupted into screams and scattering customers. Tables and displays were mowed down as people tried to flee. The police sirens were now loud and immediate. The East German burst into the traffic on 74th and made the

163

southwest corner in a full sprint. He thought he was in the clear now, running with his head held high. He was near peak speed when a slug blew away his right buttock and sent him skittering chin first thirty feet down the pavement. He writhed in pain, still clutching the brown folder. He tried to rise, but could not move his legs. Enders rolled on his stomach, screaming. Leana did not break her stride, but ran past him yelling, "Ein Geschenk von Moskau, du Verräter!"

By now the police were everywhere. Somehow, Leana, dodging through the crowd, made the two blocks to the 72nd Street IRT stop. She ran down the stairs, sprang over the turnstile and, still dressed in her baglady's clothing, leaped down onto the tracks. The crowd on the platform were agape as they saw the baglady running like an Olympic athlete down the track and into the dark southbound tunnel. As soon as she was out of view from the platform, Leana dumped the old overcoat— she had peed on it for a week for authenticity—and pulled off the gray wig. Under the old coat she wore gray workman's coveralls with a pocket pouch on her stomach. She put the heavy .45 caliber automatic in with her shoulder holster and pulled out a cap that said New York Transit Authority. She put this on, and then strapped a miner's headlamp over it.

It was only six blocks from the 72nd Street stop to the next station at 66th, one of the shortest distances in the entire transit network. Leana covered the distance in three minutes. No train had come, but if it had there would have been no special danger. There was sufficient room along the side of the tunnel for maintenance crews to stand against the wall when the trains passed. Still, she was lucky, it would have cost her time, and there was a manhunt going on over her head, in more ways than one.

Meanwhile, on the streets above, the FBI found the brown document protector on the pavement next to Horst Enders. Enders was alive but wishing he were dead. His pants were soaked in blood, he could not move his legs at all. As he lay on the cold sidewalk surrounded by FBI and police, he wondered what had gone wrong. He had no idea why this had happened. Like Voroshilov, he had recognized Leana through her disguise in that last second before she shot Kolya, their former boss and "handler." But for all he knew she was still a loyal agent of the Soviet Union. Then, after she had shot him down she screamed out, "Ein Geschenk von Moskau," a present from Moscow, and called him a traitor. A traitor to whom? In his physical agony Enders was in a mental nonplus. The only sensible explanation was that Moscow thought that Kolya Voroshilov had been turned, had become a double agent, and that somehow he, Enders, was thought to be collaborating. The KGB had sent Leana to kill Voroshilov and obviously him as well. He had survived, but next time they would get him for sure. Even if this weren't correct, even if it was Leana who was working with the Americans, he was in a miserable position. The FBI had him red-handed with the activation instructions for all the Soviet illegals, the entire Spetsnaz regiment. He had no diplomatic immunity, he was wounded, perhaps paralyzed. It was time to reassess his loyalties. Maybe the Americans would make a deal if he cooperated. Perhaps they could use a man with his knowledge and contacts. As they lifted Horst onto a stretcher, he choked back the tears from his pain and said to the man who seemed to be in charge, the one the others called O'Dwyer, "My name is Horst Enders, if you will protect me, there is much that I can tell you."

There were few people on the platform at 66th Street. It was well past rush hour, but too early for performances at Lincoln Center. There were no transfers at 66th, nothing but a quiet little IRT stop between the big stations at 72nd and Columbus Circle. So only a handful of people saw the young woman emerge from the dark tunnel. She was wearing coveralls and had a miner's lamp strapped to her head. Everyone assumed from her cap that she was a transit worker inspecting the myriad cables and rails of the subterranean city. She climbed lithely out of the tracks, went through the turnstile and disappeared into Lincoln Center. When she reemerged minutes later and hailed a cab headed south on Columbus Avenue, she had discarded the coveralls and was wearing a skirt and loose sweater. Her jet black hair was tied back in a ponytail and she wore dark glasses. Beyond her rather striking good looks she was no different from the thousands of assertive young women on the Upper West Side. The driver dropped her near 42nd Street, and she walked to the Port Authority bus terminal. In twenty minutes she had reclaimed her duffel bag from baggage, purchased her ticket out of the city, and was in the back of a bus roaring through the Lincoln Tunnel. She would pick up her car at the Morristown, New Jersey, bus station before plotting her next move. Leana took some sadistic pleasure in having killed Voroshilov with the very automatic that had been used to murder Charles Griffin. She was fully satisfied with the day's work. She had accomplished her goal, but now felt isolated and alone.

Since the preceding September the initial space station module brought into orbit by the *Constitution* had been added to by the modules brought by other space shuttles and had grown into the Space Operations Center. SOC looked by now like a giant carbon dioxide cartridge floating in space. At the very top, the nozzle of the CO_2 cartridge, was an airlock that could be used for egress to allow extravehicular mobility. The airlock was also the point at which the *Constitution*'s escape hatch was attached to SOC. Inside it was a doughnut-shaped affair. It had four floors, each about twice the size of a deck on the space shuttle. In the center of each floor was a hole through which a floating astronaut could access all the other floors. On the top floor was a control center and space suit storage. Below the control center was a health maintenance facility, complete with diagnostic equipment, a bodybag shower, and a washing machine. The third floor down was a wardroom. The galley was here, some exercise equipment, tables to work on, and a large-screen television set. On the lowest floor were six, small, pie-shaped private rooms for the crew members. It was all a very cozy arrangement.

As the zero hour for blast-off of the *Discovery* approached, Carradine and Fisher transferred from the *Constitution* to SOC. It would take *Discovery* less than half an hour from blasting off at Vandenberg to rendezvous with the *Constitution* and board SOC. Two of their fellow crew members stayed behind in the *Constitution*, sealed it off from SOC's airlock, and drifted away, allowing *Discovery* a place to dock. As the undocking and docking procedure took some time, Fisher and Carradine, who spent most of their time aboard the *Constitution*, had an opportunity to relax in the commodious wardroom. They shook off their space sloth and worked out on the stationary bicycle and aerobic equipment. They looked forward to the fresh bread and fruit the *Discovery* would bring, but since dinner was some hours away Fisher rehydrated some chili macaroni and peas with butter sauce. They talked, and inexorably the conversation turned back to comets. It was the same everywhere these days, the topic everyone in the world was thinking about most of the time.

"Where do these damn fireballs come from?" asked Fisher.

"Oh, there's something called the Oort cloud, out beyond the solar system. Basically, it just orbits the sun, but every once in a while the gravity of another large body disturbs it and a few thousand comets slow down enough to start to fall toward the sun in long elliptical orbits."

"Just what is this large body that knocks the comets out of the cloud?"

"Now that's really something," said Carradine with a grin. "Have you heard about Nemesis?"

"Whosasis?"

"Oh, it's just the wildest of many, many theories. You see, it's got to be a large body, probably a passing star, light years away, that jerks loose a few thousand comets. The problem is that stars don't pass all that often, even given the enormous size of the Oort cloud and its distance from the sun. To make it even more interesting, some say that the major disturbances seem to be about every 26 million years. You remember our talk about the dinosaurs?"

"You mean how they were wiped out by a comet?"

"Right. Well, that mass extinction was roughly 65 million years ago. The comet that hit the earth could have been kicked out of the Oort cloud at the time of this cyclical disturbance. There might have been thousands of comets pelting the solar system at that time. There seems to be a high incidence of extinction, not always so dramatic as the dinosaurs, about every 26 million years."

"So that's the pattern of extinction you were talking about. Enter Nemesis, stage left, scattering comets, comets hitting earth, scattering dinosaurs. But what is Nemesis?"

"Nemesis, my friend, is the sun's evil twin star."

"What! You're joking me."

"I said it's only a wild theory. Nobody's ever seen Nemesis."

"But how the hell could somebody miss the sun having a twin star?"

"Well, Nemesis doesn't have to be big and bright like the sun. It could be a dull, dwarf star. And remember, if you count back from the dinosaurs by 26-million-year periods, you'd get 65 million, 39 million, 13 million, which would put us right in the middle of a cycle. Meaning Nemesis is at the farthest point of its orbit away from us. Arguably, we just haven't found it. They're searching for it at one of the big observatories in California."

"They're searching for a lot of things in California," sneered Fisher.

"There are other theories," Carradine continued. "It could be planet X, the hypothesized tenth planet of the solar system. There are some wobbles in the orbits of Neptune and Uranus that could be the result of a small tenth planet, and if so, that planet could also be responsible for disturbing the Oort cloud. On the other hand, if you don't like that theory, try this one. About every thirty-plus million years all sorts of events take place on Earth, big meteorites, low sea levels, mountain building, even polarity reversals where the magnetic north pole becomes the magnetic south pole. It also just so happens that about every thirty-plus million years the whole solar system oscillates one time through our galaxy, the Milky Way."

At that point there was a noise above them in the tubular passage down from SOC's control center. Carradine and Fisher knew they were about to receive their orders. They had a general idea what the mission would be; it was obvious to them as soon as they knew the *Constitution* was to be involved. They were, however, surprised to see who had made the journey up from Vandenberg to give them their orders. Down the hatch, knocking into the walls and clearly unfamiliar with the microgravity environment, bobbed General George Lockhart, the Air Force's top man for space programs, the senior military officer at NASA.

"General Lockhart," said Fisher, floating to attention.

"If you're a bit surprised," said Lockhart, struggling to stabilize himself, "I assure you, so am I. This is my first trip into space, and I can't say I'm particularly comfortable."

"Space sickness, General?" asked Carradine.

"I suppose. Mostly just disorientation. I'm just too old for such a change. And when I think that you boys have been up here for half a year, I am in awe."

"Thank you, sir, but you do get used to it. The first week is the hardest," said Carradine.

"Fortunately, I don't have to last that long. *Discovery* will be returning in forty-eight hours, just as soon as we can transfer the external tank and flourine, and give you men your orders."

"Flourine, General? I presume that means that Shiva is to be used in the attempt to divert Halley's comet," said Carradine.

"That's right, Colonel. The president has given his final approval to use the laser to strike the comet. The plan admittedly is risky, but there is no alternative. Now please let's sit down, we've got a lot to talk about, and I'm exhausted. There wasn't time to put me through space training, and God knows I needed it."

"General," said Fisher, after they had sat down and Velcroed General Lockhart to his seat, "why was the alternative of diverting the comet by exploding a nuclear missile next to it not chosen?"

"It could just be that that is how Halley's got off course in the first place. But if so, it was when the comet was at its closest point to the sun. If the comet were still close enough we would try to blow it up and let the pieces orbit the sun until they burnt. But by the time we knew about it there was no time to get a missile all the way to the sun. You have to launch months in advance. Now the comet is too close to the earth. The risk of blowing apart the comet is too great. If it did disintegrate, some of the larger pieces would likely be pulled in by earth's strong gravity. Chunks of radioactive comet raining down on the earth is worse even than the near moon problem we're facing now. So what we need instead is one clean shot, men, one clean shot."

"Just how are we to execute the strike by Shiva?" asked Carradine.

"It will be necessary for you to proceed out to the comet and take up a firing position well beyond the moon's orbit. Our scientists feel that there will be so much electrical interference in the hydrogen cloud around the comet's coma that it will be necessary for you to penetrate all the way to the inner coma to get an effective shot. To permit you to get there we've brought up an external tank for you to carry underneath the *Constitu-*

171

tion. It's smaller than the disposable one you use for blasting off from earth, but there's enough fuel to permit you to reach escape-velocity, pass the moon, destroy the comet, fire your retro-rockets and return to this station. Just don't get going too fast toward the comet. If you do, you'll not have enough fuel to have your retro-rockets slow you for the return. There's not much margin for error. After your return to SOC, regardless of the outcome, it will be time for you to return to earth. You've been in space a long time."

"General, a chunk of rock and ice five miles across is not the normal target for a laser. What makes our people think it will work?" said Fisher.

"It has to work," said Lockhart, a little harshly. "One of the things I didn't say on my television broadcast, one of the things I came up here to discuss with you, is the very grave military threat this near moon poses to the United States and its NATO allies. I'm afraid that what we're faced with here, over and above the ecological disaster, is a drastic deterioration of Western economic and military power vis-à-vis the Soviet bloc. Not all countries will suffer equally from the effects of a near moon. The destruction of the coastline and coastal cities will have relatively little influence on landlocked countries, and the Soviet Union and its Eastern European allies are basically landlocked countries. But now, what was always their great strategic vulnerability suddenly becomes their great protection. Very few of the large Russian cities are on the sea. There are a few of course: Leningrad is on the Baltic, Murmansk is on the Barents Sea, and Vladivostok is on the Sea of Japan. Even these don't face directly onto the oceans. It's the same thing for Eastern Europe. Consider how that compares to the Western allies. The United States, England, France, Italy,

172

Japan, even West Germany, all of them have long coast-lines dotted with key cities. NATO's industrial potential will be cut in half."

"That's a pretty desperate picture," said Carradine. "Considering how beneficial this may be to the Soviet military, have our scientists been able to come up with any explanation how the comet got on the collision course in the first place?"

"Well that's the sixty-four thousand dollar question Colonel," answered Lockhart. "There is no proof, naturally, since the comet was blocked from view by the sun at the time it went off course, but as the police say, you've got to look for motive, opportunity, and method. Now I think I've made a case for the motive, that is, the destruction of the military-industrial base of the NATO countries. Opportunity would be the time that the comet was hidden from view at perihelion. That is rare, by the way. The earth could just as well have been on the same side of the sun when the comet rounded the sun and started back out. It only happens on the occasional apparition that the comet is blocked from our view.

"That gets us down to method," the general continued. "Our scientists say that a really large nuclear warhead, fired well before time in order to rendezvous with the comet behind the sun, could have caused the deflection. At the time the comet was at the nadir of its long elliptical orbit, it would have been susceptible to such diversion. Still, it would have been a formidable technical feat, especially considering that the whole plane of the orbit would have had to be altered. It would have required real daring, or recklessness as the civilians would say. Any error could have resulted in the comet's heading for the earth instead of the moon—240,000 miles is nothing in these calculations.

"The whole thing is not so far-fetched as people might think," the general went on. "A few years ago NASA sponsored a conference on this very problem, asteroid diversion, at Snowmass, Colorado. Every year, on average, a meteor fragment weighing as much as 500 tons dives into the earth's atmosphere. Fortunately, all but a few of the iron ones break up and burn before they hit the earth. We wouldn't be so lucky with a big one. Our scientists concluded that since there could be as many as 100,000 asteroids and apollo objects with orbits that threaten the earth, we had better begin to get a deflection capability in place. We were shooting for 1995. Admittedly, it is much more difficult to divert a comet or meteor into a specific flight path than out of one. Much finer calculations are required, and you need a lot more energy. If the Soviets really did pull this off it means they're about ten years ahead of us in this technology, but nobody at NASA thinks such a scheme is impossible.

"There's more," Lockhart continued. "One of the reasons I came up in person, and didn't even trust the cyfax, was because I wanted to tell you that we have a considerable amount of intelligence indicating that the Soviets have been planning for this event since at least last summer. Here again we aren't sure, but it seems that even if they didn't cause it, they at least knew it was going to happen and kept mum. The National Security Agency has told me that since last summer the Soviets have been planning for the evacuation of their coastlines. Construction on the coast was halted, except for tidal walls and floating docks—the kind of things a navy would need to deal with flooding and extreme tides. Later they started constructing whole tent cities about thirty miles inland from their populated coastal areas. For example, there are three such new cities in place on high ground outside Leningrad that, combined, can contain half of the population of that city. In retrospect all of this looks obvious, but apparently the National Security Agency didn't put all the pieces together until late February, when the comet diversion was discovered."

"Christ," said Carradine.

"It gets worse," said General Lockhart, looking fatigued. "Apparently, one of NSA's Russian translators, the man who monitored developments on the Soviet Arctic coast, did get suspicious. Some of his early reports were ignored by a jealous superior, since fired. It is now believed that the translator had perhaps cracked the whole conspiracy, but unfortunately, we'll never know."

"What happened?" asked Carradine.

"He was murdered by professional killers," said Lockhart wearily. "And it turned out, unbeknownst to the NSA, he was having a serious affair with a recent Russian émigré. She was with him on the night of the murder and has since disappeared."

"Oh, my God," sighed Carradine.

"I'm afraid the KGB burnt NSA rather badly on that one." Lockhart paused, rubbing a sore neck, then continued. "So you see, the Soviets seem to be prepared for this, and we can't ignore the possibility that in the aftermath of the tidal waves they will launch an offensive, concluding that it will not be possible for the West to resist. Given the demoralization of the populace, they might be able to occupy, say, the Persian Gulf or even Western Europe without a fight." Lockhart fell silent, seeming old and defeated.

"It still doesn't answer the technical problem of how we're going to stop this thing," said Fisher. His tone was not conciliatory.

"Major, I know you pride yourself on how much you

know about Shiva and its capabilities, but our scientists feel that if Colonel Carradine can get the *Constitution* in close to the nucleus of this thing, and if you can track it and hit it with all the energy in Shiva, then you can vaporize some of the surface and perhaps alter its course. It wouldn't take much of a change to have the comet miss the moon entirely. It's not coming in dead center. That's the whole point. The impact is going to be just a glancing blow on the far side; even a fifty-mile deflection could make all the difference. That's nothing in space. There has to be enough power in Shiva to do that much."

"Halley's comet weighs 65 billion tons!" barked Fisher.

"Listen, Major, there are a lot of men who think this will work. Now, if you don't think you can handle the job, maybe we'd be better off with one of them." Lockhart would not accept even a whiff of insubordination.

Carradine started to intercede, then checked himself. He had been cooped up with Fisher long enough to have confidence in his crewmate's ability to maneuver out of tight situations. Sure enough, the furrows on Fisher's knotted brow began to relax, and slowly his whole face eased into a winning smile. "Sorry, General Lockhart, for my exuberance. The scientists are right of course: a well-placed shot, square in the middle, could move that comet, and I'm sure I'm the man for the job."

General Lockhart immediately relaxed. "That's more like it, Major. I knew I could count on you. Now that that's settled, I'll tell the others to start the transfer of the external tank from *Discovery* to *Constitution*. Meanwhile, I've brought along some firing coordinates for the laser that I'm sure you'll want to study."

Carradine suppressed a knowing smile. He knew his

crewmate was absolutely unconvinced, but there was no way Stuart Fisher was going to get done out of a mission; not out of any mission, and certainly not out of the most important one of their lives.

APRIL

One clean shot, thought Carradine, remembering the General's words. Hit it too light and L.A. is in the drink; hit it too hard and dump 65 billion tons of radioactive comet on the earth. Nuclear winter. Extinction. One clean shot. Carradine thought through the formula from basic physics. Energy equals one-half of mass times the velocity of impact squared. How could a single bullet stop a charging elephant? The elephant was bigger than the bullet, it was ten thousand times more massive, but the bullet could still drop it cold. The bullet was faster. The quick littly guy could stop the big guy, but he had to be fast and he had to be accurate. Not only that, but the formula gave the fast guy an edge; the velocity of the impact was squared. Two became four, four became sixteen, sixteen became two hundred fifty-six. By contrast, mass took a handicap; the formula cut mass in half. Sixteen became eight, eight became four, four became two. Still, mass was in the formula; you couldn't ignore it.

178

Halley's comet was a monster. Five miles across. Wider than Manhattan. Carradine saw the brilliant ball far ahead of them. He could see it grow larger now, almost by the hour. The laser, thought Carradine, now, that had speed. It had the speed of the sun, but how about mass? Light was photons. Energy equals mass times the speed of light squared. Einstein said so. But was there enough energy in Shiva to stop a comet? One clean shot, he thought to himself.

When Carradine uncoupled from the space station and "lit the candle," he quickly raised the *Constitution*'s speed to 25,000 miles per hour. This was escape velocity, and Carradine and Fisher slowly saw their blue planet grow smaller. At this tremendous velocity, it took them only nine hours to reach the distance of the moon's orbit, 240,000 miles from the earth. Not since the Apollo missions ended in 1973 had man ventured this far from his home planet. At the time they crossed the path of the moon's orbit, the moon was far away on the other side of the earth, making its diurnal rotation. The *Constitution* did not wait for the moon to pass. Instead, Carradine and Fisher pushed beyond cislunar and out into deep space, where man had never been. They had a date with another heavenly body, which was even now bearing down on the moon from the vicinity of Venus.

"Lee? Are you asleep?"

Carradine shook from his reverie to see Fisher on the flight deck beside him. "No, Fish. My mind was wandering. What's up?"

"Look, I don't want you to think I won't give this my all. I'll follow orders, sure. But Lee, what I tried to tell that half-wit general back there is true. There's no way in hell this plan is going to work."

Carradine saw that Fisher was staring out the flight

179

deck window at the oncoming comet. Extreme distress showed on Fisher's face. "Let's hear it," said Carradine.

"I wanted to think it over, calm down a bit. I've been checking some numbers, rereading a couple of experiments on the thermal coupling of different solids. I was looking for some way to convince myself that this whole thing could work, but it's just not there. Using Shiva against that damn snowball is hopeless."

"Tell me the technical problem," said Carradine, his gaze fixed, like Fisher's, on the silvery tail covering half the sky.

"Okay, let's take it from the top, and think through the whole process. The concept of the laser is precision energy. To hit something we start off by firing the low power tracking laser. It goes out at the speed of light, reflects off the solid target, and bounces back to us. So far it's no different than radar. Then, by keeping the tracking beam on the object we pulse the laser cannon itself against the target. Since the laser travels at the speed of light there is almost no need to anticipate the target's future position. When the energy from the laser hits the target it is converted into heat. The process is called thermal coupling, but exactly what happens at that point depends on several variables, like the wavelength of the light and, maybe most important, the target material. Now, when I hit a steel or aluminum alloy, like the skin of an ICBM, the whole crystalline structure of the metal starts to deteriorate. The aluminum begins to vaporize, metal-gas pours off the fuselage, shock waves begin to tear the target apart. Meanwhile, the vaporized metal emits X-ray radiation so that all the missile's electronic components simply incandesce. Ten seconds against any missile the Soviets have, ten seconds, and it's falling out of the sky back to Minsk or Pinsk or wherever it came from."

"And what you want to tell me is that Halley's comet is vastly different in size and structure from any Soviet missile," added Carradine laconically.

"Exactly. Even if it weren't so huge, the damn thing is just a solid hunk of ablative material, one giant heat shield. Where is the thin aluminum skin to thermal couple, where are the electronic components to burn out? Oh sure, I can vaporize a little bit of it, add a little to the comet's tail. But what do they think the sun has been doing for the last eon? The same damn thing, that's what. What the hell do they think the tail is, anyway? It's just vaporizing gases from that snowball. Shiva can't out-sun the sun."

"They say a comet loses one percent of its mass each time it passes around the sun," said Carradine. Both men fell silent. After awhile Carradine added, "I suppose they feel we have to try something. Just hoping against hope."

"I think the whole thing is a big public relations gimmick. A big attention getter, to show the world what great guys the Americans are, to go out there and give it the old college try."

"Perhaps that is the reason."

"So you agree with me that this whole thing is a farce."

"No, but you have convinced me that using the laser is technically infeasible. I just don't think the public relations thing is necessarily a mistake. It might keep some people from going completely mad. Can you imagine what a strain this must be? The whole social order is being pulled apart. Perhaps we're just buying them a little time to sort things out."

"Maybe. But we're only postpoining the inevitable.

181

Tomorrow we'll fire Shiva and the world will see that against Halley's it's no better than a popgun. Anyway, I'm frustrated and beat. I'm going below to sleep."

"Oh, Fish, before you go, when will you lock on your tracking laser?"

"Oh, an hour or so before firing, just to give me a target outline. Why?"

"Nothing. Just checking. Good night."

Stuart Fisher bobbed down the hatchway, leaving Carradine alone on the flight deck. When the Orbiter middeck lights dimmed, Carradine left his commander's seat and moved around behind it to the payload station. Strapping himself in, he booted one of the shuttle's powerful onboard computers and began to calculate shuttle speeds, relative masses, fuel consumption, and vectors. Fisher had confirmed his fears. The laser would not work. Of course they would fire it, but when it failed Carradine would have a back-up plan. The computations took him the better part of an hour. He had to determine at exactly what point he must begin to accelerate, to begin to burn, so that he would hit peak velocity just before he ran out of fuel. When his calculations were through, he went to the emergency medical cabinet and pulled out a disposable syringe. Carradine took a plastic vial of a strong tranquilizer, punctured it with the needle and drew back on the plunger. The drug was for that yet-to-occur emergency of a crew member's completely losing control. It was designed to relax and numb the muscles in seconds; within a minute or two the patient would drop off to sleep and be out for eight to ten hours. Carradine spurted a few drops through the needle, which beaded up and started to float. He caught them with a small sponge, then capped the needle and put it in his flight suit. Returning to his pilot's seat,

182

he catnapped on and off, each time awakening to see the coma of Halley's comet over a larger and larger part of the emptiness of space.

A career in space had shown Carradine some beautiful sights, but the approach of the comet was the most beautiful he had ever seen. It was as if they were flying into a silver mist, a ghostly fog of brilliant light. In reality, the comet was coming at the shuttle headlong, but it appeared to be traveling sideways. This confusion between true direction and apparent direction was because the comet's tail always pointed away from the sun, regardless of the direction it was traveling. "Tail" was a misnomer; it didn't have anything to do with the direction the comet happened to be moving. Even for a space veteran like Carradine, it was hard to leave the earth-atmosphere frame of reference, where a running horse left its dust cloud or a steamship left its wake or a speeding jet left its contrail directly behind it. In the vacuum of space this was all rearranged. The comet's "tail" did not mark the place where the coma had been. It was simply the sublimation of tiny ice crystals caused by the sun's energy. These crystals and dust particles were pushed away from the sun by the pressure of the sun's radiation. It was a phenomenon independent of the path of the comet's orbit. The constant evaporation of mass only served to create a small "rocket force" on the spinning comet, which made even Halley's a little unpredictable, throwing off its calculated return by a few days every apparition.

From Carradine's vantage point through the shuttle's observation window, the tail of the comet was stretched out across space to the right of the *Constitution*, angling slightly back toward it. The comet's coma, the luminous gas ball a quarter of a million miles across, was

183

directly in front of the *Constitution*. Beyond that was the bright orb of the sun. There was no night for the shuttle here, no earth to swing behind, just the perpetual glow of the distant fireball in the inky blackness of space. Carradine could see clearly that there were two distinct tails to the comet. The longer tail, 10 million miles long and absolutely straight, was a plasma composed of electrons and molecular ions. The heavy concentration of ionized carbon monoxide made it appear pale blue. The shorter, diffuse tail was dust, released by the comet as its gases evaporated, then blown away from the nucleus by solar radiation pressure. The multitude of micron-size silicate particles gave the curved dust tail the yellow hue of reflected sunlight. Soothed by the seemingly eternal quality of sun and comet and twin tails covering the heavens, Carradine drifted off to sleep.

Hours later Stuart Fisher came up on the flight deck, climbing through the primary interdeck access just behind Carradine, who was still asleep in the shuttle commander's seat. Fisher noted a small flashing red light at his own station, the mission station, across the flight deck. It was an indication that the ship's spectroscope was detecting significant amounts of external gases. Fisher pushed himself over to his post and requested an ultraviolet spectrum analysis. A graph appeared, and the computer began to trace out on the display screen the telltale stalagmites of the resonance lines of different elements. At 1216 angstroms Fisher saw intense activity, indicating the presence of large quantities of hydrogen. He knew what this meant: they had already reached the far outer boundary of the comet, the giant hydrogen cloud, larger than the sun, that a comet emitted. This million-mile-wide invisible gas ball was the first layer of the comet's onion-like skin. Somewhere in the center of all that gas and dust was the nucleus, a pinhead by comparison. It was that nucleus that Shiva was to find and destroy.

Fisher made his way to the front of the flight deck and sat down in the pilot's seat to the right of the sleeping Carradine. He thought a long time about the floods on earth, his hometown of San Diego under water. He thought about the Russians gobbling up a few more countries, at a time when the West was too disorganized to resist. He thought about millions of people drowning or starving in the floods and dislocation.

When sometime later Carradine awoke there was little to be seen from the observation windows other than the coma of Halley's comet. The coma was not dense except for a small portion near the center. Through most of it you could see stars twinkling from behind the coma, the way you could see car lights through a light fog. When Fisher saw that Carradine was awake, he called to him, "Cup o' coffee there, sleeping beauty?"

"Yeah, please, I must have been exhausted," Carradine said, studying the changing scene before them. "We're really on top of this thing now."

"We hit the hydrogen cloud a few hours ago and got enough to get a good ultraviolet spectrum reading. I make it that by this afternoon we may hit the shock front of the oncoming nucleus. After that I suppose we can take our shot, then hightail it out of here."

The two men had breakfast in the glow of the comet. They radioed earth and although the reception was already weak from the ionized environment in the hydrogen corona, they talked for several hours. There was encouragement from Mission Control in Houston, there was a brief word from the president. They were told that the main tracking station in White Sands, New

Mexico, had a clear fix on their location, even with the interference. The world would be watching them and praying for them. They were told that the president had announced to the nation that the astronauts were flying out to the comet to see if anything could be done. Shiva was not specifically mentioned, but it was assumed that the *Constitution* had some super-weapon to deploy. They were told that from the earth, the comet's head had swollen to ten times the apparent size of the moon. People were terrified and prayed that Carradine and Fisher could do something. They were the earth's last hope. The two astronauts said a few barely audible words for the press. The only thing missing were the tears of wives and children.

As reception was lost, the fading voice of General Lockhart told them that the final readings removed any doubt that Halley's was on a collision course and would strike the moon in the next ninety-six hours if the *Constitution* could not stop it. The impact would be just a glancing blow on the far side of the moon, with the comet striking at a less than five degree angle. "It will barely graze the moon," said Lockhart, "but even that will be violent enough to do the job. If Shiva can't stop the comet, it will be a very different world when you return."

As the hours passed, Fisher and Carradine talked about everything and nothing. Carradine was amazingly loquacious, as if their camaraderie could somehow diminish the anxiety. The comet's coma steadily grew. They were too close now to distinguish the tail trailing off across space.

"So Lockhart and the big brass think the comet didn't just fall, it was pushed," said Fisher. "Do you agree that the Russians are behind this little gag?"

"There's no way to know, I suppose," answered Carradine. "But all these years that we've been working on moon landings, and then the whole space shuttle program, they've appeared to be virtually standing still. I think they must have been working on something, and maybe this was it."

As they studied the banks of gauges and dials the ship suddenly shuddered violently. "This is it," yelled Carradine, "we've hit the comet's bow wave." A host of lights and buzzers went on simultaneously. Needles began to oscillate back and forth. For the first time, man was attempting to sail through the head of a comet.

"The instruments are disoriented," said Fisher.

"We seem to be in some kind of a chaotic magnetic field," said Carradine. "Our directional indicators are all contradicting each other. We could drift off course." For the next several hours the two men tried to get a firm bearing, but with little success. The instruments had fallen under the spell of the magnetic field of the comet. Visual observation from the shuttle window did not help. All they could see was that the ship was being steadily engulfed by the thickening plasma in the outer coma of Halley's comet.

Finally Fisher said, "I can use Shiva to zero in on the nucleus." Returning to his mission station, Fisher started the hydraulic motors that opened the forward cargo bay doors. He then instructed the computer to raise the laser platform from the floor of the cargo bay. The hydraulic jacks slowly pushed up a long tube with mirrors on either end mounted on a ten-foot platform. Using the low power tracking laser, Fisher initiated the lasing reaction. Flourine gas poured into the chamber between the two mirrors of the laser, and when the reaction was sufficiently advanced, Fisher fired a thunderbolt out across the gaseous space in front of the *Constitution*. In less than a second it was back. The instruments showed that it had located the center of the fiery chariot. Knowing the speed light traveled, and the time it took for the beam to return, it was a simple matter for the computer to ascertain the exact position of the comet's nucleus in relation to the shuttle.

"I've got a bead on it, Lee," said Fisher triumphantly.

"How far away is it?" barked Carradine.

"About 500,000 miles. I'll fire again to determine the rate of speed."

Above the observation window Carradine again saw the split second of brilliant green light slice out to infinity. After a few minutes, Fisher called out, "It's going 25.79 miles per second, roughly 93,000 miles an hour."

"Analyze firing conditions," ordered Carradine.

Staring into a bank of closed-circuit TV cameras, Fisher delicately positioned the large conical shape of Shiva's cannon. It was perched on top of the opened cargo bay doors like an ungainly headdress on the space shuttle's streamlined body. Standing immediately behind the tracking laser, the cannon was fired by computer along the same path traced out by the low-power beam.

"There's a lot of dust out there, Lee. The beam is going to suffer a lot of diffusion. The nucleus appears to be spinning also. That's going to make it tough. We've got to get closer. We may need to be right on top of it."

"Okay, just keep feeding in the coordinates as we get closer. We'll have to lock the board computer on to the laser beam. We'll use it to navigate right up to the nucleus."

As the hours passed, the *Constitution* was increasingly buffeted by the waves of dust and plasma in the comet's thickening coma. The ship would be pushed off course only to be brought back on again by the arrow-straight beam of the laser.

"Listen, Fish, if we keep using the laser to track the nucleus, are we going to have enough energy to fire the damn thing?"

There was a pause before Fisher's measured response, "Sure, Cap, just enough." Carradine felt again the syringe in his flight suit, but worried whether he would be able to fly the ship, fire the engines, and navigate by laser all at the same time. His plan depended on the precision use of mass and velocity. The computers would take care of the fine tuning, but if the *Constitution* was off course at the key moment the whole sacrifice would be for nothing.

By now they had totally lost the ability to navigate by sight. From the windows all that could be seen was a curtain of multitudinous small dust particles glowing with sunlight, racing along the glass, propelled by the solar wind.

Fisher called from behind him, "We're within twenty minutes of the nucleus." Carradine set the engines for full thrust and set the automatic ignition system. All that was required was a touch of a button and a thrown ignition switch, and the *Constitution*'s three main engines would come on with all the power they had from earth lift-off. They had enough fuel for about a three-minute firing, but that would be sufficient to take their speed to over 100,000 miles an hour. After that, there would not be enough fuel to fire the retro-rockets for a slowdown. Hit, miss, or error, the *Constitution* would not be coming home. His preparations in place, Carradine said, "Are you ready to fire?"

"Ready in sixty seconds, Colonel," came Fisher's voice from behind him. "Give me a count-down."

189

Carradine was tense with concern; would he have enough time to put his alternative plan into effect? Nevertheless, they had to give the laser a try. Carradine punched the clock to initiate the countdown and brought the ship's deportment into position for firing. His face illuminated by the gleaming cloud of ionized dust, Carradine's attention was totally consumed by the shuttle's instrumentation. He grimly waited for Fisher, in the firing station behind him, to flash that emerald green ray once more through the golden dust. They would have their answer, and if it was as they both feared and predicted, Carradine would race back to Fisher and use the hypodermic. There was no other way.

At exactly the moment Fisher was to fire the laser, Carradine sensed a presence by his right ear and jerked around. Fisher lunged down on top of him and, pinning him for a second against the padded commander's chair, rammed a syringe into a thick vein along Carradine's neck. Before Carradine could push him off, Fisher slammed down the plunger.

"The laser, damn it, the laser, fire it, fire it," wailed Carradine, clutching his throat.

"I can't, Lee, I used most of the power to navigate through the coma. It wouldn't have worked anyway."

Carradine stared up at him in disbelief. Already he could feel his limbs going limp. "Jesus," he screamed, "what have you done to me?"

"It's a tranquilizer, Lee. I'm sorry, there was no other way. We've got to use the *Constitution* itself. We've got to ram the son of a bitch."

"You bastard, I'm going under."

"Lee, we can't let the Sovs get away with this. Millions will die."

190

"I know, I know, but you've got to fire the engines, you need more velocity."

"What! You agree with what I'm doing?"

"Christ, man," moaned Carradine, "I had a needle planned for you. I . . . I didn't think you had it in you. I can't lift my arms!" Carradine was on the verge of tears. "The engines, the engines, you've got to fire them. It's ready to . . . burn."

"Where, Lee, where?"

Carradine was getting woozy. "Large black . . . button. Push it in while . . . you throw the ignition . . . switch . . . other . . . panel."

"Okay, okay, Lee, hang on. I'm sorry, I'm sorry." Fisher leaned over the drowsy Carradine and pushed in the button. When he threw the switch, there was a tremendous explosion and the whole ship took off like the rocket it was. Carradine was pressed deeply into his commander's seat, but Fisher, standing and off balance, went toppling toward the back of the flight deck. The acceleration pinned him helplessly against the control panel and cargo bay windows in the back wall.

Carradine was fighting for consciousness in the commander's seat. Every few seconds the beam of the laser cut through the golden shower, the last of its energy showing the way for the *Constitution*'s computerized homing system. As the shuttle passed 100,000 miles per hour, even the microscopic dust of the comet was like a sandblaster. The very fabric of the *Constitution* tore itself apart as one warning light after another flashed on. At these speeds even the thin gases of the coma created friction; the heat tiles of the *Constitution* incandesced. Still, the fuel valve held on full open for the engines to sip their last before annihilation. The windows were ablaze

191

with the ionized vapors of the brilliant fireball of Halley's comet.

And so into oblivion. When the collision came it was totally painless, perhaps the most painless of all time; over in a microsecond, before any nerve ending could even take interest. Fisher was glued to the back wall of the shuttle, whooping like a cowboy, from fear and from excitement, daring to do what no man had ever dared. Carradine was limp in his commander's seat, still just conscious, his gaze fixed on the glowing observation window. Led in by the precision tracking of the laser beam, they hit the comet dead center. Shiva had proved its worth, even if those on earth would never know it. With one clean shot, Lee Carradine, Stuart Fisher, Shiva, and Orbiter vehicle *Constitution,* crashed, burned, and passed into eternity.

Miguel had scarcely seen Isabella since he had dumped her at the Siesta Motel, on the outskirts of Alamogordo, New Mexico, the month before. Things had happened fast for him since that morning in February when he had simultaneously sent telegrams to the Faculty of Astronomy at the University of Mexico and to his uncle at the Ministry of Internal Affairs. It had started with ridicule, then disbelief, then doubt, then interest, then concern, then alarm. By the next morning he and Isabella were on the flight from Tuxtla Gutierrez to Mexico City. They had met that night with his former professors at the university, who carefully reviewed his photographs and his calculations. By the next afternoon his uncle had him in to meet the minister, and that night Miguel had an audience with the president of Mexico. By the end of the week Miguel was in Washington, D.C., lecturing at the Smithsonian Institution. He appeared on "Nightline," "Today," "Good Morning America," and the "MacNeil-Lehrer News Hour." The world was suddenly in a crisis, and he seemed to the media to be the only recognized authority. He was asked all sorts of questions about things he could only guess at. "What will happen when the comet hits the moon?" "How did it get off course?" "Are the Russians behind this?" "What is being done to protect us?"

Isabella had rather liked all this attention. Now, her parents no longer scolded her for marrying a crazy dreamer. She was asked her opinion on the diversion of the comet. *People* magazine wanted to know what it was like being married to the world's most famous astronomer.

Miguel himself tired rather quickly of the inane questions and popping flash attachments. He therefore accepted without hesitation when NASA offered to have him visit the crisis center that had been set up at the Johnson Space Center in Houston. Apparently the NASA leadership had been impressed with him because the president of the United States himself had then called the president of Mexico to ask if Miguel could be temporarily relieved of his duties in Mexico in order to stay and assist in the tracking effort. Politics played a role in this diplomatic gesture. Considering the crisis the North American continent was facing, a little neighborly solidarity could not hurt. Miguel was taken to the ground station for the Tracking Data and Relay Satellite System (Teeders) at White Sands, New Mexico. He was put on the principal team tracking the comet's movements, and when the diversion scheme had indicated a role for the *Constitution,* Miguel had worked on methods to communicate with the shuttle via the satellite network, even as it entered the hydrogen cloud around the comet's coma.

For Isabella, this brought an abrupt halt to her brief fling with fame. The White Sands project was secret. The press was not allowed, and Isabella was to draw no attention to herself. Miguel had deposited her at the closest motel, a run-down old flea bag on route 54 between Alamogordo and El Paso. He promised her that they would fly to Mexico City every weekend, but as soon as Miguel arrived at the tracking station he began working eighteen hour days, seven days a week, arriving back at the Siesta Motel too nervous and exhausted even to eat dinner. Isabella was once again a widow to astronomy.

Miguel had been closely involved in the calculations that led to the conclusion that the collision would cause the moon's orbit to move closer to the earth. There was great concern that the moon would come so close as to pass the Roche limit, where its gravity would be overwhelmed by earth's, causing it to explode like a grenade. Miguel and others had demonstrated mathematically that this would not occur. The new orbit would be tight and fast, but would not further decay. The former distant satellite would become a permanent near moon.

When it was learned that the *Constitution* would fire a powerful laser beam at the comet to attempt to move it away from its collision course, Miguel had been skeptical. However, he realized that he knew very little about these modern weapons, and therefore reserved judgment, keeping his opinion to himself. When, in mid-April, the shuttle flew out to meet Halley's comet, Miguel was one of the many astronomers in the main tracking room following the course of Halley's and the *Constitution* across the spring sky.

As the two blips on the radar screen closed on each other far out in deep space, the tension in the tracking room was stifling. Everyone was convinced that what they were seeing on their screens was earth's last chance to maintain the status quo. If the *Constitution* failed, today would become the great watershed. The course of life on this planet would change irrevocably; all future history would trace the turning point to this day. Even after radio contact with the *Constitution* was lost in the comet's coma, White Sands was able to track the shuttle's position. When the Teeders satellites did not pick up the burst of electric energy that signaled the firing of the laser, the tracking team began to give up hope. Miguel, not an especially religious man, made a secret prayer to the Virgin of Guadeloupe. Despite the powerful air conditioners, the team was soaked with perspiration. When the *Constitution* did not turn out of the path of the comet, and continued instead deep into the inner coma, Miguel and the others knew that something had gone horribly wrong. As the interference increased, the two little electronic blips seemed to converge, and then the tracking station lost the signal for the *Constitution* altogether. No one spoke. There was just the oppresive electronic hum, the small clicks and whines of an enormous control board.

"What has happened? What has gone wrong!" said the head of station loudly but to himself, poorly suppressing his fear and bewilderment.

"Where the hell are they?" said the man at Miguel's right.

"We've had it now," said a man behind Miguel, slamming down his fist. "We blew it. It's all over. We bought the goddamn farm."

At that moment a buzzer went off, indicating that the Teeders satellites had a new signal. An enormous

195

shock wave had been detected in the vicinity of the comet.
The men stared back into their screens and the head of
station called for a recalculation of the comet's course.
A ray of hope returned to the tense faces, but it was
quickly dashed. Whatever that shock wave indicated, the
course of the comet had not been changed. The effect
of breathing hope into the exhausted tracking personnel, only to jerk it away, was to make the depression
doubly severe. Around Miguel some men grew furious,
others began to weep. There was no possibility of
redemption. The mission, the radar blips, the elec-
tronic-control room—all were forgotten. Miguel heard
the head of station talking to his counterpart in Houston, and noticed that the man could barely speak. Miguel tried to be stoic and not get caught up in the wave
of hopelessness. He stared down at the tracking scope
at the lone little blip proceeding steadily toward the moon.
Collision would be in less than four days. Some of the
team began to drift from the room to call their families.
A report was prepared for transmission to the White
House. It was brief: "No indication that laser was fired,
signal for Orbiter vehicle *Constitution* lost, Halley's comet
on course."

Miguel was worried for Mexico. Fortunately it was a
mountainous country, but Veracurz, Acapulco, and most
of Yucatan would suffer terribly. His country did not
have the land or the money that the United States had
to resettle so many millions of poor people. With a fatal-
istic curiosity Miguel again called up the plot of the comet's calculated course to the moon and projected it against
the true position shown on the tracking screen. There it
was, right on course, but perhaps a few seconds behind
schedule. *¡Caramba!* Behind schedule! Miguel thrust his
face down close to the screen as if this would help him

see it better. He typed into his console keyboard the request for information on the comet's calculated trajectory to the moon, with the exact position it should now occupy. The quadrant appeared instantly before him. He then asked the computer for an overlay window and called up the actual position of the comet as charted by the Teeders satellites. "*Santo Dios,* it is behind schedule!" yelled Miguel, jumping to his feet and then sitting down again. The other trackers looked over to see if Miguel's mind had snapped from the tragedy, but seeing his intense activity at the computer, a few of them drifted over to see what he could possibly be doing.

Miguel now asked the computer to replot the comet's actual location against the location at the moment they had detected the bow wave of energy. From these two plots and the times they were recorded, Miguel calculated a velocity. He knew instantly that it was not what they had calculated before. It seemed to be just a fraction slower. The other trackers stared down at Miguel's flying fingers on the computer keyboard. The excitement grew as the group began to perceive what Miguel had discovered. Miguel now asked for a new projection based on the slower speed the comet was moving. The course line instantly went out across the grid of space. The direction was unchanged, but when Miguel called up the time at which the comet would get to the calculated point of impact the comet was a full fifty seconds behind schedule. Other men pushed into the growing huddle around Miguel's computer terminal.

Miguel now called up the orbital path of the moon. He plotted it against the new trajectory of the comet. The two lines came so close now that on this scale Miguel could not tell if they intersected or not. He punched in for a larger scale. As if it were moving, the computer

197

screen began to blow up the image before Miguel. He moved the cursor to keep the point of intersection on the screen. It was the tensest moment of Miguel's life as the prospective descended on the point of the impact like a giant hawk diving out of the sky at a squirrel.

The computer-generated shape of the moon grew huge and then went off the screen, so you could see only the moon's edge. The moon, Miguel knew, moved sixty-four one hundredths of a mile every second, but would it have moved enough to get clear? They were down to a scale of ten miles equals one inch before they were sure. There would be no collision. The great astronomical timepiece, ticking off men's lives every seventy-six years, would come within two miles of the moon's surface, then, slingshoting off the moon's weak gravitational field, Halley's comet would be flung away into deep space, never to return.

There was wild jubilation in the tracking room. Stodgy old technicians jumped in the air like third-graders. There was whooping and hollering, and everyone pounded Miguel on the back as if he had personally decelerated the comet. It was Miguel himself who took the edge off the celebration when, after a minute, he quietly observed that the only thing that could have slowed the comet that much was a head-on collision with the American space shuttle; that is what must have caused the shock wave. The only possible conclusion was that the astronauts had deliberately sought out and rammed the comet's nucleus. As the realization of this sacrifice sunk in, someone observed that they had better correct their earlier message to the president. The hotline was actuated, and when the president of the United States was on, it was Miguel who had the honor of telling him that the *Constitution* had been lost, but that the earth had been saved.

"Eugene, Oregon?"

"Yes, near there anyway. I think you'll like it. It's a language-teaching job in a private high school; it's, well, out of the way. Athletics are first rate in the community, skiing, rafting, that kind of thing. The principal is retired military, worked in Berlin. He's one of us of course, but beyond the fact that you helped us and need a new identity, he knows nothing about you. He won't ask either. We've made up a little history for you, one that should check out just fine. You're a Volga German, grew up mostly in Russia, until your parents were permitted to immigrate to West Germany. You speak respectable German, so it makes sense. When they passed away, you decided on a new life; you came to America. If you stay away from the Russian Department at the University of Oregon, Russian films, and so on, I doubt you'll ever run across anybody you knew in New York, or for that matter in Moscow. The stylist will help you change your hair, make-up, contact lens color, wardrobe. You won't recognize yourself when she's through. If you want, we could do a little surgery, but it's usually not necessary."

"I'd like to avoid it if possible."

"With your looks, I'm not surprised." O'Dwyer did not smile when he said this. He recalled that these same good looks had so recently compromised the NSA and led to Charles Griffin's death. He was with Leana in an NSA safe-house in Cleveland, Ohio. It was a gray day, and the clouds coming off Lake Erie portended rain. It was the last day of April.

The larger world, outside the realm of spies and counterspies, was relaxed again. The man in the street, so recently convinced of his impending doom, had just as rapidly slipped into a kind of self-congratulation. Everyone viewed himself as having had a great adventure, without, in most cases, ever leaving home. Carradine and Fisher's sacrifice had made them heroes, posthumously of course, and they were truly revered at home and abroad. People were feeling pretty good about the United States too, for pulling out the chestnuts and all that. Patriotism was back in vogue.

O'Dwyer's duties were more pedestrian. It was a mop-up, a denouement, a body-counter's job after the big battle. When the comet missed the moon, Leana again called O'Dwyer. She had gotten her revenge: Griffin's killers were dead, she had dealt a heavy blow to Soviet intelligence in the United States. In the meantime, *bedá* had failed. In the end there was no reason to stay in hiding. With O'Dwyer's support she had cut herself a fair deal. The NSA had gone all the way to the White House to grant her immunity, protection, and assistance in establishing a new life. In return she would give herself up and tell everything she knew. O'Dwyer had convinced the Oval Office that her knowledge was essential, that the government was getting a bargain. When the arrangements had been made, Leana left her hiding place in the mountains of Pennsylvania and drove west to the address O'Dwyer had given her. She found the old, turreted apartment building on South Moreland Boulevard, rang the bell, and turned herself in. She had been with O'Dwyer and his assistants for several days. There was a lot to discuss.

"Of course, you'll need a new name. You could keep Leana, but it's risky. The first name could be German or

Russian, but German might be preferable. Give it some thought. The surname will be Wegen. It's a good, simple name and matches some records we're putting in place in Stuttgart, just in case anyone decides to check out your background."

O'Dwyer made some coffee, and they continued Leana's lengthy debriefing; Leana's entire life's story, and in particular, everything she knew about the KGB and its clandestine operations in America. O'Dwyer put it all on tape, slowly, meticulously, with plenty of questions. O'Dwyer tried to keep personal considerations out of it, but occasionally, at the end of a long day, when the tape recorder was off and Leana talked about Griffin, he couldn't help feeling involved and responsible.

"I just don't understand why Charlie didn't come to me when he thought he was on to something."

"I guess he felt more comfortable talking to me," said Leana without smiling. "He would have come to you soon. He was on the verge. I think he wanted to have every piece in place, to impress you." They both sat quietly for awhile, then Leana spoke again. "You know, I still don't exactly understand why the KGB decided to have him killed. I guess they thought they could buy a month, not much more than that. Once everyone knew the comet was heading for the moon, and what the collision would do to the tides, all the Soviet coastal construction and evacuation preparations would speak for themselves."

"One thing I don't understand is why the KGB wanted to kill you too."

"I've thought about that a long time. Probably because Voroshilov convinced Moscow that I was too involved with Charles, that I would have warned him or tried to protect him."

"Would you have?"

"Yes, I suppose so. Voroshilov was right; I was involved. Not romantically perhaps, but I couldn't just let them kill him. He was so defenseless. Like a little child."

"Then you weren't in love with him?"

"No . . . no, I don't think so, but I'll tell you, you can't sleep with a man for that long and not feel some emotion. It wouldn't have to be love. You could easily grow to hate someone in that situation, but there was nothing about Griffin to hate. I guess I just got used to him."

O'Dwyer brooded for awhile and rubbed his forehead. "I can't help telling you that I'll never forgive myself for this mess. It makes me and the entire agency look so damn asleep at the wheel. In retrospect, 20 / 20 hindsight, everything fits. The Sovs fired a rocket from near their base at Leninsk in Kazakhstan early last July. We didn't know what it was; we figured it was a science probe or something. Anyway, we lost it around Venus. In August, also in Kazakhstan, we suspect that they shot down one of their own transport planes near the Caspian Sea, with who knows who on board. Connected? We'll never know, but if that rocket had really been on its way around the sun to divert Halley's comet, there would have been a lot of big scientific mouths to shut. And sure enough, months later we learned through our embassy in Moscow of several separate reports that a prominent Jewish physicist had been killed, but each report mentioned a different physicist. In each case, the deceased's widow was told only that there had been a plane crash and that no details were available.

"Then all the construction," O'Dwyer continued. "I'm sure Charlie could have documented beyond doubt that this was a massive, coordinated program begun half a year before Halley's showed any indication of a course change. The Russians have practically built a fully equipped new coastline twenty miles inland. To me it's conclusive that the Soviets deliberately altered the course of the comet, knowing that the tidal changes would be devastating to the Western allies. Most of our government is convinced. There are a few left-wingers in the House who say the events are unconnected, but with those guys, you'd have to give them the original order signed by the General Secretary of the Communist Party of the Soviet Union before they'd believe you. Poor Charlie, he really hit the jackpot."

"He was a great analyst, a superb linguist," said Leana with conviction. There was another long silence. "Well, Mr. O'Dwyer, I guess I should thank you and the NSA for all you've done. Few people get a so-called new life."

"You know Leana, I'd never repeat it, but I'm just pleased as hell that you got to those sons of bitches. I was determined to use everything I had to get you pardoned. Hell, you did more for U.S. security in the last three months than our entire agency can claim in most years. And best of all, the KGB's little bastards got what they deserved. There's still one thing though that really breaks my heart. It's that with all this, with all this death, shot-down planes, professional killers, and crashed space ships, the big bastard back in the Kremlin who masterminded this so-called *bedá* fiasco is going to walk away from the whole thing *unscathed*. In fact, probably right now he's back there in Moscow thinking about a goddamn comeback."

MAY

By the second week of May most signs of winter had yielded to spring along Nevsky Prospect. It was raining, raining hard, but there was no possibility of snow. At 11:45 P.M., as Admiral Komkov's Zil limousine barreled down the broad Leningrad boulevard, the thunder boomed above. The chauffeur sped over the Fontanka canal, the bridge's beautiful bronze horses in an eternal stampede. The message had come just at twilight; take the Red Arrow to Moscow. Komkov had a meeting at the Kremlin first thing in the morning. The cable had not provided details, he didn't even know who the meeting was with, but Komkov was relieved to see it would not take long. He was to have his private plane fly at dawn to Moscow to bring him home after the meeting.

The rain became a downpour as they swung into the Square of the Revolution and the great, black car stopped in front of Moscow Station. Komkov pulled his navy greatcoat high, stepped from the car, and strode purposefully to the platform. He climbed the steps of the "soft" class sleeping car and found his compartment. Within minutes he heard the strains of the Soviet National Anthem. The conductor announced that it was exactly midnight, and Komkov felt the familiar lurch as the big locomotive pulled from the station. Of all the things in the Soviet Union, reflected Komkov, this at least, ran on time.

He slept little that night, listening to the whirr of steel wheel against steel rail, the distant horn, the slap of the rain against the window. It was a night for reflection, a night for anticipation. Komkov knew the reason for his summons to the Kremlin was *bedá*. It had to be. The events of the last month had revealed a good deal. Everyone in the country had heard on Voice of America or Radio Free Europe that Halley's comet's catastrophic collision with the moon had been diverted. He of course had unrestricted access to the foreign press and a Red Fleet dish antenna even brought him Western TV. He could understand a little English, a little German. In the hysteria over the near miss of the comet, some Western governments even accused the Soviet Union of somehow changing the course of the comet so it would hit the moon. Komkov scoffed at this, but one thing he knew for sure: even if the Soviet Union hadn't caused it, the Politburo had at least known about it well in advance. As early as September, when he got the first "white" cipher they knew. They had to know. That was what all the flood planning was about. Once the Mexicans and the Americans announced to the world that collision was imminent and that there would be massive tidal changes, all of the Soviet construction and seemingly senseless evacuation exercises since the prior summer became clear evidence of the Soviet government's foreknowledge: clear to their foes, clear to their friends, clear to the Soviet people. The Politburo had been so certain of the inevitability of the collision, that prior to the American diversion they did not even deny the accusations. Instead they had had *Pravda* tout the virtues of socialist planning. The best that could be said, even by the European left-wing parties, was that the Soviets had known in advance but had elected not to share the secret. Thinking only of their own people, the Soviets were prepared to let the rest of the world drown. More than any event since perhaps the Second World War, the impending collision of the comet with the moon had etched itself on the great collective consciousness of mankind, and while the Americans had approached the impending crisis with heroism and self-sacrifice, the Russians appeared as conniving scoundrels. *Bedá* had been a disaster all right, a disaster for the image of the Soviet Union. Komkov himself wondered why the Politburo had kept the discovery a secret. If they had announced the discovery first, last September when he had learned of it, the Soviet Union would have been heralded as the high-tech sentinel of the globe. Instead the Mexicans ended up discovering it, and the Americans saved the world, while the Soviet Union was left to suffer its worst shellacking in world opinion since the Hitler-Stalin Pact. Numerous countries had severed diplomatic relations with the Soviet Union, and mobs were attacking Soviet embassies. And, thought Komkov to himself, we have no one to blame but our own dear KGB and our dear General Secretary of the Communist Party, who will of course totally escape responsibility for their actions. Komkov felt that the greed and stupidity had been beyond belief. After the Americans had diverted the comet, the general secretary had dropped out of sight. The Kremlin had said little, retreating to claims that the Americans were trying to whip up sentiment against them. Komkov knew better.

In the far north there is little night in May as the summer solstice approaches. It was light by 5:00 A.M. and at six o'clock the conductress brought two different kinds of tea. By seven o'clock, the train was in the station, and Komkov once again, as he had so many times before, climbed down from the Red Arrow and saluted the captain of his waiting escort.

"Your trip was satisfactory, Admiral Komkov?"

"Normal, uneventful. It rained most of the way."

"Your limousine is waiting, Admiral."

Less than twenty minutes later, the limousine pulled onto Red Square. The multicolored St. Basil's cathedral loomed in front of them but the car pulled left, under the enormous Saviour's Tower with its clock and ruby star. Komkov was whisked discreetly behind the five-meter-thick Kremlin Wall. They drove past the Kremlin Theater and turned right. To the left were the cathedrals: the five squat golden domes of the Cathedral of the Dormition, the white stone Belfry of Ivan the Great, the Cathedral of the Archangel Michael where Ivan IV Vasilevich, the Terrible, was buried. They pulled up in front of the main Kremlin office building, the seat of government of the Soviet Union. It was a triangular building topped by a squat, pale green dome shaped like a contact lens. The red flag of the Soviet Union fluttered above it. It was built in the eighteenth century by Catherine II to house a parliament she never got around to calling. Lenin and his wife, Nadezhda Krupskaya, lived here for the five years he ruled the new country. Now it was used by the Council of Ministers of the USSR. Komkov went inside to building security and was met by Colonel Grishin of the KGB. They had met several times before, but for effect, and to show his power, the colonel studied Komkov's face carefully and at close range.

"This is Admiral Komkov," said the colonel shrilly for a positive identification. The captain of the guard nodded. Komkov was put through a metal detector, which immediately sounded because of the various medals and insignia on Komkov's uniform. He came back, removed his tunic, and went through again. Dressing himself, he glowered at the prim colonel of state security. The two men started upward along the broad, winding staircase, Komkov following.

"Who am I to speak with?" asked Komkov.

"You don't know, Evgenie Alexandrovich?"

"You know that I don't know, Comrade Colonel," said Komkov, trying not to show his irritation.

"Evgenie Alexandrovich, today is bestowed on you the great honor of a conversation with the General Secretary of the Communist Party, the Supreme Military Commander of the Soviet Union."

Komkov paused while this rather portentous news sunk in. "Who else will be present for this meeting?" he asked slowly.

"You will meet with him alone." The two men continued their walk in silence.

Although Komkov had met the general secretary at occasional state functions, they had never had a private meeting. Nor did they know each other in any but a cordial, professional capacity. That suited Komkov; he found nothing likable about the general secretary, and had no desire to get to know him better. The general secretary had close ties to the KGB. He was hard-core Chekist and took every opportunity to advance the interests of state security, frequently at the expense of the senior military. After a succession of political maneuvers and a series of fortuitous deaths among the Party's leaders, he had seized the top post. Getting friendly with a man like this, thought Komkov, only gave him more chances to trip you up. He felt only grim trepidation about the meeting; it could not be good news.

When the two men reached the second floor, they went through an open doorway, past another detail of emotionless young guards, and then down a wide corridor until they arrived at the offices of the general secretary. The door to these offices was steel, with a window of bulletproof glass. Another officer with the green epaulets of the KGB surveyed the two men through the window. In the corridor behind Komkov and his escort was a large convex mirror that permitted the man behind the door to make sure the entire hall was devoid of any other individual. After a moment there was the guttural whirr of an electric lock, and the door popped open. Komkov went in; Colonel Grishin remained outside.

This room was a small antechamber with a second door leading off to the left. That door was similar to the first, metal with a small, thick window. Similar too were the cold eyes of a young officer of the KGB who stared from behind it. In this first, small room, a technician sat behind a table with a small machine on it. The machine had a revolving graph and wires with clamps running from it. On the back was a small decal saying, "Made in West Germany." Komkov did not know what it was.

The KGB officer said, "Admiral Komkov, this is a polygraph, a lie detector. I am going to attach electrodes to your fingers and ask you a few questions. Answer truthfully or we will know." The technician attached two clamps to the end of Komkov's fingers. Komkov felt like a robot. Meanwhile the officer ran a hand-held metal detector along the seam of Komkov's trousers. With the electrodes in place the officer asked, "State your full name."

Komkov responded, "Admiral Evgenie Alexandrovich Komkov." The swinging plotting needle began to slowly rise and fall on the graph paper.

"Are you an admiral in the Red Fleet?"

"Yes, of course, I am an admiral in the Red Fleet," said Komkov with irritation, not fully appreciating that his answers to these obvious questions were to be used as a control, so that when he answered the key questions there would be a known, truthful response for comparison.

"Now, Admiral, do you intend to harm the general secretary in any way?"

Komkov was shocked that they would think this possible. He responded, "No, I do not."

"Do you question his right to be General Secretary of the Party and Supreme Military Commander of the Soviet Union?"

"No, I do not."

The KGB officer looked down at the tracks of the needle swinging slowly on the graph paper. He looked at the technician behind the machine and they both nodded their heads. Komkov had passed. The electrodes were removed. Not one word was spoken. No one said, "Sorry, for this inconvenience" or "Only following orders, sir." There were no apologies. It was as if the KGB thought it was only to be expected that a fleet admiral would wish to harm the general secretary. Komkov's sense of shock matured into concealed, helpless anger. He wondered how much of the general secretary's efficiency was lost by walling himself behind steel doors and lie detectors. Komkov had not heard of this little ordeal before and supposed it was introduced because of the *bedá* fiasco.

The officer behind the next window had witnessed the test and the results. Satisfied, he sprang the lock opening the inner office and Komkov went inside. This next room was perhaps forty feet long and had four desks, two on each side of the room. There were three female secretaries at work and also a man, the general secretary's aide, in well-cut business clothes. It was a normal Soviet government office room, plusher than most of course. The ceiling was high, perhaps four meters.

The aide walked over to Komkov and offered his hand. "Very good to meet you, Admiral, the general secretary is ready to see you now." The aide spoke briefly into an intercom, and a heavily padded door at the end of the office clicked. The aide pulled open this door with some effort—Komkov noted it was soundproof and probably bombproof—and ushered Komkov inside. Rising with effort from the desk was the man whose picture shone down from every office, factory, and schoolroom in the USSR. He held the triple crown of Soviet politics: not only was he General Secretary of the Party, he was also President of the Soviet Union, and commander-in-chief of the Soviet armed forces. In person he was less imposing than his title: white-haired, stout, overweight, really, considerably shorter than Komkov. He appeared as if he had not been outside since his infancy, and his infancy was a good seventy-seven years ago. His face showed considerable aging and strain since the last time, a year ago perhaps, that Komkov had seen him close up. The general secretary had not been seen in public at all since the Americans had crashed their space shuttle into Halley's comet. He had even missed the big May Day Parade in Red Square, driving the foreign press wild with speculation. He motioned for Komkov to sit down in the winged leather chair opposite him.

"Please leave us now Yuri. I may be some time with the Admiral. We will call for morning tea." The aide withdrew, pulling the big door behind him, until, with an electric hum, it locked shut.

"Tell me Evgenie, are you well?"

"Yes, Comrade Secretary, I am."

"The Red Arrow ran on time?"

"As always, Comrade Secretary."

"I am sorry for the short notice. You could have flown, of course, but with the rain I thought the Red Arrow might be more, well, reassuring."

"It was, Comrade Secretary." Komkov passed his gaze quickly over the windowless office. It was richly appointed with antiques and maps from the Czarist era. The carpet was a deep crimson, the broad desk, mahogany. There was a globe and a mirrored bar. The whole room was dark with the panelling of expensive foreign woods. It was more like a rich German's study than a government office.

"Evgenie, I want to discuss with you the rather unfortunate international situation right now, a situation that may deteriorate further if we don't take decisive action. As you know, the Americans with their contemptible space shuttle were able to divert Halley's comet. Had it not been, well, interfered with, there would have been an astronomical event the equal of which mankind has never witnessed and probably never will: the collision of the great comet with the moon, and the subsequent change in the moon's orbit." The way the general secretary described the situation was as if he were

somehow disappointed that it had not occurred. Komkov
shifted in his chair, his face expressionless.

"We held within our grasp, Evgenie, the chance to
deal our enemies a mortal blow. Had the collision
occurred, the new orbit of the moon, closer and faster,
would have had an overwhelming impact on the world's
tides. I know you have heard about these speculations
in the foreign press and they are, I assure you, accurate.
Now just so I'm sure you understand how great was my
foresight in this matter, Admiral, and why it was necessary to take certain risks, I want you to tell *me* something: tell me about Soviet geography, tell me about the
military implications of our lack of coastline." The general secretary adjusted his seat cushion and, with a smug
grin, eased back in his padded leather chair.

Komkov resented the cat and mouse game, but had
no choice but to play. He began in an even tone.

"Russia, the modern Soviet Union, has suffered, as
you know of course, Comrade Secretary, since the end
of the Middle Ages from the fact that we are basically a
landlocked power. As early as Peter the Great, the
necessity of Russia having its 'window on the sea' has
been an essential element of our foreign policy. That is
why Peter the Great took the land where Leningrad is
now situated away from the Swedes; that is why he built
the Admiralty in Leningrad and constructed a navy. What
little ocean coastline our enormous country has is either
along the Arctic Ocean, frozen and uninhabited, except
for Murmansk and Archangel, or along the Pacific, 5,000
miles from our population centers."

"Precisely so, and what has this meant for the strategic concerns of our navy?" interjected the general secretary.

"On the Pacific, the situation is satisfactory, but under

most combat conditions, the Pacific Fleet could not hope to support Atlantic operations. On the Atlantic, because we do not have direct access, we must first pass through waters controlled by hostile powers. Three of our four blue-water fleets are potentially blockaded by the NATO countries. I would have to take my ships of the Baltic Fleet out through the waters of Norway and Denmark. To the south, the Black Sea Fleet could be completely bottled up by the Turks at Istanbul and the Dardenelles. Even the Northern Fleet, our largest fleet, would have to sail from Murmansk several hundred miles along the top of Norway under NATO scrutiny in order to break out into the Atlantic in the corridor between Great Britain and Iceland. Naturally we would look to the other Soviet arms, the Red Army and Air Force, to clear our passage."

"Naturally, Admiral, naturally. I will come back to your comments on the difficulties of the Northern Fleet, but for a minute just let your imagination run. What if the great geopolitical disadvantage of our country was suddenly turned into an asset. What if the long coast-lines of our adversaries were suddenly transformed into an enormous liability?"

"It would be militarily significant," said Komkov in measured tones, puzzled and anxious about where the general secretary was leading.

"Significant, Admiral Komkov? Only significant? Can you imagine what it would be like if the ports, the ship-yards, the refueling facilities of every major NATO power were to suddenly be underwater? Can you imagine the effect if New York, Liverpool, Le Havre, Hamburg, and Genoa were caught in a tidal bore higher than the Bay of Fundy or any tide now known? What if those thieving Chinese revisionists found Canton and Shanghai, with

214

their thirty million inhabitants, uninhabitable. What if all of our enemies found their coastal cities awash, their countrymen homeless, their navies destroyed. How many fleets would that be worth, Admiral?" The old man was now shrieking at Komkov, his face flushed. "Don't you see that this idea, my idea, was a stroke of genius?"

There was a pregnant pause, and then Komkov said slowly, "If you are referring to the flood preparations, it was truly a marvel of Soviet science to be able to detect the collision fully six months before it was known to the rest of the world."

"*Detect?* My dear Admiral, do you think we are speaking here of mere *detection?* Is the military mind so unimaginative to think that I only react passively to events?"

"I do not follow, Comrade Secretary." In fact, Komkov thought that perhaps he did follow, but did not wish to leave to inference something he found so disturbing. He hoped his irate commander-in-chief would spell things out. He was not disappointed.

"I thought this would be obvious to you, Admiral, but the change in the path of Halley's comet was accomplished at my instruction, and represents the greatest achievement of Soviet rocketry."

For the moment, Komkov was speechless and sat dumb behind his poker face. It was true that, knowing what he knew about the early flood preparations, the admission was not a total surprise. Then also, the accusations of the western papers should perhaps have prepared him. Deep down he knew that, given its present leadership, his country, the Soviet Union, was capable of such a thing. However, until now, he had not had to confront his vague suspicions and had been content to shrug off the western charges as typical anti-Soviet slander. Now, however, he knew it was true, and his whole conservative nature was repulsed. Yet his emotions remained as icy as a Russian winter; he remembered his position, and said calmly and ambiguously, "How was such a thing possible?"

The general secretary, as expected, took the remark as the mere technical inquiry of a less daring mind impressed with the boldness of his plan and proceeded to explain. "For these last few years, while the Americans were focusing on moon landings and space stations, I gave instructions that a group of scientists, our 'dissident' scientists to be exact, were to develop the calculations to intercept and divert meteors and comets, including the great Halley's comet. They developed many possible trajectories of diversion, under the mistaken conception that this planning could be used, if necessary *would* be used, to deflect a comet or asteroid headed toward the earth or the moon. As you perhaps are aware, just such a large asteroid struck Siberia in 1908."

"The Tunguska blast," said Komkov.

"You know it, of course," said the general secretary. "These things are not so theoretical in this country. We are after all, one sixth of the world's land area, and this very thing has already occurred once this century. In any case, these old scientists were misled, deliberately misled. Their research was not to be used defensively as they supposed, but offensively. Naturally, their suspicions grew as the project neared completion, but I will not bore you with what happened to them. Their efforts in any case were not wasted. Last July a large rocket was fired from our base at Leninsk. Our 'disinformation' sources leaked the story that it was a science probe. Eight months later the rocket rendezvoused with Halley's comet. There was a five-hundred-megaton thermonuclear blast in the one part of the solar system where such a thing was insignificant and therefore went unnoticed—behind the sun's fireball. The entire plan, my plan, was brilliant in its simplicity and daring, and was developed right here in this office. The original signed orders, and my planning memoranda, are right in this small binder." He pointed to a leather-bound zippered document on his credenza, sat back waiting for his words to sink in, then moderated his tone and continued.

"It is after all a bit like billiards; when the cue ball starts rolling down one side of the table, the gentlest tangential impact with a cushion or another ball will produce an entirely new trajectory, an entirely new destination, by the time it reaches the far cushion. As planned, exactly as planned, the comet was diverted at perihelion into a collision course with the moon. Twenty-four hours later a Mexican astronomer in Yucatan saw Halley's was off course; forty-eight hours later the whole world knew about the impending collision, but not—and this was my masterstroke—that the Soviet Union had caused it. And all this was accomplished by the man the decadent, western press dared to call a mere preserver of the status quo!"

The general secretary raised his eyes to the ceiling, suffused with self-satisfaction. Komkov's eyes widened. He saw he was dealing with unbridled megalomania. The worst speculations of the foreign press were true. The Soviet Union had tried to destroy the world as he knew it, all to gain the geopolitical advantage of having its enemies suffer more severely than it would suffer, so that Russia would emerge from the wreckage, weaker absolutely but stronger relatively. Now that the whole plan had failed, Komkov wondered what this defeated madman would do to cover his trail. His anxiety increased

217

with the realization that this was undoubtedly why the general secretary had called him to Moscow. He steadied himself and asked, "So that, Comrade Secretary, was the plan code-named *bedá*."

"Yes, that was *bedá*. The name was unfortunate. It turned out that one of those clever old rocket scientists I had outside of Leninsk was a bit of a linguist. Some fool let them choose their own code word, and no one at first caught the significance. It turns out that one of the possible translations in English for *bedá* is the word disaster. Disaster, if you break it down into its roots is *dis* and *aster*. In Latin these words mean evil star, and as the final irony, the stupid, superstitious ancients thought that comets were evil stars, portending misfortune to heads of state. I don't know if it was a joke or an attempt to warn someone. By the time I learned of this little word game, the scientist was dead with the rest of them. Unfortunately, it didn't end there; a linguist at the American National Security Agency eventually divined the whole puzzle. I got to him too, and just in time, but this was not without cost. Given the gravity of the *bedá* plan, we had to, well, amputate part of our own limb. We had an agent in place who knew too much and was, perhaps, emotionally involved with the linguist. The whole thing was mishandled by those fools in our mission to the United Nations in New York, who hired some local incompetents. The girl escaped with revenge in her heart. Being KGB trained, she does not have the squeamish sensibilities of American justice, and I am afraid she has, single-handedly, brought our intelligence-gathering capability in the United States to a standstill. There have been several killings, blown covers, and terrified defections to the FBI. She is still at

218

large, and our few remaining people are too frightened to leave the mission building."

Komkov was appalled by these vicious acts explained in the general secretary's matter-of-fact tone, but he could not suppress his morbid curiosity about how even the KGB was able to keep such a diabolical plot secret. After all, it was a major scientific project to accomplish the behind-the-sun diversion. How many people must know?

"Comrade Secretary, how do we know what hard evidence has leaked to the outside world? It must, for example, have taken dozens of scientists and technicians to launch the rocket on the correct trajectory, and there must be dozens of others like me who were alerted in order to plan for flooding on the seacoast."

"Yes, Admiral, and now you will understand the virtue of proper training in the KGB. I think, no offense of course, that such an accomplishment would have been quite beyond the reach of the military mind." He smiled and continued. "The scientists, involved unwittingly in *bedá,* worked in isolation in a special camouflaged base near Leninsk, our Baikonur base in Soviet Central Asia. They were there a year and a half, mostly old Jews and Germans from the *Sputnik* days. There were no vacations, no visitors, and all of their mail was censored. I even had the outgoing mail brought first to Moscow to be mailed from here. The launch was last July, and after the records were all in order, the scientists headed by plane for a rest on the Black Sea. As I mentioned, the scientists on the project were told that they were only exploring the theoretical possibility of diverting comets, Halley's among them. But by early last summer some of them thought they'd been duped and we were really going to go through with it. They were curious as hell, and suspected that there was a live nuclear warhead in the July rocket. Their hearts were bursting no doubt to talk about the events of their eighteen-month desert confinement to the first person who would listen. Now, since you asked, here's the best part. Somehow they didn't make it. Fate intervened in the form of a Sukhoi interceptor; their plane just disappeared into the Caspian." The general secretary sneered sardonically and studied the admiral's reaction. When there was none, he continued, thinking he had found a kindred spirit. "As for key people along the coast such as yourself, who needed to plan for flooding, you were told to tell no one and never to mention the code name. There was only one transgression, one loud mouth in Archangel. He paid with his life. Naturally, those who followed orders, as you did, had nothing to fear."

With every revelation Komkov's disgust grew. As a commander he knew that he and his sailors were expendable. They all understood that their lives might be given for the good of the Motherland. In Komkov's mind this was the most noble of sacrifices, a thing to be treated with reverence. Now he sat before his supreme commander and heard accounts of the gratuitous execution of his loyal countrymen in a tone of nonchalance, almost disdain. He had always suspected the worst of the KGB but had not before fully appreciated that they actually took great pleasure in their work. And it wasn't just Soviet scientists and operatives; there were clearly no limits. If the comet had hit the moon, even with the advance preparations, how many thousands of Soviet citizens would have perished? And what of the Soviet allies? Cuba and Vietnam were little but seacoast. They had not been warned. What of those loyal socialists? What

220

provision had been made for them? Far worse for Komkov was the realization that the moon's stability at a closer orbit was just a theory; the moon had certainly never been moved before. What if its internal structure could not withstand the greatly increased gravity exerted by the earth? What if the earth's pull on the parts of the moon became stronger than the moon's internal gravity, the attraction that held the moon together? The moon would rip apart and come crashing into the earth, and that surely would be the end of life on this planet. Such were the risks this vicious old man, who could not have ten years left to live, was willing to force on his countrymen. Stalin at his height could not have hit on such a scheme, concluded Komkov.

"Perhaps, Admiral Komkov, you would care for some tea and cookies?" said the general secretary. "I have some tasty ones from my favorite bakery in Amsterdam. It would have been one of my few regrets, that, had our plan succeeded, that bakery would also have been underwater."

This man who coolly executed Soviet citizens and gambled the fate of mankind, thought Komkov, could joke about the loss of his foreign cookies. A lifetime of taking and giving orders kept Komkov impassive on the exterior, yet inside the Polar Bear raged. "Just a little tea for me, Comrade Secretary," he said at last.

The general secretary called his aide on the intercom, "Morning cookies, Yuri, the samovar, and my pills please."

"It's all ready, sir," came the instant reply.

"Good, I'll unlock the door." The general secretary pushed a button under the desk and the heavy door hummed and popped open a few inches. Komkov wondered what, with all the locks, would happen if the old man needed assistance. How long would it take his aide to reach him?

The heavy tray was set down on the desk between them. There was a pure silver service of cookie plate and cups, creamer and sugar, and the most beautiful samovar Komkov had ever seen. There were numerous bottles of medicine with labels saying things like nitroglycerine and digitoxin. The general secretary took one or two from each vial until he had half a handful. The aide took the Chinese-blue porcelain teapot from the top of the samovar and poured the super concentrated tea from the teapot into the bottom of each of their cups. They then, in turn, diluted the tea with near-boiling water from the samovar's silver spigot. The general secretary put one pill at a time into his mouth, punctuated by tiny sips of hot tea.

The general secretary, noticing Komkov studying the brilliantly-polished samovar, said, "You like it Admiral? Look at these little stamped medallions on the front. It was made in 1841 by the Tula works for Count Stroganoff. You no doubt know the diplomat from the famous beef and sour cream dish one of his French chefs invented. I 'requisitioned' the samovar, as we say, from the National Historical Museum on Red Square. As a matter of fact I have 'requisitioned' most of the good Count's former property. I even have his carriage at my villa in Sochi. He was a man of exquisite taste."

As the aide withdrew, Komkov speculated on how there is no such thing as absolute security, and how the effort to obtain it often left one less, not more, secure. Komkov was also sure that no guards were watching from behind a two-way mirror; no video or tape recording was being made of this conversation. The subject was *bedá,* and the KGB did not record its failures.

As the general secretary munched on his cookies, Komkov opined slowly, "Of course, had the plan been successful, there would have been some losses to our country as well, the Black Sea Coast, the Baltic, . . . Leningrad."

"A few backward provincial cities are well worth the destruction of the great metropolises of the western world," said the general secretary with conviction. "Moscow, don't forget, is on high ground, five hundred miles from the sea."

It was at this point, with the memory of his dead mother and the suffering of the 900-day blockade, that Admiral Komkov first considered whether it might theoretically be possible to kill the general secretary before the guards could prevent it. Not that he exactly saw himself as a murderer, but still, he was twenty-five years younger and much larger than the fat, white-haired man across from him. He was out of training, but how long could it take: knock him to the ground, pin him on his stomach and jerk the head around sharply. Komkov found a sudden pleasure in thinking the unthinkable, and continued his calculations while the general secretary wolfed down a quarter kilo of the little biscuits. There would be an alarm, thought Komkov, maybe more than one. He himself had one just underneath his central desk drawer. He, or rather the assailant, he corrected himself, would somehow have to get the man to raise his hands a foot or more above the level of the desk. So far, Komkov did not recall the general secretary having done so. At last the head of the Communist Party of the Soviet Union pushed aside his cookie plate and teacup and resumed their conversation.

"So I know you as a military man agree that *bedá* was

a brilliant plan that would have inalterably shifted the military balance in favor of the Soviet Union." His voice, having risen triumphantly, now died off. "But through no fault of ours, we are now faced with a somewhat different situation. Our diplomatic position is precarious. Most of the world governments and peoples believe that at a minimum the Soviet Union knew about the comet long ago and kept the secret to itself. If the comet had struck, none of their opinions would matter. However, now that the relief and the maudlin praise for the Americans have died down, the world is on a witch-hunt. Western intelligence has done everything to convince people that we were behind the initial redirection of the comet. They have had a receptive audience in some corners. Naturally, we have denied this, and frankly I am not troubled by the reaction of our enemies. They were also yelling like stuck pigs when we shot down the Korean plane in 1983, but within months the United States sold us twenty million metric tons of grain. Their sense of outrage stops at their pocketbook. The problem has come with our allies. I have here on my desk a message from the head of our KGB office in Hanoi that the Socialist Republic of Vietnam will publicly demand the expulsion of all Soviet personnel within the next forty-eight hours. We expect a similar request tomorrow from the Syrians. Even that whimpering pup Fidel has had the temerity to ask for an explanation. In the meantime he has publicly thanked the United States and requested a full review of relations. In Eastern Europe things are little better. The Poles as always are rioting, but disturbingly, the Baltic cities of East Germany have this time joined in." The general secretary paused for a minute to leaf through the telexes. "It goes on. In Sofia our ambassador was attacked with tomatoes and rotten fruit. The police let the assailants get away. This kind of thing is unheard of, impossible. If we permit this challenge to Soviet authority, the whole matrix of relationships built up in the forty years since the Great Patriotic War will crumble. And what kind of a signal would that be to our enemies abroad, and worse, here at home. I'm sure that as a military man you agree with me."

"Of course, Comrade Secretary," said Komkov, silently judging the distance from his chair to the table, then across the table to the gesticulating general secretary. His mind, he tried to convince himself, was not yet made up.

"I knew you would, Evgenie, and that is why I am giving you this opportunity to salvage the fortunes of your socialist motherland."

Komkov jerked his glance up to meet the eyes of the older man, who continued, "If the Americans deprived us of our victory by stealth, we shall have it by open robbery. I wish you to take command of the Northern Fleet at Murmansk and the Murmansk Military District and attack the NATO forces along the Soviet–Norwegian border, pushing that border back as far as Narvik."

So this was it. This was how the old bastard would redeem himself. The target was well-known. The strip of frozen Norwegian coast was sparsely settled. Norway's Finnmark County was well above the Arctic Circle; so barren and inhospitable, not even fir trees could grow there. Militarily, however, it was quite fertile, a key platform for monitoring all Soviet activity in the Arctic. Murmansk, 200 miles above the Arctic Circle, was the biggest military base in the world. The North Cape Current kept it ice-free, but forced the Red Navy into a narrow corridor south of the permanent sea ice right along the neighboring Norwegian coast.

"And if NATO tries to resist . . ." said Komkov at last.

"If the western nations wish to escalate, so be it. But they won't. What did they do about Afghanistan? Do you think their governments will want to risk nuclear war over a few hundred miles of northern Norway? I tell you what will happen is this: the West will back down, within a week the liberal parties will blame the whole thing on their own governments for hurting poor, insecure Russia's feelings with unjust accusations. When our allies see our victory and the cowardice of the West, they will flock back to us. This whole comet business will be forgotten, our allies will be back in the harness, and we will have the Barents Sea–Norwegian Sea corridor the Red Navy has always dreamed about. The West will be totally demoralized and the North Cape will be ours."

"A show of force then, Comrade Secretary."

"Precisely, Admiral, to show the whimpering capitalists that I am not the doddering old has-been they say I am."

"I presume my orders will issue from the full Politburo?"

"That won't be necessary. I have alerted certain key people, and, to be honest, after the success of your mission there will be some changes in the Politburo. Certain cowards and nay-sayers will perhaps have outlived their usefulness. Perhaps you have political ambitions yourself, Admiral, and, if you bring me a victory, we can discuss them. Since the death of Ustinov, I have been looking for a more flexible man as Minister of Armaments, for example. But for the present, Admiral Nekrasov of the Northern Fleet will receive orders today that you are arriving to take over his command. The general staff will provide whatever assistance you need. I wish a final plan of attack in the next 72 hours. This shouldn't be difficult; northern Norway has always been a tempting morsel. The file plans are here in this dossier, with my notations and opinions. Incorporate them as you see fit. You will need an airborne division. Use the one at Leningrad. It's the beginning of the North's brief summer, an ideal time for such an operation. I will contact you in Murmansk when to sail."

It occurred to the Admiral, that stripped of the cheap promises of political advancement, what the general secretary had told him was this: he was to steam out of Murmansk and attack NATO, even though the plan had not been submitted to the full Politburo, much less approved; it was simply the brainchild, the desire, of the general secretary. So little was known, even by the senior military about Kremlin politics, that the reference to the possible replacement of the Minister of Armaments was the first Komkov had heard that the minister and the general secretary had so much as a difference of opinion. The fallout from *bedá* had no doubt weakened the general secretary and his KGB clique. He wondered if the general secretary and his intimates would use Komkov's attack as a fait accompli, trapping resisting Politburo members into a pattern of action they would never have originally countenanced. There seemed to be a power struggle in progress, and Komkov saw that he was perhaps the key chess piece—to be precise, the unwilling, expendable pawn. He wondered what kind of reading the KGB would get if they gave him the polygraph test now. Murder was in his heart, but all he said was, "Comrade Secretary, why has this great honor fallen to me?"

"You are the obvious choice, Admiral. This is a large-scale naval operation in Arctic waters. Only you and old

Admiral Nekrasov of the Northern fleet were candidates. Frankly, I find you daring and imaginative, more willing to take bold risks. Then too you have known about *bedá,* some of it, since the beginning. Your only black mark is your foolish loyalty to a certain undesirable; but that relationship will in any case terminate when, after we have consolidated our victory, I am able to effect a needed cleansing of our Soviet society. Now, if there is nothing further," said the old man, slouching back in his chair, "I will have my aide show you out." He reached for the intercom on the desk.

"Just one thing, Comrade Secretary," said Komkov hurriedly.

"Yes Admiral," said the General Secretary, withdrawing his hand from the intercom.

"It's just . . . that I would find it an honor to shake the hand of the man who had devised so bold a plan," said Komkov, rising.

"Well, Admiral, of course, of course." The fat, old man rose with some difficulty, pushing himself up on the arm of the chair. He extended his right arm across the broad desk. Komkov grasped the hand firmly with his right hand and said, "For Leningrad."

"What, Admiral? What has Leningrad got to do with this?"

Komkov swung his left hand up to grasp the general secretary's right hand at the wrist, then with a ferocious tug pulled the heavy man over the broad desk on his stomach, clearing in his path telexes, documents, tea service, and samovar. Scalding water splashed high; they both shrieked and crashed over Komkov's chair to the floor. The general secretary struggled and tried to call for help. Komkov grabbed the cushion from the toppled chair and buried the old man's face in it. He had him on his back in a scissors lock, immobilizing his arms. Komkov's right arm was behind the general secretary's head, while his left arm pushed the chair cushion over the general secretary's face and nose. Komkov looked at the office door, expecting it to fly open before a squad of security men. Would he have time and strength to jerk the head around before they beat him to death on the floor? The general secretary moaned and bucked in a desperate effort, but Komkov held on. He tried to shake his head, but Komkov had him in a vice of bulging forearms.

It was almost two minutes before the struggling stopped, a good four with Komkov staring at the door, ready for the snap, before it was clear that the snap would not be necessary. The old man's cries had gone unheard through the heavily soundproofed door, further drowned out by the clatter of typewriters in the outside office. The impenetrable fortress had become an inescapable trap. Komkov loosened his grip and removed the cushion to see the blue-tinged, lifeless face of the former General Secretary of the Communist Party of the Soviet Union.

Komkov was breathing hard as he slowly unwound his legs from the dead body. It was cold in the office but he was sopping with perspiration. He became cognizant of the piercing pain of hot-water burns on his right shoulder and forearm. His uniform was soaked. He stood up in a near daze, started to pick up the samovar, and then stopped. The deed was done, yet no one had burst in. No one knew the general secretary had been killed. For the moment, no one else in the Soviet Union knew their leader was dead. Why, Komkov asked himself, had he done it? Was there a single reason? The *bedá* plot, the risk to the world, the killing of the Soviet scientists, the ordering of his fleet to war, perhaps to annihilation, on an unauthorized whim, the intimation of a new purge, the general secretary's willingness to destroy Leningrad—any of them, he supposed, was sufficient motive. He had committed murder, worse, treason, yet he felt no remorse.

His throbbing shoulder ended this brief reverie and Komkov studied the scene at his feet. There was a tipped-over chair, papers, and a samovar on the floor. There was a cookie plate, a chair cushion, and in the middle, supine, covered with cookie crumbs, was an overweight seventy-eight-year old, with glassy eyes and bluish skin. There were no bruises, there was no blood. For the first time, Komkov realized that martyrdom might perhaps be eluded. What did heart attack victims look like, anyway? The man was old, fat, he took pills, he was under a lot of strain, he hadn't been seen in public for six weeks. An autopsy, even a brief medical examination, would reveal otherwise, of course. But the people who would come rushing in were not doctors; they were secretaries, aides, and security police. They would not know it was suffocation—but would they let him go?

Komkov picked up the cookie plate, his teacup, and some of the papers and put them back on the desk so the trajectory of the general secretary's fall would not be so apparent. He set the leather chair upright, took the cushion away from the old man's face and replaced it on the chair, but then, with the recognition of a new problem, his spirit sank. He walked around the desk and dropped into the chair that moments before had contained the most powerful man in the Soviet Union, perhaps the world. At most, Komkov thought, he would have maybe six hours before the true cause of death was known, and twenty-four before the whole Soviet Union

was looking for him. If he was to evade capture he must
be out of the country at the end of that time. However,
getting out of the Soviet Union involved a little more
than buying a train ticket. The mind-numbing grip the
Soviet state held on its citizens would be inconceivable if
people could just flit back and forth across the border
as they pleased. Not even an admiral could get permission without a good reason and the approval of the KGB.
Komkov's power and rank could not help him in this;
they would only serve to heighten suspicion. Why would
a fleet commander need to go abroad suddenly and on
short notice—the mere query would invite an investigation. He thought again about the inevitability of martyrdom. As he thought, he recalled that there might be one
possibility, one tear in the curtain. Immediately he went
back into action. Komkov pulled open the drawers of
the general secretary's desk. If he was going to the West
he wasn't going empty-handed. The sheaf of annotated
plans and signed orders would probably convince western intelligence about the planned attack on Norway.
Komkov reached over to the credenza and grabbed the
signed originals of the *bedá* orders the general secretary
had pointed out to him. These, he thought, would remove
any doubt that it had been arranged by the KGB. A diary,
personnel notes, and the last two months' communiqués
and orders of the day should make interesting reading.
He picked up a military code book, then reconsidered
and returned it to the desk. It was the KGB and the
clique behind *bedá* that he wished to weaken and humil-
iate, not the Soviet military.

Komkov replaced these items in the desk drawer with
the rather more prosaic contents of his own briefcase.
He then filled his case to bursting with the general secretary's papers, no doubt the greatest haul of top secret

materials the West could ever hope to peruse. He closed the desk, ignoring the searing pain of his own burns, and picked up the general secretary's intercom.

"How the hell do I get the door open? The general secretary has had a heart attack!" screamed Komkov into the intercom.

"What?" came back the frightened, excited reply.

"Had a heart attack, damn you! He's dying! How can I open the door?"

"There's a button under the drawer." Komkov found it, paused a moment for effect, then pushed. Immediately the aide and the KGB officer poured through the door.

"Quick!" screamed Komkov to the KGB man. "Do you know cardio-pulmonary resuscitation?"

"Yes, Comrade Admiral."

"Then get to it. He was saying good-bye when he fell, pulling the samovar after him. We can save him." The officer knelt immediately, placing both hands on the dead man's heart. He began to pump. The corpse passed wind.

"There, see, he's coming around," yelled Komkov. He grabbed the aide's arm, "Where is the Kremlin doctor?"

"I will summon him," said the aide. He was in a near panic.

"No," said Komkov authoritatively, "I will have the man in the outer office do it. You must summon the Politburo. This could be serious, and nothing should be done until they give instructions. Should the worst happen, and we lose him, do not allow him to be removed from the office. Let no one leave the room until you have exact instructions from the assembled Politburo. Try to reach the Minister of Armaments first. He will

232

know what to do. Our country could be in danger if we just start yelling the news to the world. You must wait until the key people actually get to this office before you tell them. Meanwhile, I will place the military on alert. We are surrounded by enemies; we can't be too cautious. The safety of the Soviet state depends on proceeding slowly and correctly."

"Yes, Admiral," said the aide, relieved to have clear instructions from anyone. Komkov knew that in a Soviet interregnum, everyone's thoughts would fix on who the successor would be, and how this choice would affect them. Exploring the cause of the old leader's death would not be foremost in their minds, and this misplaced focus might, thought Komkov, give him the time he needed to escape. Komkov grabbed his valise and brushed by the frightened secretaries huddled about the door.

"You are not to leave this room," he barked at them, "This is a national emergency." He hurried to the exterior door and pushed the release button. In the antechamber he told the KGB officer that there was an emergency, his assistance was needed, and the general secretary's aide would tell him what to do. The officer went immediately into the main office, Komkov sprang the second door, and was again out in the corridor. In this Maginot Line of office security, all the locks faced one way. He walked with his normal authoritative stride past the corridor guards and started down the stairs. The broad staircase seemed endless, and with each step his heart raced faster. As he neared the bottom, he heard steps behind him.

"Admiral Komkov, Admiral Komkov," called Colonel Grishin.

Komkov's whole body said "run," but where would he run? He was in the Kremlin and beyond that lay the

giant fortress that was the Soviet Union. There was
nowhere to run. That was what Russia was all about.
They had him. He turned slowly to face Grishin.

"Your jet has arrived and is waiting for you at Kho-
dinka Central Airfield, Admiral. Should I signal for your
car?" said Grishin, catching up to him.

"Of course, Colonel, and thank you."

It was only five-thirty, but already quite light as the
old diesel truck chugged along the bright blue Gulf of
Finland to the north and west of Leningrad. On its side
were the markings of Len-Finn Torg, the Soviet foreign
trading company that handled all trade between Finland and Russia's second largest city. It was only a
hundred-mile drive from Leningrad to the Finnish
frontier. On the way, there were checkpoints and soldiers, but the truck excited no suspicion; someone had
to bring in dairy products to feed the city of four million. Before the Revolution, Russia and the Ukraine were
Europe's grain basket, but now the Soviet Union was
totally incapable of feeding itself.

Joseph knew the route well, knew almost every guard.
They were supposed to search his truck every time he
crossed. Interestingly though, the soldiers who were to
search had no access to the West themselves. Not that
they had any interest in what was going on in the West.
First, they couldn't read any literature not in Russian
and second, they took all the books and magazines anyone could want away from the Scandinavian tourists who
flocked into Russia along this pleasant road. No, the
guards were simple fellows; what they wanted was con-
sumer products—nothing grand, just cheap calculators
and wristwatches, blue jeans and Western records. They

saw this stuff on all the tourists, but had no pretext to confiscate it. Nor did they have anything the tourists would want to trade, and trading with a foreigner was risky anyway. Yet they were desperate for Western goods. Even something so insignificant as a flashlight battery was of much higher quality than they could get in their own country. It was here that Joseph could provide a service. Joseph was in Finland several times a week, and could pick up little mementos for the guards. At least he could if he had something to trade with the Finns. Joseph carried no rubles out of the Soviet Union; that was strictly illegal, and even if he had, they were not freely convertible. Oh, he could have gotten something for them, a fraction of their value, but there were better things to take, not so dangerous and with a ready market. There were exactly two products that were easy to get in Russia, comparatively cheap, and of great interest to the Finns. One was caviar, the other was vodka. With a few tins of Caspian beluga, a few cases of Stolichnaya or Moscovskaya, Joseph could do well in Finland, even with the obligatory "presents" to those supposed to search the van.

As Joseph rounded a turn through the pine forests along the blue Gulf of Finland, he saw the beginning of the familiar final Soviet checkpoint a mile and a half from the Finnish border. The soldiers, and there were many soldiers, all had the green epaulets of the KGB. The entire border guard was a part of the KGB, an army unto itself outside the control of the Soviet military. AK-47s bristled from every shoulder strap. Joseph stopped the truck at the checkpoint and got out. He knew the sergeant in charge of the detail.

"Good morning, Sergeant Tulipanov. Len-Finn Torg truck bound for Helsinki for dairy products. Here is my exit declaration and visa. Everything is in order, today like every other day." While Joseph spoke, a young soldier took a pole with a circular convex mirror on the lower end and began to pass it under the truck's undercarriage. Another soldier climbed up in the cab and made a routine search. Joseph knew, from long experience, that they would search carefully everywhere—except in the back where they knew the vodka to be stored.

"Joseph, listen, today I have to search the back, too," said the sergeant quietly and apologetically.

"What!" said Joseph. "I thought we had an arrangement."

"We do, we do, it's just that we got a cable just an hour ago that we were to be very thorough in searching vehicles bound for Finland. I don't know what they're looking for."

"Vodka, that's what!" cried Joseph. "Our business will be ruined."

"No, I don't think it's vodka; they're even sending a special team here to double check every vehicle. You must be just ahead of them. Listen, I'm sorry, but I think I really have to take a look this time, just a peek."

"But Misha, don't you see, what if you do find something, I mean a few cases of something, just suppose. Don't you have strict orders what to do then?"

"Well, yes, my orders say to confiscate the goods, detain the truck and driver, and report the incident."

"And if you find something, if you actually see it with your own eyes, and you don't report it, isn't that a serious offense?"

"Well, yes," said Misha haltingly, not fully understanding. "I suppose it is. Of course it is."

"So Misha, here is our situation. Right now you don't know if there is anything in the van. You have two choices.

You can search it, or not search it. If you search it, there
then follow two possibilities: either you find nothing, or
you find something. If you find nothing, OK, but if you
find something, then again you have two choices, either
you do report it, in which case I am maybe in big trouble
and we are out of business, or you do not report it, which
is serious disregard for your duty, for which you can
end up in big trouble." The KGB sergeant looked visibly
troubled. "Under the circumstances, Misha, it may be
better to exercise your reasonable discretion as a highly
trained sergeant in the people's border guard, and use
the authority granted to you to decide *not to search the
van!*"

By now the sergeant was totally nonplussed about
what he should do, so Joseph, waiting for the right
moment, decided to nail down his case with a less intellectual appeal. He said in a matter of fact tone, "Anyway, Misha, I was meaning to tell you that there is a sale
in Helsinki on those new cassette recorders from Japan,
Sony, I think, and I wanted to know if I could pick one
up for your little boy."

"Really, Joseph, you can get me a Sony?"

"Just say the word."

"Boris, Yuri, you gave the undercarriage a good look?
Okay, let's get this one out of here." The sergeant
stamped Joseph's papers and detached part of his visa.
With a wave, Joseph was back in the cab, rolling through
the checkpoint. The truck, an aging behemoth, acceler-
ated slowly, going through its gears one more time. There
was a long stretch of straight road in the "no man's land"
here, a good mile. Then it was around a bend and up a
short hill to the frontier. This final Soviet checkpoint,
the one Joseph had just cleared, was deliberately placed
before this stretch of straight road so the guards would

have a long firing lane if they wished to let rip a few parting shots. Joseph watched the rearview mirror, and it was just before the checkpoint shrunk beyond recognition that he saw three loaded jeeps flying KGB flags pull in from the Soviet side.

Joseph was well across the Finnish border and in the outskirts of Helsinki before he left the main road, drove aimlessly, doubled back on himself, and then backed into an alley. It was a few minutes before he could get the back open, climb inside, and move the first row of empty egg cartons. Then he called, "Komkov, you all right?"

"Half gassed from monoxide, but thanks to you, I'm all right." Joseph moved some cartons and helped the big admiral to his feet. "You sounded like a Talmudic scholar back there, arguing with that sergeant," said Komkov.

"Yes, well, that was my ambition, prior to going into vodka smuggling." They got down from the back of the truck. Komkov was bursting out of one of Joseph's nephew's pullovers. He had his folded uniform and his briefcase, but nothing else. He had not returned home.

"You know that it's too dangerous for you to return to Leningrad after this," said Komkov.

"Yes, well, I was thinking of emigrating some day anyway," said Joseph. "You know, a change of air." They climbed up on either side of the cab and Joseph eased the truck out of the alley and back on to the road.

"You know, Joseph, it has been some forty-five years since the last time you slipped me out of Leningrad."

"So many summers, so many winters."

"You saved my life that night too," said Komkov.

"Some things never change, Zhenya, some things never change."

The two men smiled, and together they drove the few remaining miles to the American Embassy.